19.3.2~

Hygge
and
Kisses

Clara Christensen

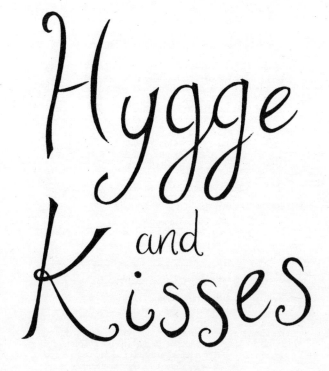

SIMON &
SCHUSTER

London · New York · Sydney · Toronto · New Delhi

A CBS COMPANY

First published in Great Britain by Simon & Schuster UK Ltd, 2017
A CBS COMPANY

3 5 7 9 10 8 6 4 2

Simon & Schuster UK Ltd
1st Floor
222 Gray's Inn Road
London WC1X 8HB

Simon & Schuster Australia, Sydney
Simon & Schuster India, New Delhi

www.simonandschuster.co.uk
www.simonandschuster.com.au
www.simonandschuster.co.in

A CIP catalogue record for this book
is available from the British Library

Paperback ISBN: 978-1-4711-6673-0
eBook ISBN: 978-1-4711-6672-3

Typeset in Bembo by M Rules
Printed and bound by CPI Group (UK) Ltd, Croydon, CR0 4YY

FSC
www.fsc.org
MIX
Paper from
responsible sources
FSC® C020471

Simon & Schuster UK Ltd are committed to sourcing paper
that is made from wood grown in sustainable forests and support the Forest
Stewardship Council, the leading international forest certification organisation.
Our books displaying the FSC logo are printed on FSC certified paper.

Part One

London

Chapter 1

As Bo Hazlehurst stood swaying on a packed tube carriage on her way to work one Monday morning, she couldn't help but worry that life just didn't feel like it was *supposed* to. The twenty-six years of her life so far had been blessed with good fortune: she had a respectable job, a loving family, and an active social life, all of which she knew she ought to feel grateful for. But she had read a feature in a magazine that weekend about the *quarter-life crisis*, and it had resonated with Bo's sense that something was not quite right; that somehow, she was not a *real* grown-up, but rather a little girl who was just faking the whole adulthood thing.

Bo lurched sideways sharply, losing her footing as the train screeched to an abrupt halt in the tunnel. Mortified, she regained her balance, adjusted her bag over her shoulder and mumbled an apology to the balding businessman whose armpit she had just face-planted into. Her fellow passengers tutted and assumed the glum expressions that were appropriate to the unexplained delay and Bo did the same, trying to take her mind off her brewing quarter-life crisis by thinking about the day ahead.

She worked in the capital's West End, for a firm which specialised in accountancy software. IT was, admittedly, not a field she had particularly aspired to during her three years studying psychology at the University of East Anglia, and she had dithered when she was offered the office assistant position at the end of her first summer after graduation. She had wondered whether something more enticing, more 'her', might come along. But her parents had encouraged her not to turn down the opportunity to get her foot in the door with a reputable firm in a secure sector ('The world will always need accountancy software,' her father – himself an accountant – had intoned sagely), and so she had accepted the job.

Mildly elated that she had found a 'proper' job so quickly (while many of her friends were making do with temping or bar work), Bo had tried to put her reservations aside and enter working life with an open mind. It may not have been the most stimulating job, but she would be working in the heart of the West End, a stone's throw from Oxford Street, which seemed like manna from heaven for a twenty-one-year-old who had spent the last three years living in student digs on a campus on the outskirts of Norwich. She envisaged lunch-hours spent browsing the clothes shops, meeting friends for lunch, or nipping into Selfridges to splurge at the make-up counter.

As the most junior member of the workforce, Bo was answerable to just about everyone in the company, and she spent her first six months at Aspect Solutions franking mail, updating the client database, fetching drinks for the company directors and, if she was lucky, taking the minutes at board meetings when one of the PAs was off sick. The job managed to be at once boring and stressful and it didn't take long for disillusionment to set in. The splurges at Selfridges were few and far between, as her modest salary did not stretch much beyond paying her rent, transport costs and chipping away at her stubbornly unyielding credit card balance. Besides, her office was located at the wrong end of Oxford Street for Selfridges, and sat squarely among the souvenir outlets and shops selling mobile phone cases. She stuck with it, however, and five years on had worked her way diligently up through the administrative ranks to the heady heights of marketing executive, with responsibility for the content and production of the company's promotional material.

The stalled tube train eventually shunted back to life and fifteen minutes later, Bo emerged into the grey November drizzle at Oxford Circus station. She rummaged inside her handbag for her umbrella and shook it open on the pavement, waiting amid a surly crowd of commuters at the pedestrian crossing. At the appearance of the flashing green man, the throng surged forward, moving en masse in front of the line of buses and taxis waiting impatiently for the lights to change. Lowering her head to avoid the umbrella spokes of oncoming pedestrians, Bo turned right in front of the flagship Topshop store. She stole a fleeting glance at its huge glass-fronted displays, in which one of the androgynous white mannequins was wearing a cropped top and skin-tight jeans so low cut that its plastic hip bones protruded above the waistband. 'She'll catch her death in those,' Bo muttered under her breath, before realising, with a flash of embarrassment, that she sounded just like her mother.

Bo took a left down a side street, keen to leave the busy thoroughfare behind, and held her breath as she darted between a line of queuing taxis, trying not to inhale the black fumes belching from their exhaust pipes. She hopped up onto the kerb to avoid being clipped by a Lycra-clad courier weaving recklessly on and off the pavement, and inadvertently stepped into an oil-slicked puddle which had filled the dip in a cracked paving stone. She tutted, feeling the squelch of water inside her shoe and the cold dampness spreading up her tights.

Taking shelter under a coffee shop awning to shake the grimy water out of her shoe, she caught sight of her scowling reflection in the tinted window. It seemed to have become her habitual expression of late, to the point where Bo had noticed the beginnings of a permanent wrinkle forming between her eyebrows. It struck Bo as ironic that she was already developing wrinkles when, inside, she still felt that she was not yet a proper grown-up. Perhaps 'premature ageing' was another woe to add to her list of quarter-life concerns.

Bo generally rated herself a solid seven in terms of attractiveness, stretching to an eight and a half if she had made a particular effort. She was not especially tall, but had been blessed with a naturally slim figure, clear skin and blue-grey eyes, and hair which, though naturally curly, could be tamed into elegant waves with the help of straighteners. There was no denying, however, that she was not looking her best on this particular Monday morning. Dressed in the drab office-worker uniform of grey trench coat and black trousers, she looked pallid and washed out. She raised a gloved hand to smooth the strands of hair clinging to her clammy forehead back into place, cursing the genetic inheritance that had given her hair that turned to frizz at the merest hint of moisture in the air.

Bo slipped her foot back inside her wet shoe and continued to weave north towards the ugly grey office block which housed Aspect Solutions. There she pushed open the heavy glass door and walked across the tiled lobby to the lift, letting her eyes rest on the list of companies located on each floor. Most of them had names which gave away nothing about what purpose they served or even what sector they were in. Several professed to be 'agencies' or 'consultancies', with meaningless abstract names that sounded to Bo more like the names of characters in Science Fiction than they did business organisations: Zeneca, Sentralis, Clostridia (this last one, on reflection, sounded to Bo more like a sexually transmitted disease than an alien overlord).

An electronic ping indicated that the lift had arrived at the fourth floor and, as the metal doors slid open, Bo steeled herself for another week at work.

'Morning, Bo,' chirped Chloe, the receptionist. Chloe had platinum hair, eyelash extensions and eyebrows which looked as if they'd been etched onto her forehead with a stencil.

'Morning, Chloe,' Bo smiled in reply, dropping her umbrella into the stand beside the water cooler. 'Good weekend?' She knew that Chloe liked nothing more on a Monday morning than to talk about her weekend's antics.

'Yeah, good, thanks,' beamed Chloe. 'Out with the girls Saturday night for Kelly's birthday. Oh. My. God. That girl can drink.'

Bo had met some of Chloe's friends, when they had come along to her birthday drinks in the wine bar which served as Aspect's regular after-work haunt. They had all been equally as groomed as Chloe, their hair primped and teased to within an inch of its life, their skin an alarming shade of orange. Bo had felt positively middle-aged and prudish by comparison, especially once they had had a few drinks and got on to the subject of their boyfriends and their sex lives (loudly and in graphic detail).

'It was Jägerbombs all round,' Chloe continued proudly. 'Ended up getting a bit messy, y'know?'

Bo nodded, inwardly grimacing at the thought of what a messy night out involving Chloe, her girlfriends and Jägerbombs might involve.

'Kelly was sick in the cab on the way home,' Chloe went on, as if answering Bo's unvoiced question. '"Oh my God, Kels," I said. "Are you for real?" It was running all over the floor, under the seats, got on my shoes and everything. I went *ape-shit*. Those shoes were brand-new!' Chloe looked at Bo for outraged sympathy and Bo tried to assume an expression of empathy rather than revulsion.

'Oh no,' she murmured half-heartedly.

'I ran them under the tap, when I got home, and they look all right now,' she went on breezily. 'Might need some deodorant on them to get rid of the smell, though,' Chloe concluded with an air of practicality, rifling through the morning's mail to find the wad of envelopes destined for the marketing department. 'How 'bout you anyway? Get up to anything nice at the weekend?' she asked, handing over the stack of mail.

'Um, nothing special,' answered Bo, flicking distractedly through the wedge of post.

'Oh, right.' Chloe looked disappointed, as if Bo had let her down by not having at least one scandalous anecdote with which to liven up her morning duties of answering phones and greeting visitors.

'Well, see you later,' Bo said with a faintly apologetic smile and a 'must be getting on' tone of voice.

'See ya,' Chloe chirruped in reply, distracted by the electronic ping which heralded the arrival of the next lift-load of Aspect workers.

Conscious of her left shoe squelching with every step, Bo made her way through the open-plan office to the bank of desks which comprised the marketing department. The first of her team to arrive, she pulled off her coat, switched on her computer and sank onto her swivel chair. Above the faint electrical hum of her computer, she heard a phone was ringing and, beyond the triple-glazed windows, she could make out the distant pounding of a pneumatic drill from the Crossrail site on Oxford Street. It was the familiar soundtrack of the office, virtually unchanged since she had started working at the company five years earlier. Would it be the same five years from now, she wondered, and would she still be here to find out?

Claire, the marketing manager, arrived at her desk just as Bo had begun to scroll through the thirty-seven emails which had arrived since she had shut her computer down at six o'clock on Friday.

'Morning, Claire, good weekend?' Bo asked.

Claire was in her late thirties, with two children under three and a perpetual air of harassed anxiety. This morning, she looked exhausted.

'Don't ask,' Claire answered, grimacing. 'Sick bug. Coming out of both ends of both children.' Bo pulled a sympathetic face and fleetingly wondered whether she could ever love a child enough to be sick-nurse in such circumstances, or whether, when faced with a projectile-vomiting infant, she would simply recoil in horror and run from the room. She suspected the latter.

'That can't have been much fun,' she said.

Claire took a deep, stoical breath. 'Well, you know what they say,' she replied in a long-suffering voice, 'you're not a real mother until you've had to wash your child's puke out of your cleavage.'

'Tea?' asked Bo, standing up abruptly. There was only so much vomit-based chat she could handle first thing on a Monday morning.

'Oh, yes please, Bo,' Claire whimpered gratefully. Natasha, the department's other executive, and the assistant, Hayley, had arrived together and were removing their scarves and coats at the desks opposite. 'Tea?' Bo mouthed across the royal-blue desk dividers, and they both nodded.

The acrid aroma of burnt toast greeted Bo before she entered the office kitchen. Inside, Becky and Alison, two administrators from payroll, were side by side at the worktop. Becky was scraping a layer of black crumbs off the incinerated slice of Mothers Pride, while Alison watched, sipping tea. The women were in their mid-thirties, one dark-haired and the other fair, but they had the same stocky build and surly expression, which had always made Bo feel slightly nervous around them. They reminded her of the girls she used to come up against in netball matches at school, who seemed to be all elbows and fingernails and would think nothing of flattening a smaller, slighter opponent such as Bo.

Bo gave a friendly nod of greeting, but the two women made no effort to let her pass, obliging Bo to squeeze past in the few spare inches between their combined width and the units on the other side of the narrow, windowless kitchen. Having salvaged the unburnt core of her slice of toast, Becky began to spread margarine liberally over it. She and Alison were chatting about their weekends, and they both steadfastly ignored Bo as she filled the kettle at the sink.

'Good morning, ladies.' Bo turned round to see Ben, one of the account managers, stride into the kitchen with the relaxed, lithe movements befitting a twenty-nine-year-old who was confident of his appeal to women.

'Morning, Ben,' Alison and Becky replied in unison, instinctively moving aside to make space for him to pass. Bo said nothing, but turned back to face the kettle, concentrating on watching the plume of steam which was now issuing urgently from the spout.

'Morning,' Ben repeated in a quieter voice, as he arrived at the sink beside Bo and reached up to take a mug from the cupboard above her head. Bo glanced sideways at him.

'Oh, hi,' she mumbled. Ben dropped a tea bag into his empty mug then placed it at the end of the row of four she had neatly lined up on the worktop, watching in silence as Bo filled the cups with boiling water. Bo sensed he was about to say something, when Becky's voice piped up.

'Good weekend, Ben?' she asked, taking a bite of her jam-smeared slice of toast.

Bo's back was to the room but her hand faltered momentarily in mid-pour and she splashed a puddle of boiling water onto the Formica. She tutted and reached for a cloth to wipe it up.

'Great weekend, thank you,' Ben replied, stepping away from the sink to reach for the plastic bottle of milk which he passed to Bo without making eye contact. She took it from him in silence. 'Yourself?' he asked Becky. 'Get up to anything *exciting* on Saturday?'

Bo thought she detected a hint of sarcasm in his tone, but his rapt audience seemed not to have noticed.

'Oh, nothing really, just a quiet night in in front of *Strictly*,' answered Becky dejectedly.

'Hey, don't knock *Strictly*,' Ben shot back in a tone of mock-reproach. 'I won't hear a bad word said against that show. Best thing on television.' His charm offensive was working: Becky and Alison tittered. Stirring milk into the tea with her back to the room, Bo rolled her eyes.

'I wouldn't have had you down as a *Strictly* man, Ben,' Alison chipped in. There was no mistaking the flirtatiousness in her voice.

Ben had heard it too, and reacted accordingly. 'I'm a *huge* fan!' he protested earnestly. 'Dancing, celebrities, what's not to love? And then of course there's Tess Daly . . .' Ben trailed off and, as if on cue, the two women started to giggle girlishly.

Bo dropped the used teaspoon into the sink where it clattered noisily against the stainless steel.

'Ooh, fancy Tess Daly, do you, Ben?' Becky asked coquettishly.

Oh, for God's sake, thought Bo. She glanced sideways and caught the unmistakable glint of enjoyment in Ben's eye.

Ben feigned concentration for a few seconds. 'Well, of course she's the wrong side of forty,' he said regretfully, making Alison and Becky gasp in horror, 'but she *is* still fit.' His face contorted as if he was tortured by indecision. 'On balance, I think . . . I probably would.'

The two administrators erupted in a cacophony of 'you can't say that', 'she's a married woman' and other admonishments. Delighted by their reaction, Ben gave a 'just being honest' shrug. Bo yanked a battered plastic tray out from the cupboard beneath the sink and roughly assembled her four mugs onto it.

'Your tea's there,' she said crisply, without looking at Ben. Then she picked up her tray and left, with the sound of Alison and Becky's cackling laughter still ringing in her ears.

Bo returned to her bank of desks and distributed the teas to her team, to a chorus of grateful noises. She felt irrationally cross with Becky and Alison for being so easily manipulated by Ben, and for behaving like silly schoolgirls around him. Couldn't they see that they had played into his hands? She dropped into her chair and stared blankly at her dormant computer screen. It wasn't just Becky and Alison she was cross with. It was Ben, for his hypocrisy. Bo knew Ben's real feelings about *Strictly*. They had discussed it that very weekend, in fact. She had mentioned the show in passing, on their way back to Ben's flat after dinner, and he had given a scathing laugh and teased her for being prematurely middle-aged. Bo had become used to Ben's acerbic sense of humour, which had a tendency to verge on spiteful. It was one of several things which had begun to bother Bo about their relationship, which had been going on, in secret, for the past eight months.

Chapter 2

Bo nudged her mouse to bring her monitor back to life, then absent-mindedly clicked open the first email in her inbox, an all-users' missive from human resources regarding company restructuring. She frowned at the screen, hoping to look like she hadn't noticed Ben carrying his tea past her desk on his way back to his department. A couple of minutes later, a flashing icon indicated that she had received a message. *Looking hot this morning*, it read. *Fancy being my plus one for a cocktail bar launch on Friday?*

Bo stared at Ben's message in a state of indecision. She felt indignant about the scene she had just witnessed in the kitchen, and knew that to accept Ben's offer would be a tacit acknowledgement that she had let him off the hook. And yet the pragmatic part of her considered the possible alternatives for her Friday night, knowing that the most likely scenario would be a solitary take-away on the sofa, in front of *Gogglebox*.

This, she thought ruefully, was surely evidence of her quarter-life crisis, further proof that her outwardly grown-up life was just a charade. Nine months into their relationship, she and Ben were (at his insistence) still hiding their relationship from their colleagues, sending each other secret messages like teenagers and ignoring each other around the office. She often wondered whether Ben enjoyed the power it afforded him, whether he got a thrill from being able to flirt with other women in front of her, knowing she was powerless to react.

Tess Daly turn you down, did she? she tapped out, lips pursed. Dating Ben sometimes felt like playing a game of poker, where every move they made was designed to call the other's bluff. Bo had never particularly enjoyed card games, least of all poker. Her opponents always seemed to be able to see right through her poker-face, just like Ben could, no doubt, see right through this attempt to play it cool. She took a sip of tea and waited for Ben's response.

Tess has got nothing on you. You were my first choice.

Her shoulders sagged slightly, and she put her hands to her keyboard. Who was she trying to kid? They both knew how this would end, and she had work to be getting on with.

Okay. Where and when? she typed.

Ben Wilkinson had joined Aspect ten months earlier, appearing in the office on a grey day in January, the first day back after the Christmas break. Bo had, as usual, spent Christmas at her parents' house, a detached property on an estate full of similar, expensively maintained houses on the outskirts of a prosperous commuter town in Buckinghamshire.

Going home for Christmas as a twenty-something was a mixed experience for Bo, a slightly jarring collision of her current life and her past. She slept in what had been her childhood bedroom, but which had long since been redecorated as a guest room, to her mother's taste. The walls that had been covered in music posters throughout Bo's teenage years had been repainted a delicate primrose yellow, and the duvet cover and matching scatter cushions were a lavender paisley.

Since leaving home, Bo had come to appreciate the luxury of her parents' house which, as a child, she had always taken for granted: the comfortable furniture, the spacious rooms, and the well-stocked fridge. There was an undeniable pleasure in returning, albeit briefly, to a lifestyle devoid of responsibility, where all her meals were provided and she had nothing to think about other than which Christmas movie to watch on TV. But the price that had to be paid for that return to carefree indolence was the simultaneous regression to the family dynamics of her youth, whereby her parents tended towards being overly anxious about her, and in return she assumed the demeanour of a sulky adolescent.

That Christmas, Bo had been more than usually evasive in response to her parents' enquiries about whether she was 'seeing anyone special', being unwilling to disclose that most of her recent dates had come via Tinder. She was quite certain that they would be horrified, and convinced that she would end up being groomed by a predatory online psychopath, the likes of which they had read about in the newspapers. It was quite possible they would not let her return to London until she had promised never to use the app again.

In truth, Bo had been reluctant to try Tinder but set up a profile under the influence of a bottle of wine and her flatmate Kirsten, who had reassured her that it was perfectly normal for millennials to use dating apps, and that she had nothing to lose by giving it a try. Her scandalised shock at the lewd images and crass propositions which popped up on her phone with alarming regularity had soon worn off, and once Bo had perfected the art of swiftly deleting unwanted matches, she threw herself into the Tinder dating scene with gusto.

After six months of frenetic swiping and messaging, however, Bo became disillusioned. She had been on numerous dates, but none had led to any relationship lasting longer than a few weeks. She was increasingly plagued by the sense that there was simply too much choice out there, too many single people her age in London, and that even if she liked a man she had matched with, the chances were that he was keeping his options open lest he get a better offer. She began to tire of the Tinder mindset, in which people were as disposable as the free newspapers which were thrust into her hand on the steps of Oxford Circus tube station every evening. She had switched off the app while she was at home for Christmas, and felt a blissful relief to be free of its incessant demands for attention.

Bo had returned to work on a particularly grim, sleety day just after New Year, a few pounds heavier, a bank balance at the brink of her overdraft limit, and bracing herself for the onset of January blues. She had just begun a half-hearted attempt to sort through the towering stack of paperwork in her in-tray when Matt, the company's accounts director, appeared at her desk.

'Bo, I'd like to introduce you to our new senior account manager, Ben.' Bo had looked up to see a young man smiling at her, his hand outstretched to shake hers. He wore the unofficial uniform of the men in the office – a collared shirt open at the neck and smart trousers – but she couldn't help noticing that his shirt looked beautifully tailored and the watch on his wrist discreetly expensive.

'Nice to meet you, Bo,' he said, his confident manner and well-spoken voice instantly conveying to Bo an expensive education. (She had encountered enough men of his type at university to recognise a public schoolboy when she met one.)

Bo felt a flutter in her stomach as she shook Ben's hand, and the words 'he's nice' flashed through her mind as she noted his green eyes, dark wavy hair, and the toned but slim physique which spoke of summer weekends spent playing tennis and cricket. They exchanged pleasantries across the top of Bo's filing tray for a couple of minutes, until Matt had steered Ben away to continue his tour of the office. Bo sat down and gazed vacantly at her computer screen for a few moments, with a wad of buff-coloured folders still clutched between her hands. She couldn't help smiling to herself, suddenly feeling as if January might not be such a bad month after all.

Over the next few weeks, the winter gloom had been considerably lessened by Bo's burgeoning flirtation with Ben. The way his eyes followed her across the office let her know that he was attracted to her, and she seemed to find herself in the kitchen at the same time as him with uncanny frequency, but his attentiveness stayed on the right side of acceptable office etiquette. (Bo had experienced the wrong side of acceptable the previous year, in the form of a rather forlorn-looking member of the tech team who had taken to following her into the lift at lunchtime every day, only giving up once he had been given a formal warning by HR).

Ben began calling her by the nickname 'Blu-ray' when she had explained that Bo was short for Boughay, a family name which her mother had been keen to pass on to another generation. In truth, Bo had never been keen on 'Blu-ray', but she tolerated it in the hope that his use of a nickname suggested a certain intimacy between them. (She tried not to dwell on the fact that, in her experience, ex-public schoolboys rarely addressed anyone in their social circle by their actual name.)

Through their chats in the kitchen, Bo learned that Ben's background was similar to hers: a solidly middle-class upbringing in the Home Counties followed by a degree at one of the respected universities. His fondness for nicknames notwithstanding, Ben seemed a good match in terms of both their temperaments and their aspirations. He was humorous and urbane and soon Bo had pretty much made up her mind that Ben Wilkinson was what her mother would term 'perfect boyfriend material'.

Bo was in no doubt that Ben was attracted to her. The only hitch was that he seemed to be taking his time to do anything about it. He continued to flirt with her throughout January in the office kitchen or waiting for the lift, or in chatty messages over the intranet in which they shared conspiratorially gossipy exchanges about their colleagues. But by the end of the month, Bo was beginning to wonder if Ben was ever going to make a move.

'But why hasn't he asked me out?' she wailed to her flat-mate Kirsten as January turned to February. Kirsten was a level-headed girl whom Bo had known since university when they had adjoining rooms in their residence hall.

'Why don't you ask him out?' Kirsten had riposted with a shrug. 'This isn't the 1950s, you know.' A wrinkle formed between Bo's brows. She knew Kirsten had a point, but the fact remained that she didn't want to have to ask Ben out. She had done enough to signal her interest and, in her opinion, it was up to him to do the rest.

'You're so English,' Kirsten chastised her. Kirsten was half-Danish on her mother's side and, although she had been born and raised in Godalming, had inherited her mother's tendency towards plain-speaking. 'Why does he have to do the asking? Whatever happened to gender equality?' Kirsten flicked her brown hair away from her face and gave Bo a challenging look over the rims of her metal-framed glasses. Bo's shoulders sagged.

'I know, I know,' she murmured sheepishly, knowing full well that – traitor to her gender though it might make her – she would never, ever, ask Ben Wilkinson out.

Instead, Bo did the next best thing and went clothes shopping. She spent a pleasurable Saturday afternoon trawling the shops for a new outfit to wear to work which would look professional and irresistibly seductive at the same time. One snugly fitting cream sweater and a pair of high-heeled boots later, Bo felt ready to up her game in the flirtation stakes and call Ben's bluff. In poker terms, she was ready to play her royal flush.

Whether it was the sweater or the heels that did it, Bo's

strategy worked, and at five to six one Friday evening in February, she had just placed her empty mug in the dishwasher when Ben sauntered into the kitchen, a half-empty bottle of beer dangling from one hand.

'Evening, Blu-ray,' he drawled, and Bo immediately spotted his relaxed, unguarded manner.

'Evening, Ben. You've started early,' Bo replied with a smile, glancing at the bottle.

'I'm celebrating,' Ben grinned. 'I landed a new account today.' Ben beamed and, for a split second, Bo glimpsed a little boy brimming with pride.

'That's great news. Well done, you!' she answered, before wondering whether her words had made her sound like a proud mother rather than an impressed potential girlfriend. But she didn't have time to dwell on the question. With one seamless movement Ben placed his bottle on the worktop and stepped across the cramped kitchen, cornering her in front of the microwave.

'You're looking *particularly* fit today, Blu-ray,' he leered, and Bo smiled demurely whilst inwardly congratulating herself on her choice of ensemble. 'What would you do if I kissed you?' he asked, pinning her against the Formica worktop.

She tilted her head coquettishly and replied, 'I'd kiss you back.' *Finally*, Bo thought, as she allowed Ben's arm to circle her waist and pull her towards him.

Bo still got a fluttery feeling in her stomach as she remembered the illicit thrill of that first kiss in the kitchen, the scent of his aftershave and the faint taste of Sol on his breath. It was every bit as enjoyable as she had hoped, and made even more thrilling by the knowledge that they could be discovered at any moment by their co-workers. They had gone out for impromptu drinks to celebrate Ben's new account, crossing Oxford Street to disappear into the crowds and rickshaws thronging the narrow streets of Soho. Drinks led to a late-night meal in Chinatown, followed by a giggly journey on the tube back to Clapham and an energetic if somewhat drunken night at Ben's flat.

The following morning, however, when Bo was putting her previous day's clothes back on, Ben had said, 'Best to keep this quiet, at work, don't you think?' and she had felt it would be churlish to disagree. As she sat chewing the limp slice of buttered toast Ben had made for her, she wondered whether she had been naïve to assume that what had happened would automatically take their *entente* into the clear-cut realm of 'relationship'.

During the tube ride back to north London, Bo had sat in a trance-like state, obsessively analysing the events of the previous night (at least, what she could remember of them) and trying to work out what Ben's comment over breakfast had meant. Perhaps he was keen to protect their privacy in the early stages of their relationship, reluctant to face the intrusive curiosity of their colleagues while they were still getting to know each other. But by the time her tube train rattled to a halt at Holloway Road station, Bo was riven with doubt, convinced that she had misread the situation and that Ben intended to keep their assignation a secret not because he wanted to allow the relationship to develop in private, but because, as far as he was concerned, it had been a one-off.

Any glow of triumphant happiness that Bo had felt when she stumbled into Ben's flat at one o'clock that morning had well and truly worn off by the time she unlocked the front door of her flat.

'Good morning,' Kirsten said, stepping out of the bath-room in her dressing gown. 'New clothes did the trick, then?' she grinned. Bo checked her reflection in the hall mirror. Her eyes were smudged with the remains of yester-day's make-up, her cheeks were deathly pale, and wayward frizz had sprung up around her hairline.

'I guess so,' she answered half-heartedly, belatedly trying to smooth her hair back into position.

For the rest of the day, Bo could not settle to anything. She performed her usual chores, going to the supermar-ket, tidying her bedroom and changing her bedding. She climbed into bed, checked her phone for the umpteenth time, in case she had missed a message from Ben, and stared out of the window.

Her bedroom was at the rear of the Victorian terraced

house, the lower ground floor of which she and Kirsten rented. A glass-panelled door next to her bed opened onto a rectangle of concrete surrounded by a six-foot-high retaining wall. The letting agent had optimistically described this damp, moss-covered area as a 'walled courtyard garden' and, when they had first moved in, Bo had attempted to improve it with an arrangement of planted terracotta pots. But her green-fingered efforts had been thwarted by the permanent lack of sunlight in that sunken area, and the garden herbs and patio roses had withered and died within weeks. Now the pots remained in their positions, cracked and neglected. They stood as a faintly accusatory reminder to Bo, every time she yanked open her blind, that she wasn't yet enough of a grown-up to be able to take responsibility for anything living.

Bo's doubts about Ben intensified as the weekend dragged on, and on Sunday her phone remained stubbornly silent. Instead of feeling elated that she had finally progressed from 'flirtee' to 'girlfriend', Bo was tortured by the suspicion that she had spent the past six weeks laying the groundwork for a one-night stand.

By Sunday evening, Bo's anxiety had morphed into trepidation about how to behave around Ben at work the next day. Should she act like nothing had happened? Or ignore Ben completely? It was almost midnight and Bo had just drifted into a light doze when her phone buzzed and lit up the room with the green glow of an incoming text message. Bo sat bolt upright, instantly wide awake.

Really enjoyed Friday night, Blu-ray. We should do it again some time. Bo felt her stomach flip with relief. She stared at Ben's message for a few moments, a smile spreading across her face.

Me too. I'd like that. Night night, she tapped out. Then she put the phone down, plumped up her pillows and went to sleep.

Chapter 3

While she was at university, Bo had dreamed of living and working in London. She had envisaged the kind of cosmopolitan lifestyle in which nights out at the capital's trendy bars would be *de rigueur,* and eating at the best restaurants would be a regular occurrence. The reality, however, was that her dining habits in London had hardly changed since her student days in Norwich: on the rare occasions that she could afford to eat out, her options were dictated by a restaurant's cost and proximity to her flat, rather than by its reputation. In Bo's mind, being a 'proper' grown-up meant being able to order from the à la carte menu rather than the *prix fixe*, and choosing a bottle of wine that wasn't prefaced by the word 'house', but, for the first five years of her working life, such luxuries had remained, infuriatingly, out of her reach.

That all changed when she started dating Ben, however.

Ben's best friend was a PR consultant to the restaurant trade, whose job involved ensuring that launch nights for new bars and restaurants were well attended by a young, attractive clientele. Ben could add his name to the guest list for a seemingly endless succession of launch nights of new food venues across the capital. This was a fact which he had been quick to drop into conversation with Bo early on in their flirtation and, although she knew it might make her shallow, Bo could not help but be impressed.

For one of their early dates, Ben had taken her to a restaurant launch in Shoreditch. The venue was underground, accessed by an inauspicious flight of stone steps which led into a cavernous space. The walls were covered in industrial concrete and rows of exposed-filament light bulbs dangled from the ceiling on long wires. The menu was so sparsely written that it seemed, to Bo at least, to be virtually unfit for purpose. She stared at the handwritten sheet she had been handed by a youthful, bespectacled waiter, wondering how on earth she could make an informed choice when there were dishes that included 'burnt pig' and 'beetroot, beetroot and more beetroot'.

Bo had never been in a restaurant quite like it before, and felt terribly out of place and *suburban*. Ben, however, seemed to take it all in his stride, asking the waiter to explain the more gnomic-sounding dishes so that Bo had at least a vague notion of what to order. Ben's confidence and good humour had put her at ease, and with the help of a few cocktails, Bo started to enjoy herself. By the time the main courses arrived she felt relaxed enough to suggest, with a giggle, that Ben should grow a beard and handlebar moustache in order to fit in with the hipster male clientele. Ben had met the suggestion with a raised eyebrow and a wry smile, before calling the waiter over and ordering a second bottle of wine.

Soon a month had passed, then another. Bo had accompanied Ben to the launches of bars and restaurants in all the trendier parts of London, sampling dining concepts which ran the gamut from 'nose-to-tail eating' (featuring an unpleasantly high proportion of offal) to raw cuisine (lots of wheatgrass and uncooked vegetables). Bo threw herself into each experience with enthusiasm, relishing the feeling that, not only was she enjoying the best that London's culinary scene had to offer, but she was doing so with a good-looking, charmingly attentive companion.

Bo was in no doubt that Ben liked her: she could see the way his eyes lit up when she removed her coat to reveal a tight-fitting dress, and there was no question that they got on well, never running out of conversation, whether the topic was food or venue, or work. Her only reservation was that, in spite of the fun they had together, Ben remained stubbornly reluctant to make their relationship public.

The element of office subterfuge had added a certain frisson to the early phase of their romance – meeting in secret outside the office after work; surreptitious messages on the company intranet; the thrill Bo felt when Ben casually brushed past her in the kitchen. But by the time they had been seeing each other for three months (a period of time which Bo had always considered to be an unofficial relationship milestone), the novelty of conducting a secret office romance had begun to wear off. Any pleasure that she had derived from deceiving her colleagues had long since evaporated, and Bo found the need for secrecy impractical, inconvenient and immature.

But when she raised the issue, at a pop-up restaurant in the shadow of London Bridge one night in April, Ben's boyish features assumed a tortured expression, making her feel like a critical mother unfairly chastising a small child. He placed his drink on the table and, in a low, confiding tone, explained that he had been in a relationship with a colleague at his previous employer's, a fellow account manager who had turned out to be needy and controlling, and she had begun bad-mouthing Ben to their colleagues when the relationship turned sour. He had ended up leaving the company to get away from her.

'I guess I got my fingers burnt,' he said, reaching over to sweep away a stray curl that had fallen in front of Bo's face. 'I swore I'd never date anyone from work again. But then I met you . . .' He gave her a coy smile, and took her hand in his. This time, he wanted to keep office politics out of it, he explained. Ben had chosen his words carefully, and Bo had felt flattered by the implication that, unlike his ex, she was not needy and controlling.

'Don't worry, I get it,' Bo reassured him, squeezing his hand. And, in that moment, she did.

Nevertheless, when Bo was alone, she found that her niggling doubts returned. She sought Kirsten's opinion one night, over a bowl of pasta and a bottle of wine in the flat.

'Do you think it's weird that he still doesn't want anyone to know about us?' she said. Kirsten narrowed her eyes thoughtfully. As a recently qualified solicitor, she liked to reserve judgement until she knew the relevant facts.

'How long have you been seeing each other?' she asked.

'Three months.'

Kirsten nodded. 'What's his relationship status on Facebook?'

'Single,' Bo said morosely, pushing a piece of soggy pasta around her bowl.

'Hmm,' Kirsten replied, sensing her friend's disappointment. 'Maybe he's just not ready for something serious yet,' she said gently.

'I'm not expecting him to propose,' Bo protested, refilling her wine glass. 'Just to acknowledge that we're a couple. Is that too much to ask?'

'Of course you're a couple!' Kirsten riposted. 'You're always out with him—'

'Yes, but all we ever do together is eat out then go back to his place!' Bo cut in, her eyes gleaming with frustration. Kirsten's brow furrowed.

'Food and sex. Sounds like an ideal relationship to me. What's your point?'

Bo sighed and took a gulp of wine. She was beginning to feel like she was being cross-examined in court and her defence was crumbling. 'Don't you think it's just all a bit too much ... fun?' she pleaded. Kirsten considered her friend thoughtfully across the rim of her wine glass.

'You're worried because you're having too much fun?' Kirsten said, with a puzzled smile.

'Well, no, of course not,' Bo replied exasperatedly. 'It's just – don't you think it's weird that we don't ever do any of the *normal* stuff couples do, like spend an evening in front of the TV, or go to the supermarket together? And he's never *once* spent a night here.' Kirsten inclined her head in acknowledgement. She had often hoped for an opportunity to meet the elusive Ben for herself, but Bo had never managed to persuade him to come back to N7.

'The older I get, the further away from a grown-up relationship I seem to be,' Bo said dejectedly. 'Do you remember Miles? Can you believe we actually used to talk about getting married?' Kirsten slapped her forehead in mock despair. Miles had been a boy Bo spent (or 'wasted' as she now realised) her final year at university dating: an English literature student who had excellent bone structure, was sensitive and thoughtful, and had ultimately turned out to be gay. (He had broken the news to her as they sat in a minibus en route to their graduation ball). Kirsten had borne witness to the relationship and its abrupt, mortifying ending.

'I rest my case!' Kirsten shrieked. 'Just think what your life would have been like if you had married Miles.' Bo winced.

'But the fact remains, the only man who has ever expressed a remote interest in wanting to marry me was gay!'

'So what?' Kirsten shot back with a derisory snort. 'You're twenty-six, Bo! Too young to get married. And you're having fun with Ben, aren't you? Just enjoy it.'

Bo agreed, in theory, that she was too young to get married, and she couldn't deny she was having fun with Ben. But there remained a part of her which believed that a relationship should follow a certain trajectory, and that if two people enjoyed each other's company as much as she and Ben did, the natural next step was to become more involved in each other's day-to-day lives. And that could only happen if their relationship was public knowledge.

She knew that it was perfectly normal for millennials to have relationships which didn't conform to traditional patterns. Most of their friends, Kirsten had reminded her, were involved in romantic dalliances which did not fit the conventional 'couple' mould: variations on the 'friends with benefits' set-up, or the emotional minefield offered by Tinder. But, much as she tried to tell herself that what she had with Ben was perfectly compatible with the millennial mindset, the lingering suspicion persisted that something was missing from their relationship and that Ben was reluctant to commit. At least, reluctant to commit *to her*.

Bo's doubts persisted, but she kept them quiet from Ben, fearing that it would be somehow unreasonable to challenge him. He had been honest and open about his reasons for keeping their relationship secret, after all, and perhaps it would be immature or needy of her to complain. So, rather than voice her concerns to Ben, she had silently nursed them into a full-blown grudge that he was dictating the terms of their relationship to suit his own needs rather than hers.

Bo's growing ill-feeling was not helped by Ben's tendency to flirt with other women in front of her. When they were out on a date, her heart would sink if a pretty waitress approached their table, as she knew that Ben would be unable to resist engaging the girl in mildly flirtatious banter. The boyish smile on his face suggested he considered his behaviour charming, but Bo found it tedious and irritating. His repartee with the payroll women in the office kitchen that Monday was a case in point. Bo knew that she had no reason to feel threatened by his flirtatiousness with Becky and Alison, and – that he was no more likely to date either of them than he was to date Tess Daly – but she suspected that the real purpose of the exchange had been to make her feel jealous, and that it was his way of reminding her that he was in control.

Bo cursed her own complicity in his behaviour. The truth was she had chosen to put up with Ben's flaws because the alternative – singledom, and finding herself back on the dating scene, perhaps even reactivating the dreaded Tinder – seemed infinitely worse. Her frustration was as much with herself as it was with Ben, and she berated her shallow lack of resolve as soon as the lure of a new cocktail bar was dangled in front of her.

When Friday arrived, the bad mood which had been festering all week was exacerbated by having to sit through a particularly boring meeting with her team. The marketing department was preparing for an upcoming trade fair, at which Bo would be responsible for greeting the hundreds of delegates who would mill through the draughty conference centre over the course of the day, encouraging them to take a leaflet and Aspect-branded pen, before shepherding them towards one of the suited techies for a software demonstration. The very thought of it filled her with bone-crushing boredom.

The hours dragged by until finally it was six o'clock, and around the office people began switching off their computers and putting on their coats. Bo stayed at her desk, pretending to be busy at her keyboard until quarter past six, when the rest of her team had made their farewells and she was able to slip to the Ladies to fix her hair and make-up without having to submit to their chatty queries about what her plans were for the evening. Ten minutes later, she slipped out of the office to catch the tube to Farringdon. Ben had been out all day with a client, and she was to meet him at the cocktail bar.

It was a blustery, grey evening, threatening rain. When she emerged at Farringdon station, Bo tightened the belt on her trench coat and lowered her head against the wind, and would have walked straight past the venue were it not for Ben pulling up in a taxi as she arrived. He jumped out of the car and gave her a perfunctory kiss on the cheek.

'Is this it?' Bo asked, baffled. The venue bore no name over its dark front door and its blacked-out windows gave no indication of what was inside. Ben nodded, but Bo detected a slight frostiness in his manner and wondered if he, too, was in a bad mood.

Bo pushed open the door and stepped into what appeared to be a Prohibition-era speakeasy. Tiny spotlights on the ceiling cast pools of light onto small, round tables, and the walls were lined with black leather banquettes. A bow-tied man was playing jazz at an upright piano, and white-jacketed waiters glided between the wooden tables with elegant-looking concoctions in glasses.

A beautiful young woman with a glossy mane of chestnut

hair wafted in front of them clutching a clipboard. She was wearing a silky black dress with a neckline which revealed the pale curve of her cleavage. Bo's heart sank.

'Hi, good evening,' the woman intoned huskily. 'Are you on our guest list this evening?'

'Ben Wilkinson plus guest,' Ben replied smoothly. Bo couldn't help but notice how his bad mood seemed to have evaporated in the brunette's presence. The woman checked the sheet of A4 on her clipboard.

'I'll show you to your table,' she purred, looking up at Ben with an ingratiating smile. She led them past the bar, behind which a row of mixologists were assembling complicated drinks with expressions of utmost seriousness. Bo was aware of the eyes of some of the overly attractive young people at the bar following them as they walked past.

They sat down at a tiny dark wood table near the bar and the brunette handed them each a cocktail menu.

'Enjoy your evening,' she said, holding Ben's gaze for a fraction longer than was necessary. Bo noticed Ben's eyes drift to a space over her shoulder and wondered if he was checking out the rear view of the woman as she sashayed away.

'What do you fancy?' she asked snippily, glaring at him over her menu.

'Sorry?' Ben said, his eyes sliding back to her face with a faintly guilty look.

'Which cocktail?' she clarified. Bo had been hoping that an evening out would lift her spirits after a dismal week, but was beginning to realise that being in this phony speakeasy full of beautiful people was making her feel worse rather than better. Perhaps she just needed to start drinking, she reasoned. She was bound to feel better after a cocktail or two. Bo scanned the menu in front of her, not recognising a single cocktail on the list. Each one seemed to involve ingredients, botanicals and even spirits she had never heard of, and she felt too tired and hungry to know which one to choose.

'Would it kill them to do a Cosmopolitan?' she muttered crossly. Across the table, Ben pulled a face.

'A *Cosmo*?' he repeated sardonically. 'Very *Sex and the City*.' Then he raised his head and cupped his hand around his mouth as if about to shout. 'Hey, Blu-ray, the Noughties called. They want their cocktail back!' he mocked. Opposite him, Bo stared at her menu in simmering silence.

'I'll have a Hoxton Martini,' Ben said nonchalantly to the white-jacketed waiter who had appeared beside them.

'I'll have the same,' murmured Bo, pointedly avoiding Ben's eyeline. The waiter nodded, scribbled on his pad, then left.

Drinks ordered, Bo glanced over her shoulder at the cluster of gorgeous girls posing and preening at the bar. They seemed mesmerised by their mobile phones, compulsively photographing themselves and their surroundings without really interacting with each other. It was the same behaviour she had witnessed at countless other launch nights, and she knew that it was part of the deal at events like this – that posting shots of the event on Instagram was, in truth, why they had all been invited in the first place. But tonight, Bo was suddenly struck by the utter hypocrisy of it all, and the fact that how much fun you were having was much less important than how much fun you *appeared* to be having.

She slid her gaze back to Ben, who had also picked up his phone, and was scrolling distractedly across the screen with his thumb, scowling slightly in its blue light. Bo drummed her fingers on the lacquered wood table, waiting for him to finish.

'So, good day at work?' she asked dutifully, once Ben had returned his phone to the table.

'Not really, no,' came his curt response. 'It was fucking tedious.' Ben's eyeline hovered above Bo's shoulder again, and she suspected he was checking out the girls at the bar. The waiter returned and reverentially placed two martini glasses on paper coasters in front of them.

'Well, cheers,' Bo said tetchily, and took a grateful sip from the glass. The cocktail was delicious, herbal and sweet without being sickly, and she savoured the ice-cold chill of the liquid in her throat. Bo took another sip, waiting for Ben either to elaborate on the nature of the day's tedium, or reciprocate by asking how her day had been. But Ben did not seem predisposed to say anything at all. 'How's the new client?' she persevered. With a wince, Ben let her know that he had no desire to talk about the new client.

The sound of female laughter at the bar mingled with the tinkling jazz at the piano and, almost in spite of herself, Bo felt her mood soften. The iciness of her first few sips had given way to a warming sensation, and a pleasant fuzziness filled her head, as if someone had removed the sharp, jagged edges and replaced them with tufts of cotton wool. Feeling her animosity fall away, she leaned across the table and took Ben's hand.

'Look, I'm starving. Shall we finish these and go and get something to eat?' she suggested, her voice conciliatory. 'Nothing fancy. There's a Pizza Express over the road.'

'We've only just got here,' replied Ben, his mouth forming a petulant pout. 'Besides, I think we could do better than *Pizza Express*,' he sneered, draining his glass. Wounded, Bo withdrew her hand sharply and sat back in her seat.

'I'm hungry, that's all, and I could murder a pizza,' she said defensively, aware that her eyes were starting to prickle. Across the table, Ben continued to look appalled, as if he had taken the suggestion of pizza as a personal slight. She felt a sudden flash of irritation and, galvanised by the cocktail, decided to seize the moment.

'It's just that – haven't you noticed how all we ever do is go out?' she said. Ben's eyes met hers with an expression caught between appalled and dumbfounded.

'And your point is ...?' he replied, looking genuinely baffled.

'We're always eating out, or going to places like this, but we've never eaten a single meal at home together, either at your place or mine. Don't you sometimes just want to ... cook up a big bowl of spag bol and just chill out?'

'Wow, Blu-ray. I had no idea you were so ... conventional,' Ben said, after a stunned pause. The barb stung, and his use of the nickname during a row rankled.

'Well, if I am, what's wrong with that?' she countered defiantly. Ben's lip curled upwards into a sneer.

'Besides,' she went on, incensed, 'I thought you liked nothing better than a Saturday night on the sofa in front of *Strictly*. Or was that just some bullshit you made up for the benefit of the payroll girls?' Ben looked momentarily caught out, but he quickly recovered his composure.

'Horses for courses,' he shrugged, giving a snide little laugh. 'I was just messing around.'

The awkwardness between them was broken by the reappearance of the waiter at Ben's shoulder. 'Same again for me,' Ben said, without consulting Bo. She could feel her rumbling stomach crying out for something solid and sustaining, but she nodded at the waiter to indicate likewise.

'This isn't really a relationship at all, is it?' she said, once the waiter had left. With the merest flicker of his facial muscles, Ben managed to convey how disinclined he was to answer. The halogen spotlight above them cast shadows across his face, emphasising his prominent cheekbones and jawline. Bo continued to glower at him, determined to wait for his response.

'I don't know what kind of relationship you want, babe,' he said at last, with an injured, martyr-like tone. 'I thought we were having fun together.'

'But fun only gets you so far, doesn't it?' she replied. 'Life can't *always* be fun, can it? There's the boring stuff too. Chatting about work, doing the laundry, cooking dinner. That's real life.' Bo was warming to her theme, ignoring Ben's evident discomfort. 'Going to non-stop restaurant launches and drinking ludicrously expensive cocktails isn't real life.' As if on cue, the waiter reappeared and placed the fresh drinks in front of them with professional seriousness.

'Well, they look pretty real to me,' Ben replied, lifting his glass and holding it towards her in a parody of a toast. 'Cheers!' he grinned. Bo watched him take his first sip, feeling frustration rise like bile in her throat. She stared at the cocktail in front of her, taking in the condensation running down the sides of the glass, and the delicate twist of orange zest which had been painstakingly placed on the meniscus of liquid. For a split second, she fought the urge to pick up the drink and pour it over Ben. But even in her fury, she couldn't bring herself to cause a scene and endure the embarrassment and commotion that would surely follow.

Instead she did the next best thing, rising from the leather banquette and extricating herself and her belongings, with some difficulty, from behind the table.

'Where are you going?' Ben asked, shock written plainly across his face.

'Home,' answered Bo. She pulled on her coat, strode past the bar and headed out into the damp chill of the city streets.

Chapter 4

Bo was woken the following morning by the shrieking siren of a passing ambulance. She rolled onto her side and blinked in the grey light of her bedroom. As she stared blankly at the woodchip-covered wall beside her bed, a succession of images, each one more mortifying than the last, flashed through her mind: the supercilious smile of the brunette with the clipboard; Ben's expression of appalled disbelief during her fumbled attempt to extract her things from behind the little table; the bitchy, sidelong glances from the preening girls at the bar as she strode past, pink-cheeked and flustered. She cringed and buried her face in her pillow, as if hoping to eradicate the memories by physical force.

Bo's rumbling stomach forced her, eventually, to lift her head from the pillow and glance at her alarm clock. It was eleven o'clock and, apart from a packet of crisps she had picked up on her way back from Farringdon, she had not eaten since lunch almost twenty-four hours earlier. With a groan, she flung an arm sideways to the bedside table and fumbled amongst the clutter for her phone, torn between hope and dread that Ben might have tried to contact her. There were no messages or missed calls, however, so she kicked off her duvet and reached for her dressing gown.

The flat in Holloway did not have much of a kitchen – certainly nothing like the spacious, country-style kitchen-diner in her parents' house, with its bespoke, solid wood units, granite worktops and Aga. Instead, Bo and Kirsten made do with a cramped L-shape of shabby units, a tarnished sink, and a low-grade freestanding oven with a clunky gas hob and smoke-stained glass door. The window behind the sink was inaccessible behind a metal security grille that had been screwed to the frame, itself caked in the greasy residue generated by years of cooking in the poky space. As if to compensate for the lack of ventilation, an old-fashioned circular extractor fan had been built into the window pane, a simple contraption of spinning plastic blades operated by a string pull, which proved totally ineffective at extracting either steam or smells, but was highly effective at allowing draughts in.

Bo peered inside the bread bin, which was empty but for the remnants of a loaf of supermarket white, the crusts dotted with green spots of pin-mould. With a sigh, she filled the kettle and leaned back against the worktop, allowing her eyes to settle on the wall-shelf which heaved with recipe books, takeaway menus and countless out-of-date coupons and vouchers. Sensing that she needed something to take her mind off Ben and the humiliations of the previous evening, she plucked a cookbook from the shelf and laid it out on the worktop. She made herself a cup of coffee and flipped through the grease-spattered pages in search of a recipe to cheer herself up.

Bo had discovered the joys of baking as a twelve-year-old when, faced with the prospect of a never-ending school summer holiday, she decided to attempt a simple Victoria sponge recipe from her mother's well-thumbed edition of Delia. There was something about the activity of baking which Bo had found intensely rewarding; she could still remember the glow of satisfaction she had felt as she smeared the circles of sponge neatly with jam and whipped cream before placing them together and dusting the golden dome with icing sugar. She was hooked, and spent the rest of that summer working her way diligently through her mother's cookbook collection, trying her hand at everything from plain scones to profiteroles. When she was a teen, baking had seemed to offer an escape from the emotional turmoil of adolescence, with its insecurities, anxieties and constantly shifting friendships. As an adult, Bo still found baking the ideal displacement activity to take her mind off her problems.

'Morning.' Kirsten stood in the doorway in her pyjamas, her mussed-up hair and pillow-creased face indicating that she had not long woken up. 'God, I feel rough this morning,' she croaked, shielding a yawn with her forearm.

'Heavy night?' Bo enquired, measuring out a teaspoon of vanilla extract and tipping it into a bowl of eggs and sugar. Kirsten nodded.

'Impromptu office drinks. We went to a new Brazilian place in Islington. The caipirinhas went down *very* easily,' she said with a grimace. 'Something smells good,' she murmured, peering hopefully past Bo at the bowl of melted butter and chocolate simmering over the hob. 'What're you making?'

'Chocolate brownies,' replied Bo, whisking the eggs and sugar together in a mixing bowl. Kirsten looked visibly cheered by the prospect of freshly baked brownies for breakfast. She dropped a tea bag into a mug and poured in water from the kettle.

'You didn't stay over at Ben's last night, then?' she asked.

'Nope,' Bo replied crisply, adding flour and cocoa to the egg mixture before tipping in the melted chocolate.

'Everything okay with you two?' Kirsten probed, stirring her tea. Bo fought with the urge to confess to Kirsten that, although she wasn't sure if things were okay with Ben, she was certain she had made a fool of herself at an achingly trendy cocktail bar. But instead she poured the glossy brownie batter into the baking tray, forcing back the tears which she could feel ready to spring to her eyes.

'Nothing that a gooey chocolate brownie won't fix,' she said at last, with a shaky, sideways smile. There followed a moment's silence, during which Kirsten watched as Bo slid the baking tray into the oven and slammed the glass door shut with a flourish.

'Pleased to hear it,' Kirsten said, with a supportive look.

A little later, while the brownies were in the oven and the sink was filling with hot, soapy water, Bo's mobile phone buzzed on the worktop. Her heart racing, she hastily wiped her hands on a grubby tea towel and grabbed her phone.

I was an arse last night. Been a shit week. Sorry.

She stared at the text in a state of inner turmoil. This was what Ben did when he knew he had pushed her too far; he apologised (invariably by text), blamed his behaviour on work stress, or tiredness, then moved on as if nothing had happened. In the early days of their relationship she had seen his willingness to apologise as an encouraging sign. At least he was willing to acknowledge his own shortcomings, she reasoned. She had, in turn, been quick to forgive.

'That's one of the things I like about you, Blu-ray,' he'd told her once, when she had agreed to overlook a blithely dismissive remark about the work done by her department. 'You're easy-going. You're not one of those girls who hold on to a grudge, festering over something trivial for months.' Although intended as a compliment, the comment had left Bo feeling as if she had no choice but to accept Ben's apologies, because not to do so would make her unreasonable – another one of *those girls*.

The oven timer started to beep, and Bo set her phone back

down on the worktop, leaving Ben's message unanswered. She removed the baking tray from the oven and gave it a gentle shake. The mixture didn't wobble, so she lifted the brownies carefully out of the tray and placed them gently onto a cooling rack, before picking up her phone to stare at Ben's text again. She recalled his brazen appraisal of the brunette with the clipboard, his contemptuous comment about the women from payroll and his casual dismissal of her suggestion that they go for a pizza. He had indeed been an arse, and it riled her that he thought an offhand apology by text would be sufficient to make up for it. She had begun to suspect that Ben's apologies were merely a means to an end – the price he needed to pay for her acquiescence – and that he didn't feel any genuine remorse for his behaviour at all. She leaned over the slab of brownie and inhaled its warm cocoa aroma. Perhaps, she thought ruefully, she had identified the problem: Ben wanted to have his cake and eat it.

Galvanised by the thought, she wiped her hands and picked up her phone. *Yes, you were*, she tapped out, pressing send before she could lose her nerve. Craving reassurance, Bo grabbed a knife from the wooden block on the counter and cut herself a generous slice from the corner. She took a big bite, feeling the crumbly top layer give way to the warm gooey middle. She closed her eyes as she chewed, allowing the taste and texture of the brownie to envelop her like a warm hug.

Momentarily soothed, she set about washing up the bowls

and utensils but, like drips from a leaky tap, her conviction that she had done the right thing began to drain away as she scrubbed and rinsed. On the worktop, her phone remained stubbornly silent. She paused to gaze through the grimy window, and the image of Ben's appalled face when she had stood up to leave came unbidden to her mind. She felt a sudden stab of panic to the stomach. Had her text been too harsh? He had apologised, after all, and maybe he really had had a shit week.

Only now did she recall her irritable mood when she left the office, that she had been tired and bad-tempered before she even stepped foot inside the speakeasy. The preening girls at the bar had irritated her long before she had noticed Ben checking them out over her shoulder. She felt queasy, as if the brownie she had just eaten was on the verge of coming back up. She was still cross with Ben for his snide dismissiveness and brazen disregard for her feelings but, in the cold light of day, she felt embarrassed about the way the evening had ended, and suspected that she might have overreacted.

'Shit,' she hissed, wiping her hands on a tea towel and grabbing her phone.

I was in a bad mood too, she typed. *Sorry for walking out.*

Almost immediately, three dots began to flash inside a speech bubble on her screen, indicating that Ben was typing. Nervously, she bit her lip, riven with doubt as to whether she had been mature to accept her share of the blame for the evening's disastrous denouement, or whether she had merely backed down for the sake of keeping the peace, just like she always did. Seconds later, the phone buzzed.

Never seen you throw a strop like that before, Blu-ray. Kind of sexy.

Bo felt a jab of some intense emotion, but whether it was relief, desire, or anger she wasn't entirely sure.

Later that morning, when she had showered, dressed, and eaten a second slice of brownie, Bo pulled on her trainers and coat and headed out. She slammed the front door shut and climbed the steps to the neglected area of crazy paving which passed for the house's front garden, although it functioned primarily as a storage area for the many wheelie bins and recycling boxes belonging to the property. In the four years that she and Kirsten had occupied the house's basement, Bo had frequently bumped into their neighbours when they were emptying their bins. They had exchanged nods and smiles in the way that seemed to be considered sufficient by Londoners, but neighbourly relations had never progressed further than polite civility, and she had never set foot inside any of the other flats.

The autumn sun was weak and watery, and low clouds scudded across the sky, throwing sections of the pavement into shade as she walked towards Holloway Road. There, she crossed at the pelican crossing and headed into the bright orange frontage of Sainsbury's. A blast of warm air from an overhead vent greeted her when she stepped through the sliding doors causing perspiration to prickle uncomfortably on the back of her neck.

As Bo loosened her scarf, a toddler with a shock of blonde curls wailed nearby, her back arched and limbs rigid as she tried to resist her mother's attempts to force her into the plastic seat of a supermarket trolley. The girl's mortified mother attempted to bribe her into compliance with a plastic pot full of grapes, which the toddler met with a howl of rage. The mother, with a shamefaced expression, whisked a packet of Iced Gems out of her bag, at which the howling infant immediately fell silent, holding out her hand to claim her prize. The now-quiescent toddler triumphantly shoved a fistful of tiny biscuits into her mouth and Bo smiled, recognising something of her own fondness for sugar and carbohydrate in times of distress.

Sainsbury's was full of the usual diverse crowd characteristic of her part of north London: Asian women in headscarves, moustachioed Turkish men, and stout Afro-Caribbean grandmothers, all of them wearing expressions suggesting they would rather be doing anything other than their weekly shop. Bo meandered between the aisles, absent-mindedly throwing bread, milk and other essentials into her basket whilst mulling over Ben's text. She wanted to strike the right tone with her reply, something light enough to show that she acknowledged her own share of the blame, whilst at the same time letting him know he was not off the hook entirely. Dropping a roll of cling film into her basket, she wondered whether Ben ever agonised to the same extent about the texts he sent her. She suspected not.

Back at the flat, she dumped the plastic shopping bags on the dining table and drew her phone from her bag.

Call that a strop? That was nothing ;-)

An anxious few moments followed, then the phone buzzed.

Is that a promise?

With the lines of communication open once again, they continued to text back and forth throughout the afternoon. When Ben asked what her what she was up to, she sent him a photo of her brownies, cut into neat squares and stacked in a pretty Cath Kidston cake tin (one of many items borrowed from her mother's kitchen).

Quality time with these bad boys, she typed. *I made them this morning.*

I had no idea you were a domestic goddess, Blu-ray, came Ben's response, followed quickly by, *Save some for me.*

Bo felt a glow of gratification. She had never told Ben about her passion for baking, assuming he would laugh and make some scornful allusion to her being a frumpy housewife.

I'll bring one into the office Monday, she promised.

Are you free for dinner after work? he replied. *How does Pizza Express sound?*

Bo smiled at her phone, feeling happier than she had done for weeks. Maybe this time, Ben had listened to her after all.

Chapter 5

On her journey into work the following morning, squeezed between an overweight tourist and a youth with white earphones which were leaking a frantic drumbeat, Bo felt cautiously optimistic about her evening's plans with Ben. She had devoted a great deal of thought to analysing the events of Friday night and their subsequent exchange of texts, and felt hopeful that Ben had, for once, taken her frustrations seriously. Why else would he have suggested going to Pizza Express? That, surely, had been intended as an olive branch.

As if to reward his efforts, Bo had selected one of the choicest brownies from the batch for Ben: a corner slice, with two sides of crispy edges. It was nestled inside her handbag, and every now and then she heard the rustle of its foil wrapping as the tube rattled on through the dark tunnel.

'Morning, Chloe. Good weekend?' she asked, stepping out of the lift into the Aspect reception area.

'*Epic* weekend, thanks,' Chloe replied brightly, her orange-tinged face lighting up. 'It was Gemma's twenty-first. We got a VIP table at Legends in Loughton. Her boyfriend's the bar manager. He laid on cocktails, champagne – the lot!' Chloe's heavily made-up eyes were wide to emphasise the magnanimity of the gesture. 'We were rat-arsed by nine o'clock!' she giggled, sliding her chair sideways to retrieve the day's mail from the far side of the curved desk. Bo mouthed a silent 'Wow!' to indicate that she, too, was impressed by Gemma's boyfriend's generosity.

Bo headed past reception into the office, noticing immediately that Ben's chair was empty and his computer was switched off. Trying to quell the stab of disappointment, she carried on to her own department, where she found Hayley perched on the corner of Natasha's desk. They were speaking in low, urgent voices.

'Have you heard?' Hayley demanded immediately upon catching sight of Bo. 'Tash thinks marketing is on the hit-list for redundancies.' Hayley was a gregarious twenty-three-year-old who had spent a year working on reception prior to her promotion to marketing assistant. She thrived on putting herself at the hub of office gossip and was permanently on the lookout for snippets of intelligence with which to alarm her co-workers. She was, in Bo's opinion, prone to over-dramatics.

'Oh, really?' Bo answered distractedly, her mind still on Ben's vacant desk. 'What makes you say that?'

'Something Claire said on Friday,' Natasha chipped in, with the grave air of one imparting worrying news, 'about how she was having to "fight our corner" with the directors.' Bo had been unzipping her coat but paused momentarily to glance at her colleagues. Natasha was an earnest-looking, studious sort of girl, and Bo was inclined to pay more heed to her concern than to Hayley's.

'Is Claire in today?' Bo asked, clocking the empty desk next to her own. Hayley shook her head and flicked her long dark hair off her shoulder.

'She phoned in earlier. She's working from home. Rosie's got chickenpox, *apparently*. Either that or she doesn't want to answer awkward questions.' She gave Bo a significant look. 'I'm shitting myself,' Hayley concluded bluntly. 'I was made redundant at my last place. If it happens again people are going to start thinking there's something wrong with me.' Bo began to unwind her scarf, conscious that her colleagues were both turned towards her expectantly, awaiting her opinion. Bo draped the scarf over the back of her chair and gave a slightly helpless shrug.

'I guess we just have to wait and see,' she said mildly. Hayley's wrinkled nose conveyed her dissatisfaction with Bo's response, and she turned back to Natasha. Bo dropped onto her swivel chair and started up her computer, keen to put Natasha and Hayley's preoccupation with redundancy out of her mind.

By half past nine, Ben had still not arrived at his desk, and a growing unease began to gnaw at the pit of Bo's stomach. At quarter to ten Bo heard her phone ring from the depths of her handbag. She retrieved it, to see an incoming call from Ben's number. Perplexed, she put the phone to her ear, her hand cupped over it for discretion.

'Hello,' she said quietly, acutely conscious of her colleagues' proximity on the other side of the desk-dividers.

'Hi, it's me.' Ben's voice had the tinny, echoing quality that indicated he was using his phone hands-free. She could hear the thrum of a car engine and the distant roar of passing traffic. 'Listen, babe, gotta take a rain check tonight,' Ben said, sounding stressed. 'The shit's hit the fan with the Milton Keynes client. Matt's there already. I'm on my way there now. I'll probably have to stay the night . . .' Ben trailed off and a pause followed, during which Bo stared blankly out through the window at the anonymous figures sitting at their desks in the building opposite. She wondered, idly, if any of the people she could see were also conducting a secret affair with a colleague.

'Right,' she replied flatly, sensing that he was waiting for her to say something.

'It's a pain in the arse,' Ben continued. 'Client thinks he knows more about the software than we do—' Ben broke off mid-sentence, then she heard him mutter 'Wanker', although whether he was talking about his client or another driver was unclear. 'And the M25 is a fucking nightmare.'

'Oh dear,' Bo murmured. She could hear the rhythmic click of the indicator and the surge of the engine, and could picture Ben impatiently pushing his foot to the floor of his nippy Audi. 'Don't worry, it's fine,' she replied in the blandest tone she could muster, with a glance at Hayley, who had returned to her seat directly opposite Bo's. A crackle, then the line abruptly went dead, whether because Ben had hung up or because he had lost signal she wasn't sure. She sat with the phone to her ear for a few seconds longer, before mumbling, 'Okay, bye,' down the silent line. Then she dropped her phone back inside her handbag, hearing the reproachful rustle of the foil-wrapped brownie as it landed.

She feigned interest in her monitor, inwardly raging with hurt and disappointment. She was simultaneously angry with Ben for cancelling and cross with herself for allowing him to do this to her, again. She had foolishly read some non-existent significance into his suggestion of dinner at Pizza Express, in the hope that it represented some sort of turning point in their relationship, the moment when they progressed from just having fun together to being a 'proper' couple. Whereas, in reality, it had been merely an off-the-cuff suggestion that he hoped would calm the waters between them. He had probably known he would need to cancel all along, she thought bitterly.

The morning wore on, and Bo's wretched mood persisted.

She was quiet and subdued, tapping away at her keyboard whilst achieving hardly anything.

'You okay, hon?' Hayley asked, placing a mug of tea on Bo's desk at eleven o'clock. 'I'm sure you'll be all right; they wouldn't let you go,' she said reassuringly, mistaking Bo's sullen expression for anxiety about her job.

'I'm fine, thanks,' Bo answered lightly, arranging her face into a pleasant smile. But inside, she was seething.

When an email pinged into her inbox from the head of human resources, asking if she could pop in for a chat, Bo did not feel unduly alarmed. If anything, she felt relieved to have an excuse to escape the concerned looks of her colleagues, not to mention the relentless, torturing thoughts about Ben that showed no signs of abating.

Half an hour later, Bo sat in a cubicle of the ladies' loos, dabbing her eyes with toilet paper. The HR manager, a jowly, middle-aged blonde called Cheryl, had worn a mask of professional sympathy as she broke the news to Bo that the company directors had taken the difficult decision to let her go. Bo had sat in blank-faced shock, hardly taking in a word that was said to her, cursing her stupidity for not paying more heed to her colleagues' warnings, and aware of the irony that only an hour earlier she had thought a cancelled date with Ben was the worst of her worries. With a voice tinged with professional regret, Cheryl had reassured Bo that this was not a sacking and explained that a company-wide reorganisation meant that Bo's current role was no longer required. Financial conditions meant that all departments would need to make efficiencies, she added.

'Efficiencies?' Bo had repeated dumbly, feeling her chin start to wobble. Cheryl had tilted her head sympathetically and in a deft, well-practised movement, passed a box of tissues across the desk.

After allowing Bo a few moments to compose herself, Cheryl had pressed the tips of her fingers together and glanced down at the open lever-arch folder in front of her. Bo tried to concentrate as she listened to the details of her redundancy, but her mind had started to race with thoughts about her future, how long it might take her to find another job, and whether she would be able to afford her rent payments. Cheryl rambled on about severance packages, notice pay, and share option refunds, but the words were like white noise to Bo's ears.

'And we will of course, provide you with a good reference,' Cheryl concluded, with an encouraging smile.

'Thank you,' Bo replied meekly, at a loss for anything else to say.

Cheryl closed her lever-arch file and handed Bo a copy of the severance agreement. 'If you have any questions, do just pop in,' she said, coming around the side of the desk to steer Bo by the elbow towards the door.

'Okay, thanks,' answered Bo obediently.

Bo allowed herself ten minutes of hot, silent tears in the toilet cubicle, before blowing her nose on a strip of toilet paper and telling herself sternly to get a grip. Worrying about her future would have to wait till she got home. Her immediate priority was not to embarrass herself in front of her colleagues. She took a deep breath and unlocked the cubicle door, peering out gingerly to make sure the bathroom was empty, before stepping up to the row of washbasins to check her reflection in the wall mirror. Her eyes were red and puffy, her make-up had run, and there were pink blotches across her neck. She splashed cold water on her face and did her best to wipe the smudges of mascara from underneath her eyes.

'You're fucking kidding me!' said Hayley. In spite of Bo's efforts in the bathroom, Hayley had spotted the telltale signs that Bo had been crying before she had even reached her desk, and had sprung to her feet and practically pinned Bo against a filing cabinet. A dramatic gasp had greeted Bo's announcement that she would be leaving the company on Friday.

'I can't *believe* they've let you go, Bo. I thought you were the safest of all of us!' Hayley said, her mouth forming an O of scandalised outrage. Bo couldn't help but think that Hayley's shock seemed disproportionate, given her certainty a few hours earlier that redundancies in their department were inevitable. 'I mean, you've been here longer than either me or Tash. Doesn't that count for anything?' Hayley ploughed on, looking over her shoulder at Natasha, who was hovering behind her, looking grave.

'Obviously not,' Bo murmured bitterly, trying to compose her face into a stoical mask to conceal her discomfort.

'I knew something was up when Claire phoned in,' Hayley muttered conspiratorially. 'I'm sure Rosie's already had chickenpox. She just didn't want to be around when you got the news. Guilty conscience.' Hayley's eyes narrowed in disgust, but Bo felt numb. Even if Hayley was right about Claire's absence, Bo didn't have the energy to feel aggrieved about it.

'I think I'd better get on. I've got to make a start on my handover notes,' she said, faintly apologetically. With a final pitying pout and lung-crushing hug from Hayley, Bo was released from the filing cabinet. She cast a surreptitious glance around the office on her way back to her desk. All around her, heads were lowered and keyboards were being tapped. Everyone seemed absorbed in their work, but the uncharacteristic lull in conversation and averted eyes merely confirmed Bo's suspicion that everyone within earshot had heard her conversation with Hayley, and that news of her redundancy would be common knowledge within seconds. Cheeks burning, Bo sat down and busied herself with sorting through the contents of her in-tray. Her one consolation was that at least Ben hadn't been in the office to witness her humiliation.

That evening, Bo and Kirsten sat on the sagging tartan-print sofa in their living room, a bottle of Cabernet Sauvignon and two glasses on the coffee table in front of them.

'Oh, Kirst, it was *excruciating*,' Bo groaned, taking a sip of wine, while Kirsten glanced over Bo's contract and severance agreement with a professional lawyer's eye. 'Can you believe I actually *thanked* the HR manager?' She cringed. 'Like I was *grateful* to her or something. I mean, what kind of loser says "thank you" for being fired?' Kirsten looked up from the paperwork to give Bo a sympathetic smile.

'Don't stress about it, Bo. I'm sure that's what everyone does, in those circumstances.' Her eyes returned to the page. 'And besides, you haven't been fired, you've been made redundant. Big difference.'

'Of course,' Bo said drily. 'At least they've promised me a *good reference*. That'll make all the difference.' Bo slumped listlessly against the sofa arm, cradling her wine glass between both hands.

Bo's rather maudlin mood was interrupted by a distant rumble of drums followed by the *EastEnders* theme tune reverberating through the ceiling from the upstairs flat. Their neighbours had bought a state-of-the-art television in the summer. Bo had seen the set arrive in a John Lewis lorry one Saturday morning in August, and her heart had sunk slightly at the sight of the multiple boxes of speakers and sound bars being carried up the steps to the front door. Since then, Bo and Kirsten had become intimately familiar with their neighbours' viewing habits, which centred largely on soap operas and medical dramas.

'Well,' Kirsten said at last, flipping the stapled A4 sheets back into position, and pushing her glasses back onto her head, 'the good news is, what with your share options refund, redundancy and severance pay, you could be in line for a decent pay-off.'

'Just as well,' replied Bo morosely, leaning forwards to slosh more Cabernet Sauvignon into her glass. 'It might have to last me for months. I can't see another job coming along before Christmas.'

'You don't know that,' Kirsten said, doing her best to sound upbeat.

'Yes, I do,' Bo countered. 'Another couple of weeks and we'll be into Christmas party season. Nobody will be doing interviews or making job offers until well into January.'

Kirsten sipped her wine in supportive silence. 'Have you told Ben?' she asked tentatively.

Bo inhaled sharply. 'Not yet. He was in Milton Keynes all day.'

In truth, Bo had considered calling Ben from the toilet cubicle, in the hope that he would know what to say to console her, or even just be willing to listen to and reassure her. She had pulled her phone from her bag and found his number, but then she had remembered their conversation that morning as he drove to Milton Keynes, his stressed, impatient tone, and the blasé way he had cancelled their dinner plans. How would he react if she interrupted him at his client's office, tearfully distraught, to tell him she had been made redundant? At best, he would be evasive and brittle, telling her not to worry and that he would call her back later. More likely, he would screen her call and let it go to voicemail. She had stared at his number on her phone, until eventually the screen went dark, and then she had dropped the phone back inside her bag.

'I dare say he'll find out soon enough anyway,' Bo said, resigned to the fact that she would be the subject of office gossip for the next few days.

'Wouldn't you rather tell him in person?' Kirsten asked tactfully. Bo leaned back against the sofa and took a long slug of wine.

'I'm not sure I would,' she replied. 'He's all about having fun, isn't he? Consoling your girlfriend through redundancy wouldn't be many people's idea of fun. Least of all Ben's.'

Chapter 6

Bo stood in front of the Aspect reception desk, a fake smile on her lips and a bunch of flowers under her arm. Her colleagues milled around, clutching bottles of beer and watching patiently as she peeled open the bright yellow envelope Claire had just handed her. *Sorry You're Leaving*, the card announced in a sparkly font. The inside of the card was scribbled over with the bland farewell messages from her co-workers: 'Best of luck for the future'; 'We'll miss you'; 'Keep in touch, Bo!'.

'Thanks everyone,' Bo murmured, taking out the John Lewis voucher which had been tucked inside the card. The ceremonial presentation of card, flowers and voucher took place, as was office tradition, at six o'clock on Bo's last day. It was the final hurdle to be faced at the end of a week which had seemed to drag on for ever, managing to be both mind-numbingly boring (thanks to the drafting of a comprehensive handover document) and an exercise in forbearance, as she endured the well-meant but occasionally misjudged sympathy of her colleagues.

Bo had been dreading the leaving do all week, and the prospect of having to smile politely and reassure her colleagues that she was sure everything would be fine, whilst knowing that they were all thinking, *Thank God it wasn't me.* Now the moment had arrived, she was relying on the company's beer supply to help her get through it, and was already on to her fourth bottle by the time Claire said a few words of thanks and thrust the card and flowers into her hands.

From her vantage point by the reception desk, Bo had a clear view of Ben. He was standing by the water cooler amid a group of fellow account managers. He was sipping from a bottle of Sol with his back to her, although every now and then she caught him glancing over his shoulder in her direction. Things had been tense between them since his return to the office on Wednesday. As she had anticipated, news of her redundancy had reached him in Milton Keynes, and he had texted her from his client's office on Monday afternoon:

Just heard you've been culled, Blu-ray. Gutted. Won't be the same in the office without you.

Even though she had told herself not to expect much by way of support from Ben, Bo nevertheless felt a twinge of irritation at the glib tone of his message which, as she dutifully worked on her handover notes, she duly nursed into something more akin to rage. It was not just his flippancy that riled her, but the fact that Ben seemed only to be thinking about her leaving in terms of how it would affect him, rather than what it meant for her. She left the text unanswered and, when he returned to the office the following day, she pointedly avoided him, ignoring his intranet messages and walking away if he attempted to follow her into the kitchen or the lift. Sensing her frostiness, Ben had reacted in kind, and by Thursday they were in a mutual sulk and had ceased to communicate at all. Now he seemed determined to spend the duration of her leaving do with his back to her.

Bo stood in front of the curved reception desk, flanked by Hayley and Chloe.

'Account management might be next in line, apparently,' Bo heard Hayley say at her shoulder, and her attention instantly snapped back to her surroundings.

'Who'd'ya think'll go?' Chloe said, her eyes wide. Hayley, relishing the role of office know-it-all, tossed her dark hair back over her shoulders and glanced around to make sure no one was within earshot.

'My money's on Charlotte,' Hayley whispered. 'She lost a client last month.' Bo's eyes flicked back to the cluster of account managers around Ben. Charlotte was standing to his right, blissfully unaware that her professional shortcomings and possible redundancy were being discussed just a few feet away. She was a mousey, insipid-looking girl who had joined the company a year earlier as a junior account manager. Bo had never really paid her much attention, finding her timid demeanour made her easy to overlook.

'Poor Charlotte!' Chloe sighed pityingly. Then Hayley's eyes narrowed and she leaned closer in. Bo and Chloe instinctively mirrored her body language, until all three heads were almost touching.

'I know,' Hayley agreed, 'and just as things were getting interesting on the office romance front, too.' There was a glint of mischief in her eye.

'What do you mean, interesting?' Chloe asked breathily, her stencilled eyebrows climbing up her forehead. Hayley smirked, gratified by her response.

'According to my sources,' she whispered gleefully, 'Ben made a pass at her.'

'At Charlotte?' Chloe gasped. Hayley nodded. Bo looked between the two of them, feeling as if the temperature in the room had suddenly dropped.

'When?' Bo asked in the mildest, most disinterested voice she could muster.

'Tuesday,' Hayley intoned sombrely, before taking a swig from her beer. 'While they were staying at that Travelodge in Milton Keynes.'

'In Milton Keynes?' Bo repeated dumbly. She had not been aware that Charlotte had been in Milton Keynes – she was certain Ben hadn't mentioned it.

'I know, not very glamorous, is it? Anyway,' Hayley went

on triumphantly, 'she friend-zoned him. Not interested, apparently.' Hayley grinned and Chloe gave a short cackling laugh.

Bo had a strange feeling of dislocation, as if the floor had just shifted beneath her and she wasn't sure if she was still upright. She stared across the room at Charlotte and felt as if she was seeing her with fresh eyes. Charlotte was standing between Ben and Matt. She looked subdued and faintly uncomfortable, and kept glancing at the clock above the door as if she was wondering how soon it would be acceptable to leave. Bo forced herself to try and appraise Charlotte's looks from a male perspective. Although she was undeniably at the mousey end of the spectrum, Bo had to admit that she was not *unattractive,* per se. As if sensing she was being watched, Charlotte glanced sideways and caught Bo staring at her. She gave Bo a vapid smile, to which Bo responded with a slow half-nod of acknowledgement.

'You okay, Bo?' Hayley sounded concerned. Bo could feel a flush beginning to spread from her neck to her cheeks.

'I think I might have had too many of these,' Bo said, swinging her empty beer bottle by the neck. Chloe snorted.

'Easily done, babe, easily done,' she said, understandingly. 'What you need is a Maccy D's on your way home, to line your stomach,' she advised.

'Actually, I think I'd better make a move, I'm not feeling very well.' Hayley and Chloe exchanged a worried look but Bo was resolute. Her face was burning and she had an urgent need to escape the office as quickly as possible, to be away from the pity and concern of her soon-to-be-ex colleagues, to digest in privacy the revelation that had just been sprung on her.

She sensed heads turning as she pulled on her coat and gathered her things. She knew it was bad form to pull a disappearing act at her own leaving do, but she couldn't face doing a tour of farewell hugs, not least because to do so she would have to acknowledge Ben and Charlotte. Instead, she bade an apologetic goodbye to Hayley and Chloe, tucked her bunch of flowers under her elbow and slipped out of the office.

Waiting for the lift doors to close, she caught sight of Ben beside the water cooler. He had broken off his conversation, and looked stunned. She held his gaze as the metal doors slid closed, then as the lift whirred into motion she squeezed her eyes shut, fighting the tears that she had been holding back all week, tears of frustration, anger and humiliation all rolled into one.

'Were you going to leave without saying goodbye?' Ben asked, as the lift doors opened on the ground floor. He was out of breath and beads of sweat had formed on his brow.

'I didn't want to interrupt your conversation with Charlotte,' she said snappishly, stepping past him and striding through the foyer towards the entrance doors. He jogged a few paces to catch up with her, and she felt a twinge of gratification that Ben was still panting from the exertion of racing down four flights of stairs. 'G'night, Bill,' she said sweetly to the grey-haired security guard perched on a stool behind the bank of monitors. He nodded amiably, and raised one arm from his bulging belly in a waving gesture. At the office's heavy glass and metal doors she fumbled with her flowers and bag, but Ben reached her side just in time to pull the door open for her. 'Thanks,' she mumbled begrudgingly.

Outside, a light drizzle was falling and the night air was chilly, but the street had the unmistakable buzz of a Friday night in the West End. Hoots of laughter and the clink of glasses drifted over from a pub further along the street, where a crowd of suited workers had gathered on the pavement to smoke cigarettes in the warm glow of a paraffin heater. Bo pulled the zip of her coat up to her chin and started walking.

'What was that supposed to mean?' Ben asked, stepping in front of Bo on the pavement in order to block her path. He was wearing his open-necked shirt, the sleeves still rolled up, and when he raised his hand to push his hair out of his eyes, Bo noticed goose-bumps on his forearm.

'It means, wouldn't you rather be back inside with Charlotte?' she repeated in a slow, deliberate voice, as if talking to a small child.

'With Charlotte?' he echoed incredulously. His surprise appeared genuine and she felt a wobble of uncertainty – was it possible Hayley had made a mistake? But she decided that, having gone this far, she might as well continue.

'The whole office knows what happened in Milton Keynes,' she persisted, determined not to betray her doubt. Ben looked gobsmacked. He gave a short, mirthless laugh. 'Nothing happened in Milton Keynes.'

'That's not what I heard,' hissed Bo. A chorus of blokeish laughter heralded the appearance of a group of leery young men coming along the pavement towards them.

'Mind out,' Ben muttered, taking Bo by the arm and leading her into the relative shelter of a recessed doorway further along the street. 'Look,' he said, fixing her with an intent stare, 'I don't know who's been gossiping, or what you've heard, but I can guarantee it's bullshit.' His gaze was steady, and Bo felt her nerve wavering once more.

'So you didn't try it on with Charlotte, while you were in Milton Keynes?' she asked, figuring there was nothing to lose by being blunt.

'With Charlotte? Are you kidding?' he replied. Then he laughed, but there seemed to be genuine affection in his eyes. 'Is that why you've been ignoring me all week?' he asked.

'No,' Bo admitted. 'That was because you cancelled our trip to Pizza Express,' she said morosely. Ben's eyes creased in amusement and Bo found herself trying to stifle a smile at how childish her words had sounded. 'I only heard about Charlotte just now,' she added meekly.

'Let me, guess. Hayley?' he asked.

She nodded, feeling a pang of guilt for her disloyalty to her former colleague. Her head was foggy from the beers she had downed, and she was aware that the emotion of the week was beginning to catch up with her. She felt drained, confused, and on the verge of tears.

Ben lifted a hand to stroke a stray strand of hair away from her face. 'You shouldn't believe everything you hear. Especially not from some shit-stirring assistant with nothing better to do than spread rumours.'

'Why didn't you tell me that Charlotte was there, too?' Bo asked, as if grasping for evidence that suggested he had something to hide.

'Why would I mention it?' he replied, baffled. He placed his fingertips beneath her chin and tilted her face up so that he could look her in the eye. 'It was me, Matt and Charlotte. We spent the day slogging our guts out for an arsey client, then went back to a third-rate hotel, had a couple of drinks in the bar, then went to bed. Separately.' His face softened. 'Besides,' he said, a tender smile playing around his lips, 'why would I make a move on Charlotte? She's got nothing on you.'

Bo felt the warmth of Ben's hand on her face, and part of her wanted nothing more than to lean into his arms in the damp doorway and let him comfort her. She longed to believe him, but from somewhere in the recesses of her mind a voice urged caution, reminding her that she was tired, a little drunk, and emotionally overwrought. Even if Ben was telling the truth about Charlotte, did that excuse the way he had treated her over the past week?

'Shall we go and get something to eat?' Ben asked softly. 'Pizza, perhaps?' He gave a boyish smile, but his face looked orange in the neon glow of a nearby street lamp.

'Actually, I think I might just head home,' she said after a moment's silence. 'It's been a long week. I think I need an early night.' She dropped her head and adjusted the bunch of flowers under her arm. He took a step back, and there was no mistaking his hurt feelings.

'Okay, if you're sure,' he said matter-of-factly, crossing his arms in front of his body to rub them. 'It's freezing out here,' he added, with a look which brought to mind a schoolboy waiting to be dismissed at the end of a lesson.

'You'd better get back inside, you'll catch pneumonia if you stay out here any longer,' she said, taking the hint. Ben smiled and leaned forward to give her a kiss. His lips felt cold and dry. Then he turned and dashed back along the pavement towards the office, bounded up the stone steps and disappeared inside. Bo watched until the door had swung shut behind him, then she pulled her handbag more securely onto her shoulder, stepped out from the doorway, and began to make her way slowly towards the tube.

Chapter 7

Bo arrived home to find the flat unlit and empty. Clutching a boxed pizza she had picked up at the local takeaway, she grabbed a bottle of wine and a glass from the kitchen and went through to the living room. There, she collapsed onto the sofa, poured herself a large glass, and opened the cardboard lid. The pizza was oily and unappetising but, with the Shiraz to wash it down, Bo found the meal was palatable enough. Soon a pleasing numbness started to spread through her, softening the painful recollections of the evening's events, and by the time the pizza was finished and the bottle was almost empty, Bo had convinced herself that she didn't care whether Ben *had* made a pass at Charlotte in Milton Keynes.

When Kirsten let herself into the flat at just gone midnight, she found Bo passed out on the sofa, the empty wine bottle by her feet and the grease-stained pizza box still open on her lap.

'Been partying by yourself, I see,' Kirsten teased, shaking Bo by the shoulder. Bo groggily pushed herself upright.

''S'my leaving do,' she slurred, rubbing her eyes, 'I'll do what I like.'

'Did you speak to Ben?' Kirsten asked, helping to lever Bo off the sofa and onto her feet. Bo's mouth twisted.

'I did. Says izn't true. But 'e's prob'ly with Charlotte now. Eating *pizza*.' Bo emitted a hysterical giggle.

'What isn't true? Who's Charlotte?' Kirsten asked, confused.

'She'z in Milton Keynes too, but's got *nothing* on me, 'pparently.' Bo let go of Kirsten's arm momentarily to reach for her phone on the coffee table, almost losing her balance and falling back onto the sofa in the process. Kirsten deftly grabbed her by the elbow, pulled her upright once more, and began to lead her slowly towards her bedroom.

'Tell me about it in the morning,' Kirsten said soothingly. 'I think you need to get to bed.'

'Fucking Milton Keynes,' Bo muttered as she shuffled compliantly down the hallway.

Kirsten deposited Bo on her bed and fetched her a glass of water and a packet of ibuprofen.

'Thanks, Kirst,' Bo mumbled, shoving a box of tissues onto the floor in order to make room on the bedside table for her glass.

'No problem. Get some sleep,' Kirsten said, closing the bedroom door softly behind her.

Bo remained slumped on the edge of her bed, watching the furniture in the room swim back and forth in front of her eyes, before allowing her body to topple sideways. With a groan, she swung her legs up onto the mattress and within seconds she sank into the blissful oblivion of sleep.

The next morning, she woke with a pounding head, stale mouth and contact lenses that felt welded to her eyes. She moaned with discomfort, as the realisation sank in that she was still dressed in yesterday's work clothes. She gingerly groped at the bedside table for the glass of water and propped herself up on her elbow to take several long gulps and swallow two ibuprofen. The movement made her head spin and she dropped back onto her pillow and lay motionless for several minutes, shielding her eyes with her forearm. It was not until she picked up her phone and saw the notification message that she remembered she had promised to go to her parents' house for lunch.

A couple of hours later, Bo was sitting on a train bound for Buckinghamshire. She had not yet broken the news of her redundancy to her parents, telling herself that it would be better to tell them face to face, but now that the moment was approaching, she was beginning to regret not having laid the groundwork for her announcement. She slumped low in her seat and allowed the rocking motion of the train to soothe her throbbing head, and let her eyes wander across the vista of grotty estates and industrial buildings that was sliding by outside the scratched train window.

Drinking alone was something she had never done before and it felt vaguely seedy and shameful; it was something she associated with lonely alcoholics rather than cosmopolitan twenty-somethings. She rested her forehead against the cold glass of the window and wondered whether her drinking habits were something else she ought to worry about, as further evidence of her quarter-life crisis.

Against her will, she found her thoughts shifting to the reason for last night's drinking: Hayley's gossipy revelation about Milton Keynes, and Ben's subsequent denial. Although, he had seemed genuinely affronted by the accusation, and his insistence that he, Charlotte and Matt had simply shared a few comradely drinks after a difficult day sounded plausible. Now that Bo had left Aspect, however, it would be virtually impossible for her to find out the truth. Any enquiry to her former colleagues about this particular piece of office gossip would give away her personal involvement.

The train rattled on, and the urban vista of north London gradually gave way to the well-kept gardens and low-rise housing of outer suburbia, and eventually to the fields of green belt beyond the M25. Leaving the city behind, Bo tried to put thoughts of Ben and Charlotte out of her mind in order to prepare for the task ahead.

*

'Here she is.' It was her father's habitual greeting, and he didn't deviate from tradition when he opened the wooden front door of their Tudor-style house. Clive Hazlehurst was a benevolent-looking fifty-something with greying hair and a physique that betrayed his penchant for a gentle round of golf followed by several more rounds of drinks at the club bar.

'Hi, Dad,' Bo said, giving him an affectionate peck on the cheek. She took her coat off and removed her shoes, accustomed to her mother's horror of finding dirty footprints on her beige carpets.

'Your sister's here,' her father said, leading her down the hallway to the kitchen. 'She's brought the twins,' he added, in a slightly strained tone.

Following her father into the kitchen, Bo was met by the sight of her parents' cat tearing towards her, its tail fluffed in alarm, hotly pursued by her shrieking niece and nephew. Bo stood aside to allow the whirlwind of rampaging toddlers and terrified cat safe passage into the hallway. Seconds later she heard a tumult of paws and feet as all three scrambled up the stairway to the bedrooms, where the cat would escape by vanishing underneath one of the beds.

'Amelie! Freddy! Careful on the stairs!' her sister Lauren called wearily, emerging from the kitchen in their wake, with a resigned 'here we go again' expression.

Lauren was older than Bo by two years, taller and with

hair the same honey-blonde shade as Bo's but without its tendency to curl (a cause of envy in Bo since childhood). The sisters had been close in their youth but their lives had diverged in adulthood, with Lauren giving up her job as an office manager to start a family in a leafy part of Berkshire near to her husband's office in Reading.

In some respects, Bo envied the financial and emotional stability of her sister's lifestyle, but at times she felt that Lauren had somehow *opted out* by giving up her career to become a housewife and full-time mother. Bo sometimes found it difficult to disguise her irritation when Lauren talked about the challenge of finding a good builder for their next phase of home improvement, or the dilemma of whether she ought to buy the twins an iPad each or make them share. Bo knew it was disloyal, but she couldn't help but feel that her sister had it easy. Although she had never said anything out loud, she sometimes suspected that Lauren knew that was how she felt, and that it had driven a wedge between them.

Nevertheless, Bo felt a glimmer of relief that Lauren and the twins were present, if only to deflect some of the attention that might otherwise fall, exclusively, on Bo's announcement.

The kitchen smelled mouth-wateringly of roast beef, and pans of vegetables were steaming and bubbling on the Aga's hotplates. 'You'll have a glass of Rioja, won't you, Bo?' Clive asked, uncorking a bottle of red wine at the granite-topped kitchen island.

'Maybe just one,' Bo murmured, knowing that wine was the last thing she should be drinking after last night's exploits, but also that it would undeniably help her cope with what was to come.

The prospect of telling her parents about her redundancy was not one she relished. In truth, a part of Bo would have liked nothing more than to open up and admit to her parents that she had spent five years working in a sector that she had never really felt passionate about, doing a job that had ceased to challenge her a long time ago, but that now she had lost it she felt rejected and rudderless, as if she had just been cast out into open seas in a dinghy. But she knew that if she did so, the price would be to endure her parents' alarm and anxiety that she was not coping with the stresses of living and working in London. She had resolved that she would rather put on a brave face and play down her own fears than have to endure that.

'Hello, darling,' her mother said, stepping away from the Aga to give Bo a hug. A cooking apron covered her loosely tailored trousers and silky blouse, in Bo's opinion an unnecessarily formal ensemble for a family lunch at home, but then Barbara had always instilled in her daughters the importance of *making an effort*. (Bo was fairly confident that her mother would rather lose a limb than be seen wearing jeans.)

'Something smells good,' Bo said appreciatively, her grumbling stomach reminding her that, other than coffee and ibuprofen, she had consumed nothing all morning. Bo picked up the crystal wine glass which her father had placed in front of her and took a sip, appreciating, even in her hung-over state, the wine's rounded, full-bodied flavour.

'Is Nick here?' Bo asked, glancing across the open-plan kitchen to the dining table, which was meticulously laid for lunch, complete with folded linen napkins, side-plates, and a china tray bearing a selection of condiments in bowls, each one with its own tiny silver spoon. Nick was Lauren's husband. He worked as something in insurance, and Bo had always found him on the pompous side of pleasant ('thirty-four going on sixty-four', was how she had once described him to Ben), so she felt slightly relieved when her mother answered in the negative, explaining that Nick was play-ing golf in Newbury. At least, Bo thought gratefully, she wouldn't have to endure her brother-in-law's advice when she broke the news of her redundancy.

Over lunch, the task of persuading the twins to remain seated at the table long enough to eat their meal, and to refrain from smearing food across the tablecloth and chairs, demanded everyone's attention. Bo allowed her father to top up her wine glass which, combined with the deliciousness of her mother's roast beef and the low autumn sunshine stream-ing through the conservatory windows, induced a relaxed state, verging on sleepy. It was not until Bo was sitting on the Liberty-print sofa of her parents' comfortable living room, cradling a cup of coffee on her lap, that she realised she could put off her task no longer. The children had been released into the garden to play on the ageing swing and slide set that dated from Bo's own childhood, and Lauren had gone out to supervise them.

Bo took a deep breath. 'So, anyway, I was made redundant this week.'

In the pause that followed, Bo was aware of the ticking of the gold-plated carriage clock on the mantelpiece, and a distant shriek from one of the children in the garden beyond the French doors. Barbara, who was perched on the edge of the sofa cushion with her coffee cup halfway to her mouth, took a deep breath which verged on a gasp. Bo knew what was coming.

'Redundant?' her mother repeated, returning her coffee cup with slow precision to its saucer. 'But . . . You've worked there for five years. Surely they can't do that?' Barbara worked as an administrator at a primary school. In her mind, if you worked hard, were punctual and polite, there was no reason to think that your services might no longer be required.

'Yes, they can, Mum,' Bo demurred, feeling the first knot of discomfort in the pit of her stomach. 'They haven't fired me,' she clarified, aware that her voice was becoming brittle.

'They're not saying I've done anything wrong. They're just ... restructuring the organisation, that's all.'

'But, why would they ...' Her mother trailed off helplessly. Although Barbara had always professed pride in Bo for being what she termed a *career girl,* Bo had always sensed her unspoken anxiety that the pressures of living and working in London might prove to be *too much* for her daughter. There had always been an anxious tone to her questions about work, or the flat, as if she was convinced that, sooner or later, something was bound to go wrong. For five years, Bo had been able to reassure her mother that everything was fine and that she was still gainfully employed. But the look of panic in Barbara's eyes said, as clearly as if she had spoken the words out loud, *I knew this would happen.*

'Clive?' she bleated, shooting her husband a look which communicated that paternal intervention was required to help deal with this crisis. Bo*'s* father placed his coffee on the occasional table beside his chair with careful deliberation.

'Don't panic, Barbara,' he said quietly, before turning towards Bo with an expression of benign concern. 'If you like, Boughay,' he began solicitously, 'I'll put out feelers at work on Monday. One of the PAs is retiring soon. I could put in a good word for you.' Bo's heart sank. The thought of being the personal assistant to one of her dad's cardigan-wearing colleagues made her want to crawl under her duvet and never come out.

'Thanks, Dad, but I'm not that desperate,' she replied, but the hurt look on her father's face immediately made her regret her snarky tone. 'I mean, thank you but – I don't think that'll be necessary. I only finished at Aspect yesterday. There's plenty of time to find something else.' Another silence, during which Barbara continued to stare urgently at Clive in a way that conveyed her conviction that Bo had failed to grasp the seriousness of her situation and needed to have it spelled out to her.

'It's all right, Mum, really. I should be in line for a decent pay-off. I'll be okay,' Bo said defensively. Her mother's thinly veiled panic, although not unexpected, was beginning to rile her. 'Actually, I'm thinking of going travelling,' Bo heard herself say. She knew it was a peevish, provocative comment – travelling was not something that had even crossed her mind before now – but she was beginning to resent the way she was having to reassure her mother, and her tongue had been loosened by her father's Rioja.

Barbara's eyes widened and her mouth dropped open. 'Travelling? Where? For how long?'

'Don't know yet,' Bo replied airily.

At that moment, the French doors swung open and a gust of chilly air heralded the return of Lauren and the twins. As they noisily set about unzipping their coats and peeling off their gloves, Barbara jumped up to help remove the children's shoes before they could tread mud and dirt all over the carpet, giving Bo a welcome respite from her concerned scrutiny. Once the twins were disrobed of their outerwear and occupied with juice cartons and electronic devices, Barbara returned to her seat.

'Bo's been made redundant,' she said in a stage whisper as Lauren dropped onto the sofa beside her. Bo glowered into her coffee and braced herself for her sister's pity. Given Lauren's comfortable, cosseted lifestyle, Bo could not expect any genuine empathy or understanding for her situation.

'Oh, no,' Lauren murmured, leaning sideways to rescue a half-full juice carton which was about to topple off the sofa arm.

'It's okay, really,' Bo said, with a tight smile. 'They've got to make efficiencies across the company; it's not just me they're letting go. And I'll get a decent redundancy package.' The stock phrases of reassurance rolled easily off her tongue.

'She's thinking of going travelling!' her mother continued, unwilling to let the subject drop.

'Who with, Bo?' Lauren asked, turning to face her sister with an expression of curiosity.

'On my own, probably,' she replied lightly.

Lauren continued to look at her sister shrewdly, prompting Bo self-consciously to raise her cup to her lips even though the dregs of coffee lying at the bottom were now stone cold. It was a fair question, but it rankled that her sister had assumed that she would have to go travelling *with* somebody. Was Lauren so entrenched in the married-with-kids mindset that she couldn't contemplate the thought of a woman travelling alone? Bo was disappointed but not surprised, thinking peevishly that there was only so much solidarity she could expect from someone who didn't work, and whose husband earned enough to pay for a fortnight in Florida plus a week's skiing every year.

She wondered whether the question had, in fact, been Lauren's way of trying to flush out her romantic status. Bo had never mentioned Ben to her family. It wasn't that she didn't think they would like him – in fact, she knew her parents would be charmed by his social poise and well-spoken confidence – but Ben had never expressed any interest in her family or desire to be introduced to them. And, given the semi-secret nature of their relationship, it had never felt appropriate to suggest a meeting. She had decided early on that the simplest thing was not to mention Ben's existence to her family at all.

Feeling that whatever she said was probably going to make the situation worse, Bo sank into a sullen silence, so her parents had no choice but to let the subject of her redundancy and travel plans drop. She submitted to another hour or so of small-talk before getting up to leave at five o'clock, insisting that she had a train to catch.

'You know, you could always stay the night,' Barbara said with a meaningful look as Bo pulled on her coat. Bo smiled through gritted teeth and submitted to the hug which accompanied the offer.

'Thanks, Mum, but I've got stuff to do tomorrow,' she replied. In fact, there was nowhere she needed to be, but were Bo to agree to spend the night, in light of her recent announcement, she would feel obscurely as if she was admitting defeat, and that somehow this was the thin end of the wedge. Bo might not have any clear sense of what she was going to do next, but she was certain that she was not ready to give up on her London life yet.

Chapter 8

Although the afternoon spent with her family had been tense, it had motivated Bo to prove them wrong, and to show that she was able to cope with the adversity that life had thrown at her.

'What are you doing up?' Kirsten asked through a mouthful of Cheerios, as Bo walked past the sitting room at a quarter to eight on Monday morning.

'Lots to do today,' Bo trilled, not stopping on her way to the bathroom.

Showered and dressed, Bo sat down with tea and toast at the glass dining table which pretty much filled one side of the living-cum-dining room. As she chewed, her eyes wandered across the dusty surfaces around her, and she resolved that her first job of the day would be to clean the flat from top to bottom. Once breakfast was cleared away, she delved underneath the kitchen sink for the various sponges, cloths and sprays she needed, then pulled on the musty pair of Marigold gloves she found lurking at the back beneath the water pipes.

The furniture in the flat had been provided by the land-lord and looked, Bo thought, as if it had been purchased in a hurry at a jumble sale. The bulky tartan sofa filled one wall of the living area and, on the other side of the handsome cast-iron fireplace, stood a rattan armchair which looked as if it belonged in a conservatory and an old-fashioned pine side-board complete with grooved shelves for displaying plates. When they first moved in, the girls had done their best to personalise the place with accessories purchased during a trip to Ikea in Kirsten's parents' Volvo estate. But the addition of their brightly coloured rugs, prints and soft furnishings merely added to the flat's bizarre, mismatched appearance (or 'eclectic aesthetic', as Kirsten somewhat optimistically described it). After a few months, however, Bo had ceased to care about the décor. What with work and her social life, she was rarely in the flat long enough to let it bother her.

Bo turned the radio on and set to work. There was some-thing surprisingly rewarding about spending a morning cleaning. It was certainly more pleasurable than the Monday team meeting, she told herself with a glimmer of satisfac-tion. After a morning of dusting, wiping and hoovering, however, Bo's back ached and her hands reeked of sweaty rubber, and she concluded that she had reached the limit of her domesticity.

She made herself a sandwich for lunch then opened up her laptop on the glass table and spent a couple of hours updating her CV, playing around with different fonts and layouts until she had produced a resumé which made her sound professional, diligent, and eminently employable. She rewarded herself with a cup of tea and an episode of *Countdown*.

'Bloody hell, you've been busy!' Kirsten exclaimed when she got home from work that evening and saw the gleaming surfaces and track marks of the vacuum cleaner on the rug. 'I don't think I've ever seen this place so clean. Unemployment clearly suits you,' she teased.

'Not for much longer, hopefully,' Bo replied with a nervous laugh.

'You've earned a glass of wine,' Kirsten said, pulling a bottle out of the plastic carrier emblazoned with the logo of their nearest off-licence, but Bo shook her head.

'Nope, not for me. I'm detoxing.' Kirsten's eyebrows shot up.

'Since when?' she asked, incredulously.

'Well, since today,' Bo replied a little sheepishly. 'I've had too many hangovers recently, and now seems like a good time for a fresh start.'

'Good for you,' Kirsten said, with an admiring, if dubious, nod.

In spite of her initial optimism, Bo grew increasingly disheartened as the week went on. On Tuesday, she emailed her CV to numerous recruitment agencies, but her mail-shot yielded nothing more than automated responses saying the agency would be in touch if anything suitable came up. It seemed there was nothing she could do except wait and, with time on her hands, she found herself struggling to fill the days.

On Thursday night Kirsten got home to find Bo kneeling on the floor in her bedroom, the contents of her bookcase spread across the carpet before her.

'Good day?' Kirsten enquired with a concerned air. With a manic look in her eye, Bo explained that she couldn't decide whether to shelve her fiction collection alphabetically or chronologically.

'What do you think?' she demanded. Kirsten looked at her intently.

'Bo, have you actually left the flat this week?' she asked. Bo was nonplussed.

'I put the bins out on Tuesday,' she replied.

'Right, come on,' Kirsten said authoritatively. 'We're going out.'

'This is a nightmare,' Bo admitted, as she and Kirsten tucked into a selection of meze at their local Greek restaurant. It was a cheap and cheerful place, with framed prints of the Greek Islands on the walls, and artificial trailing plants in the windows. 'I'm going out of my mind. There's nothing I can do except wait.'

Clara Christensen

'It's only been a few days,' Kirsten reassured her, helping herself to a chunk of grilled halloumi. 'Give it time.' At that moment, Bo's phone vibrated on the wooden table. It was a text from Barbara: *Any news on the job front?* Bo rolled her eyes.

'You were saying?' she said archly, showing the screen to Kirsten.

The girls continued to eat in silence. 'Heard anything from Ben?' Kirsten prompted at last. Bo shook her head. They had not spoken since the conversation on the street on Friday night, and she suspected that he considered himself the aggrieved party and was waiting for her to apologise.

'And you haven't called him because . . .?' Kirsten asked, as if she had read Bo's mind.

'Because why should I?' Bo countered defiantly. 'I'm the one who's been made redundant. He's the one who supposedly made a pass at another colleague. I shouldn't *have* to call him! If he was a *proper* boyfriend he would have called to see how I am. Wouldn't he?' It felt good finally to air out loud some of the grievances she had been dwelling on all week.

'Supposedly?' Kirsten repeated, eyeing Bo over a forkful of grilled fish. Bo returned a puzzled frown, not catching her friend's meaning. 'You said he *supposedly* made a pass at another colleague,' Kirsten elaborated. 'That suggests an element of doubt.'

Bo groaned. 'You're *such* a lawyer, Kirst,' she complained.

She speared a chunk of calamari and popped it in her mouth. 'He said nothing happened, but . . .'

'But you don't believe him?' Kirsten volunteered.

'I don't know what I believe any more,' Bo admitted. 'I never know where I stand with him. He can't get enough of me one minute, and doesn't want to know the next. I think I'm just . . . tired of it all.' Kirsten gave her a consoling smile.

'Maybe you need to get away, to take your mind off everything,' Kirsten suggested brightly.

'Funnily enough, I told my parents I was thinking of going travelling. Alone. Mum nearly had a heart attack,' replied Bo. Kirsten chuckled; she had met Barbara enough times to know how she would have reacted to the idea of Bo setting off on an independent travel adventure. 'Thing is,' Bo sighed, 'I don't really fancy going anywhere on my own, and I can't afford it anyway. Not till I know I've got a job lined up.' The truth was that Bo had always found the thought of independent travel slightly scary. The closest she had come to it was a couple of all-inclusive holidays with her friends during their summer breaks at university and she knew that didn't really count. Bo took a sip of water and, not for the first time that evening, eyed Kirsten's wine glass enviously.

'Look, here's an idea,' Kirsten said, in a resolutely upbeat tone. 'I've got some annual leave left over – we could go and stay in my mum's summerhouse in Denmark for a few days. We could make a girly trip of it.' Bo looked dubious.

'It wouldn't cost you anything except the flights, and at this time of year they won't cost much,' Kirsten went on.

Bo wavered, torn between yearning to get away, to escape her relentless torturing thoughts about Ben, and worrying that it would be irresponsible to go on holiday when she should be looking for work.

'A change of scene might do you good,' Kirsten urged. 'Besides, you said yourself, there's not much more you can do than wait.'

Bo appreciated the effort Kirsten was going to to cheer her up, and did not want to seem ungrateful. But in her despondent mood, she was finding it hard to feel enthusiastic about anything. 'Thanks, Kirst. That's really kind of you. But I'm not sure,' she demurred.

Their conversation was interrupted by the appearance of the restaurant's owner, a portly, convivial Greek man, to clear the table. He chattily engaged Bo and Kirsten in conversation, asking whether they lived locally, were they sisters, and so on, in the harmlessly flirtatious way that seemed customary for Mediterranean men of his age. Bo answered his questions as politely as she could, fleetingly wondering how he would respond if she told him the truth: that she had just lost her job, that she suspected her boyfriend of cheating on her, and that she had no idea what she was going to do with her life.

The restaurant owner finally ambled away, laden with their

empty plates, and Kirsten headed for the Ladies. Alone at the table, Bo picked up her phone, opened her mother's text message and tapped out *Nothing yet* by way of a reply. Then, while she waited for Kirsten to return from the loos, she scrolled through her Facebook timeline. Her stomach gave a small jolt when she saw that Ben had been tagged in a photo captioned 'Team night out'. It was a casual snapshot taken in the wine bar near the office. Ben was standing at the bar with the half-dozen other account managers from Aspect. They all had the uninhibited body language and glassy-eyed looks which betokened an evening spent drinking. Ben was in the middle of the group, his face animated and his eyes glittering, as if he was in the middle of telling a joke. One hand held a half-empty pint glass, but his other arm was draped casually around the shoulder of a petite woman beside him.

Feeling her pulse start to race, Bo pinched the image on her screen, zooming in on the female figure next to Ben. Her face was partially obscured by someone's raised hand in the foreground, but Bo recognised the mouse-coloured ponytail and pale blue cardigan as Charlotte's. She slid her finger across her screen to look more closely at Ben's face, trying to read his expression in the grainy pixels of the enlarged image. Ben looked drunk, no question, but would drunkenness alone explain the casual intimacy of his pose, the presumptuously proprietorial way his arm was draped around Charlotte's shoulder?

She placed her phone back on the table in a state of shock. By the time Kirsten returned from the Ladies, Bo was staring into the middle distance, pale-faced and impassive.

'Everything okay?' Kirsten asked, sitting down opposite Bo.

'Absolutely fine,' Bo replied briskly. 'I've been thinking about Denmark,' she said decisively, fixing Kirsten with an intense stare. 'Let's do it.'

When Bo woke up the following morning she felt fully alert, as though she had hardly slept. She lay for a few moments staring at the ceiling, before twisting onto her side to grab her phone to look again at the photo on Facebook. Surely, Bo reasoned, Ben would not be so openly demonstrative towards Charlotte if something had happened between them? If her own experience was anything to go by, if something was going on between Ben and Charlotte, he would want to keep it secret. Bo stared at the image until her eyes began to ache, then abruptly exited Facebook, turned the phone off and pulled the duvet up over her head.

Facing another day alone in the flat, Bo knew she needed something to distract her from the doggedly persistent mental image of Ben's arm around Charlotte's shoulder, and researching her forthcoming trip to Denmark with Kirsten presented her with the perfect displacement activity. Kirsten had not said much about the location of her family's summerhouse other than that it was in a seaside village called Skagen in Northern Jutland. She spoke about it with the mild complacency bred from countless family holidays in the same place, and teenaged summers spent wishing she was somewhere hotter and more exciting. Bo recognised the sentiment, having felt a similar ennui about her annual visits to the same cottage in Devon throughout her adolescence. But for Bo, the summerhouse in Skagen sounded like the perfect antidote to everything that was wrong with her life in London, being remote, quiet, and several hundred miles away from Ben.

On Saturday morning, Bo and Kirsten sat down together at the laptop.

'What's the weather going to be like over there?' Bo asked, scrolling her cursor across the airline webpage, her credit card in front of her on the table.

'Shit,' Kirsten replied matter-of-factly. 'London is Mediterranean by comparison, and of course it's November so it'll be dark fifteen hours a day. Stock up on thermals before we go.' Bo nodded, undeterred. 'Oh and by the way, there might be a couple of other people staying at the house at the same time as us,' Kirsten added. Bo glanced up from the laptop. 'Just a couple of my mum's ex-students. She's always offering the place up to people. She says it makes sense for it not to stand empty all winter.'

Kirsten's mother, Pernille, was a ceramics tutor at an art

college in south London, a bohemian-looking lady with hennaed hair and a penchant for bold jewellery. Although Bo felt a mild misgiving at the thought of sharing the house with strangers, she knew it would be churlish to begrudge anyone else the same hospitality she was being offered. Besides, even if there were other people staying at the house, that didn't mean she and Kirsten would be required to socialise with them.

A few clicks later, she had booked their flights for a week's time. 'Done!' she announced. As if in answer, her phone beeped, announcing an incoming text message: *You free tonight, Blu-ray? Dinner?*

Bo frowned, then passed the phone to Kirsten.

'What do you think?' she asked. Kirsten gave a diplomatic shrug.

'D'you think he realised you would've seen the photo on Facebook?' she asked.

'Probably,' Bo replied.

'Maybe he wants to make amends,' Kirsten added hopefully.

'Perhaps.' Bo gave a wry half-smile. 'I guess there's only one way to find out.' With a deep breath, she opened the text message and clicked reply.

Okay, she typed. *What did you have in mind?*

Chapter 9

Ben had booked a table at an expensive restaurant in Soho, a fact which Bo spent much of the afternoon analysing, wondering if it was a sign that he had a guilty conscience, or that he wanted to make amends, or even if this was going to be a precursor to breaking up with her – a treat to sweeten the bitter pill of hearing that he had found someone else.

She wanted to look her best so that, if Ben was about to tell her that he was dumping her for Charlotte, he would at least be reminded of what he would be missing. It was of the utmost importance, however, that she did not appear to have gone to any special effort; the last thing she wanted was for Ben to think she was desperate to lure him back. She had more self-respect than that, she reminded herself sternly, as she set to work with her hair straighteners. Achieving a look of effortless sexiness entailed emptying her wardrobe onto her bed, and ruling out any items that she deemed either too frumpy or overtly sexy. Eventually, after much trying on and discarding of outfits, Bo settled on her best clingy jeans with a black blouse and long boots.

Her hair straightened and make-up applied, Bo set off for the West End. It had only been a week since she left Aspect, but she felt an uncomfortable jolt of disconnection, of having become an outsider in what had used to be her manor. She strode through the maze of Soho streets, telling herself to stay calm and keep an open mind, but by the time she reached the restaurant she was in a state of such heightened anticipation that she pushed the glossy front door open with enough force to make the windows rattle and several diners looked up, startled by the noise.

Ben, who had been sitting at the bar to the right of the entrance, turned and looked at her over his shoulder. He was wearing an open-collared shirt underneath a well-tailored, close-fitting waistcoat, the charcoal-grey silk panel taut across his shoulders, emphasising the well-toned muscles underneath. Bo tried to ignore the flutter of attraction in her stomach, reminding herself sternly not to allow physical attraction to override her principles. Ben stepped down from his bar stool and advanced towards her, smiling.

'That was quite an entrance,' he murmured, moving in for a kiss. She averted her face, and his fractional hesitation before brushing his lips against her cheek communicated his wounded pride.

At the bar, Bo ordered a gin and tonic without further ado. She had decided, with Kirsten's encouragement, that tonight was not a night to be endured sober. (In fact, she had already soothed her nerves with a vodka and tonic before leaving home.) Ben sat beside her, sipping his whisky and ginger ale, while they watched the barman prepare her drink. The restaurant had a discreetly affluent ambience which felt far more *grown-up* than most of the places she and Ben had frequented. There was not a preening Instagramer in sight, but Bo found herself feeling faintly self-conscious, and uncharacteristically at a loss for something to say.

'So, how's life as a lady of leisure?' was Ben's opener, when the barman had placed Bo's drink in front of her. Bo winced at the phrase, resenting its implicit suggestion that redundancy would give her time for leisurely *pursuits*, such as flower arranging or needlework. She took a fortifying sip from the tall glass at her elbow.

'Okay so far,' she said demurely, deciding it would be ungracious to slap down Ben's attempt – albeit a poorly phrased one – to show an interest in her. Besides, she was determined to put a brave face on what had, in truth, been a resoundingly disheartening and dispiriting week.

'I've been in touch with a few contacts, and picked up some good leads,' she went on, hoping to give the impression that her redundancy was no more than a blip, a temporary setback which she was confident would come to an end imminently. She picked up her glass to take another sip, surreptitiously glancing at Ben out of the corner of her eye, wondering if he could tell she was lying.

'I'm sure you'll get snapped up soon,' he said with a flash of his straight, white teeth. Something about his tone inclined Bo to think that Ben had seen through her attempt to appear blasé. She gave a tight smile, and there followed a slightly awkward silence, during which they both sipped their drinks.

'Actually, I can't take on anything immediately,' she said finally, 'I'm off to Denmark next week.' She raised her glass to take another slug of gin, and was surprised to find that her glass was empty, but for a mound of ice cubes. The attentive barman wasted no time in gliding over to offer her another. 'Yes please,' Bo replied without hesitation.

'Denmark? How come?' Ben raised a quizzical eyebrow.

'I'm going with Kirsten, to stay in her family's summerhouse.'

Ben let out a noise which Bo felt to be dangerously close to a snigger. 'A summerhouse?' he repeated, trying to contain a smile. 'In Denmark? In *November*? Don't forget your sunblock, will you?' He started to laugh. She felt a flash of rage sweep through her.

'I'm not going there to get a tan,' she said self-righteously.

'I just thought it would be good to get away, and Kirsten offered, and—' Ben was still smirking, but Bo's self-justification was cut short by the appearance of a suited waiter at their side, informing them in deferential tones that their table was ready. Bo stepped down unsteadily from her stool, and picked up the replacement G&T which had just been put in front of her. As she swayed along behind the waiter through the hushed, elegant restaurant, Bo suspected that she was doing a poor job of masking the effect of the gin and vodka swilling around her otherwise empty stomach.

Their table was in the middle of a row of others already occupied by diners, most of whom, Bo couldn't help noticing, were older couples, the women all sporting expensively maintained hair-dos, their wrists and necks draped with *serious* jewellery. Bo had the unpleasant sensation of feeling like a child who had been admitted, erroneously, to a grown-up party, and felt acutely conscious of her high-street clothes and beaded choker from Accessorize. *Get a grip, Bo*, she told herself, making an effort to project mature sophistication rather than the wobbly tipsiness she really felt as the waiter pulled back her chair for her to sit down.

Once the formalities of perusing the menu and ordering food were completed, Bo launched into an account of her planned trip to Denmark, partly to prove to Ben that she had made an informed choice to go there, but also because she didn't yet feel ready to tackle the conversational elephant in the room: the photo on Facebook.

'It's a place called Skagen at the northernmost tip of the country,' she explained, 'a former fishing village, now a popular holiday destination for the Danes. It also used to be an international meeting place for artists, because of the quality of the light. It's known as the Land of Light, in fact.' She was aware that she was talking fast, and suspected that she was furnishing Ben with more detail than was strictly necessary, but she had a point to prove, and the gin had loosened her tongue. Ben leaned back in his chair as she talked, looking faintly amused.

'Surely more the Land of Cold and Dark at this time of year?' he quipped. His comment took the wind out of her sails.

'Well, yes, it probably is. But that's not really the point,' she mumbled petulantly. The conversation ground to a halt and in the silence, Bo took a long slug of her second gin and tonic. 'So, what have I missed at Aspect? Have any more redundancies been announced?' Bo asked with a forced lightness, taking a forkful of the seared scallop which the waiter had placed on the table in front of her. Ben pulled a face that suggested he was racking his brains, before eventually volunteering the names of a couple of techies and someone from sales who had been given their notice.

'What about account management? Are you all safe?' she

probed, with a veneer of concern which belied her itching curiosity to know whether Hayley had been right about Charlotte being lined up for redundancy.

'Yeah, we've made a few changes, too,' he replied evasively.

'Oh, really?' she prompted, sipping white wine whilst waiting for him to elaborate.

'Matt's gone, for starters.' Bo's eyes widened in surprise; as well as being the accounts director, Matt had been one of the founders of the company. 'He can afford not to work. Took early retirement, basically. Plans to see out his days on a golf course. Lucky bastard,' Ben muttered, a touch bitterly.

'Have they found someone to replace him?' she asked, doing her best to sound like she cared about Matt, whilst in fact she was trying to formulate a way of asking about Charlotte's fate without being too obvious. Ben looked down at his plate and began to push his food around with his fork.

'Yeah, actually, they have,' he said, avoiding her gaze.

It took a moment for Bo to process Ben's sudden, uncharacteristic bashfulness, and to realise what it meant. Then, in a moment of stunning clarity, the photo from Facebook flashed into her mind – the assembled group of workers, a laughing Ben at its heart, his hand proprietorially around one of his colleagues as if he were a king holding court. Suddenly, it was obvious: the occasion wasn't just the usual after-work drinks; it was a celebration. For Ben. Bo felt a flush start to rise from her neck to her cheeks.

'It's you,' she said. It was a statement rather than a question. Ben glanced up at her through a strand of wavy dark hair which had slipped forward over his right eye, and nodded. Bo felt her face set into a rigid, artificial smile.

'Wow, congratulations,' she said. 'Accounts director at twenty-nine. That's amazing.'

Ben smiled bashfully. 'Thanks,' he replied.

As an afterthought, she asked, 'How long have you known?' Ben looked down at his dinner plate.

'Matt was negotiating his leaving settlement for a while. They first sounded me out about replacing him a month ago.' It was taking all the self-control Bo had to maintain her calm, civil façade, but inside she was raging. Not just at the irony that whilst she had worked her way up through the ranks for five years, just to find the door slammed in her face due to 'efficiencies', Ben had landed a massive promotion after less than a year at the company. She felt the beginnings of a feminist rant brewing, and was looking forward to getting home and offloading to Kirsten who, being half-Danish, was fiercely egalitarian in her workplace attitudes. But what stung most was that Ben had kept his promotion secret from her.

'You never mentioned it,' she said lightly, taking a rather larger sip of wine than she had intended. Ben gave a little shrug of his shoulders.

'Well, it wasn't official till this week,' he said, 'and besides, it was confidential, and—'

'And you couldn't trust me not to blab to the whole office,' Bo cut in, fixing him with a stare. Ben gave a small, brittle laugh.

'Course not, babe, but you know how these things go. If word had got out, they'd have known it had come from me. The whole deal could have gone tits up.'

'Mmm-hmm,' Bo concurred, draining her wine glass. God forbid that Ben's gilded promotion might have been in jeopardy because he trusted her – his *girlfriend* – enough to confide in about it. At that moment, the suited waiter re-appeared at her shoulder to clear away their starters.

'Can we get another one of these, please?' she asked sweetly, grabbing the empty wine bottle by the neck.

'Of course, madam,' the waiter purred, before disappearing in the same silent, gliding motion that had brought him to the table.

'So, when do you start?' Bo asked.

'Monday,' he answered. She nodded slowly.

'Are they bringing in anyone to replace you?'

'Not as such,' Ben answered. Bo detected a reluctance to elaborate, but continued to look at him expectantly.

'Charlotte's taking over my accounts, the day-to-day stuff,' he said, finally.

'Of course she is,' Bo whispered, a rueful smile spreading across her lips. 'So you'll be working pretty closely with her from now on, I guess. *Showing her the ropes.*' Her eyes glittered harshly and there was an unmistakably sardonic emphasis on the final phrase. A slight frown clouded Ben's brow.

'Well, we're doing a handover, if that's what you mean,' he said, noticeably on the defensive. Bo gave a sudden, un-ladylike snort, which caused the grey-haired couple at the next table to stop, mid-conversation, and look at her.

'A handover?' she sneered. 'Sh'rly leg-over would be closer to the truth?' Bo was hazily aware of the slurred quality of her speech, and the curious glances from the neighbouring tables gave her reason to think she might be speaking more loudly than normal. Opposite her, Ben was sitting perfectly motionless. Even though his meal was only half eaten, he seemed to have lost interest in his food. 'Had enough?' Bo asked, gesturing with her knife towards his half-finished sea bass.

'You could say that,' Ben replied quietly, pushing his cutlery neatly together at the edge of his plate.

'Oh! Where did you come from?' Bo exclaimed tip-sily, upon noticing the waiter who had reappeared at the side of their table. He inclined his head and proffered the replacement bottle of wine, presenting the label for Bo's approval. 'Lovely, thank you,' Bo said with an attempt at suave sophistication. The waiter smiled and deftly uncorked the bottle, wrapped the base in a linen napkin and poured a splash of wine into Bo's glass for her to taste. Beginning to tire of the display of wine-based reverence and ritual, Bo made an impatient, flicking gesture with her hand. 'No need, I'm sh'r'ze fine. Fill her up!' Another slight incline of the waiter's head. Ben glared at the tablecloth while the waiter filled both their glasses.

When they were alone again, Ben leaned forwards and placed his hand on Bo's arm as she was about to lift the glass to her mouth.

'Don't you think you should slow down, Bo? That's a fifty-quid bottle of wine and you're drinking it like Ribena.' The jibe, and the implication that she was behaving immaturely, stung, but Bo was not in the mood for accepting criticism.

'And *very* lovely wine it is too,' she grinned. 'Besides, I'd have thought an *accounts director* could afford to splash out on a decent bottle of wine. Or two.' She removed her arm from underneath his hand, and lifted the wine glass to her lips. Ben's jaw tensed, but he said nothing until she had returned her glass to the table.

'Look,' he said seriously, leaning closer, in an attempt to encourage Bo to speak at a more discreet volume.

'Charlotte's taking over my accounts, that's all.' His voice was a low-pitched monotone, and Bo fleetingly wondered if he was trying to hypnotise her.

'Is that why you had your arm round her shoulder?' Her gaze was steady, and Ben gave a slight double-take.

'If you're referring to Dan's photo, it's not what it looked like,' he said in a tight, buttoned-up voice. Bo tilted her head to one side.

'Really? What was it then?'

'It wasn't anything,' Ben said, with a look that, through Bo's increasingly blurred vision, seemed almost pleading. 'It was our team night out, I was celebrating my new job, she was celebrating hers. It was just ... high spirits. I was pissed ... and Charlotte was just – there. That's all.'

'Well, of course, if she was *just there*, that makes it okay ...' Bo trailed off and sat back in her chair, looking Ben in the eye as she took another defiant gulp of wine. Ben's face was set hard: she had never seen him look so uncomfortable. Even though she had a growing sense that she would regret what she was doing in the morning, for the moment at least, she was enjoying herself. It felt good to behave recklessly, for once, to say what she was really thinking without worrying about the consequences. When the waiter reappeared to clear their plates and hand them each a dessert menu, she smiled warmly and leaned back against her padded dining chair to peruse the menu studiously.

'Oh look, Ben,' she exclaimed. 'There's a chocolate brownie on here. I know how much you like them.' She flashed a saccharine smile. Ben held her gaze for a moment then glanced at his watch.

'I think maybe we should just get the bill,' he said sulkily.

Bo sat in the back seat of the taxi Ben had called for her, aware that the motion and hum of the engine were at the same time lulling her to sleep and making her feel slightly nauseous. The feeling of triumph she had enjoyed at the table was beginning to seep away, to be replaced by the clammy fear that she had almost certainly just made a fool of herself. She tried to recall the details of their conversation – had Ben conclusively denied that anything was going on with Charlotte? Infuriatingly, she couldn't remember, and it now seemed like a major oversight on her part that she had not pressed him for a definitive answer one way or the other.

She drifted into a light doze and was woken only when the driver pulled up outside her house. She stumbled out of the taxi and staggered down the short flight of stone steps to the flat's front door, where it took several attempts to get her key into the lock.

'Hi, Kirst,' she called, when she had finally gained access. 'Just wait till you hear about my *epically* shit night with Ben.' She was met with silence, although the lights were on. 'Kirst?' Bo repeated, removing her coat and thrusting it in the general direction of the hooks on the wall, oblivious to the fact that she missed and her coat had landed in a heap on the floor. She walked down the hallway and pushed open the living-room door, to find Kirsten curled up on the sofa, red-eyed and sniffing.

'Oh my God,' Bo gasped. 'What's happened?' She felt instantly sober and sat down beside her friend. Kirsten's eyes were puffy and her face was blotchy.

'It's my grandfather,' Kirsten croaked, wiping at her eyes with a tissue. 'He's been rushed to hospital. They think he might have had a stroke.'

'Oh, I'm sorry,' Bo murmured compassionately, stroking Kirsten's shoulder.

'He's in intensive care,' Kirsten went on, her eyes filling with fresh tears.

'Are you going back to your mum and dad's?' Bo asked gently.

Kirsten nodded. 'Tomorrow.' She blew her nose noisily into a tissue while Bo sat beside her in silence, allowing the full implication of Kirsten's news to sink in. The same thought seemed to occur to Kirsten, and she looked at Bo through red-rimmed eyes. 'I might not be able to come to Denmark after all.'

Part Two

Skagen

Chapter 10

Monday morning found Bo drinking coffee at the edge of a cavernous departure lounge in Gatwick airport. The place seemed designed to be as unpleasant an environment as possible, with harsh neon strip lights above rows of uncomfortable metal seats surrounded by shops and fast-food outlets. With two hours still to wait until her flight, she had already made two circuits of the tax-free shop, popped into Boots, and picked up an armful of magazines from WHSmith. Now, at a loss for something to do, she had sought out the relative comfort of a Costa Coffee.

Bo sipped her cappuccino and took a bite of limp croissant, allowing her eyes to wander around the busy lounge on the other side of the red rope dividers. It had the frenetic air characteristic of airport terminals, full of passengers rushing to departure gates or staring blankly at the boarding-gate screens, all wearing looks of thinly veiled impatience to be anywhere other than in this soulless, limbo-like space.

Wiping the grease from her fingers with a paper napkin, Bo sighed, then pushed back her sleeve to look at her watch. It was just gone nine-thirty, and her mind drifted automatically to the Aspect office. She pictured her former colleagues going about the usual Monday morning routine: the exchange of pleasantries about their weekends, the first tea-round of the working week, the catch-up meetings and checking of emails.

Of course, this was also Ben's first day as Aspect's newly appointed accounts director. Bo imagined him striding from the lift into the office, enjoying the sheen of glamour and power afforded by his promotion. Frances, the matronly PA who managed the directors' diaries, would pop her head around the door of his glass-walled office to offer him a hot drink, and Ben would smile winningly and ask for tea, relishing the fact that he had reached the professional milestone of having someone else make drinks for him. Bo shuddered and tried to be thankful that redundancy had, at least, spared her the ordeal of having to witness his triumphant inauguration in the flesh.

Bo was still no closer to knowing what, if anything, was going on between Ben and Charlotte. She had taken his word for it that nothing had happened in Milton Keynes, but now there was the photo on Facebook too . . . Could the arm draped around Charlotte's shoulder *really* be excused by drunken high spirits? She would rather know for certain one way or the other – even if the truth was hurtful – than have to deal with this infuriating uncertainty. Instead, she was left doubting her own judgement. To doubt Ben's innocence might be a sign of her paranoia and neediness, but to believe him might make her gullibly naïve.

She stared at her phone, debating whether to send Ben a message. But to say what? To apologise for the way she had behaved in the restaurant? To ask how his first day in the new job was going? To ask him outright whether he fancied Charlotte? She sighed, deciding that the best course of action was probably to do nothing. She had arranged this holiday, in part, to put some distance between herself and Ben, and to give herself space to work out how she felt about him. Texting him from the airport would mean she had fallen at the first hurdle. Besides, if curiosity got the better of her, she would be able to find out what Ben was up to via social media. And that, she reasoned, could be done just as easily from Denmark as it could from London.

Determined to drive thoughts of Ben from her mind, she tried to focus on the trip that lay ahead. In truth, she was feeling more apprehensive than excited. She had very nearly lost her nerve about the whole enterprise over the weekend. When Kirsten had set off for Godalming first thing on

Sunday, pale-faced and tearful, she had no idea how serious her grandfather's condition was. Bo had kept her own anxieties to herself, knowing it would be crassly insensitive to bring up the subject of their trip at such a moment of crisis. She spent the rest of the day alone in the flat waiting to hear from Kirsten, unsure whether their plans were about to fall through.

When Kirsten finally called on Sunday night, Bo could immediately hear the relief in her friend's voice. Her grandfather had suffered a stroke, Kirsten said, but a mild one. The hospital wanted to keep him in for observation, but the doctors were hopeful he would make a good recovery.

'Thank goodness,' Bo murmured, thinking not just about Kirsten's grandfather, but also (a touch selfishly, she knew) about their holiday plans.

'Dad wants me to stay here until Grandad's been discharged, though.'

'Oh, okay,' Bo replied, trying to hide her disappointment behind an upbeat tone.

'It should only be a day or so till he's got the all-clear,' Kirsten added. 'There's no point both of us changing our flights. Why don't you go tomorrow as planned and I'll join you in a couple of days?'

Bo exhaled slowly, feeling her nerve wavering. When she had booked their flights, Bo had blithely assumed that Kirsten would take responsibility for all the niggly, anxiety-provoking aspects of travelling abroad: speaking the language, knowing the route, being familiar with the house. Instead, she faced the prospect of travelling to the remote reaches of a strange country on her own.

'The house won't be empty when you arrive,' Kirsten urged, as if sensing her friend's discomfort. 'Mum says one of her ex-students is already there.'

'Oh, right. Anyone you know?' Bo enquired.

'Someone called Florence. An artist. I've never met her. But she's stayed in the house before, so she'll know how everything works.'

To Bo, the thought of an artist named Florence conjured up an image of a woman in late middle age, a willowy, ex-hippy-type, fond of batik-print dresses. Bo couldn't imagine that they would have much in common. If she and Florence didn't get on, then what exactly would she do to fill her time until Kirsten arrived, in a seaside town in the depths of a cold, dark Scandinavian winter? She pictured awkward silences at the dinner table, desperately trying to think of something intelligent to say about art, while Florence looked on haughtily.

But even if sharing the house with a stranger were awkward for a day or so, what was the alternative? To cancel her flight, pay for a replacement plane ticket and sit in the empty flat for another day, checking job sites and obsessing about what may or may not be going on between Ben and

Charlotte? Hardly an appetising prospect. She took a deep breath and told herself (in one of Ben's favourite phrases), to *man-up*.

'Okay, that sounds like a good plan,' she had told Kirsten.

'Great,' Kirsten said happily. 'Anyway I'd better go, we're about to eat. Have a good trip, and I'll keep you updated.'

Bo leaned back in the faded coffee-shop armchair, feeling apprehensive. This was not going to be the relaxing holiday with her best friend that she had planned, at least not for the first day or two. She drained the dregs of her coffee, wiped a residue of milky froth from her lip, and checked her watch again. It was nine-forty-five. On a whim, she picked up her phone, found the contact details for one of the recruitment agencies, and dialled the number. She drummed her fingers on the table-top, listening to the ring-tone.

'B&D Employment Services. How may I help you?' demanded a shrill voice on the line.

'Oh, hello,' Bo said with forced brightness. 'This is Bo Hazlehurst. I sent you my CV last week and I was just wondering—'

'Please hold,' the voice cut her off mid-sentence. A blast of The Four Seasons followed, then – 'Can I take your name, please?'

'Bo Hazlehurst,' repeated Bo, trying to keep exasperation out of her voice. After several more minutes of Vivaldi, which Bo quickly discovered was the first eight bars only, played on a loop, she was eventually put through to a girl who sounded no more than eighteen but introduced herself as a consultant. The girl chirpily informed Bo that, yes, she had received Bo's email and CV, but there was nothing suited to Bo's experience at the moment. But she would *definitely* be in touch as soon as the situation changed.

'Okay, thank you, I'd appreciate that,' Bo said through a clenched jaw.

The interminable preamble to the flight dragged on with a tense wait in front of the departures screen for her gate number. Eventually, feeling as if she was already exhausted and ready for bed, Bo stood in line with her passport and boarding pass, queuing for her flight to Aalborg in the endless grey corridor that housed the departure gates.

Scanning the faces in the queue, she guessed that the majority of her fellow travellers were Danish. There was a noticeable amount of tall blondes, with just the occasional Brit among them, recognisable by being stockier, mousier, and carrying an English newspaper. She noticed with mild alarm that the Danes were also, without exception, dressed in high-tech outer layers or goose-down jackets. Bo glanced at her own woollen coat with slight misgiving, wondering if she should have paid greater heed to Kirsten's warnings about the severity of the Danish weather.

On board the aircraft, she edged her way patiently along

the aisle, stowed her wheeled suitcase in the overhead locker, then clambered into the cramped, rigid seat. She wondered how long it would be until the Viking-esque cabin crew came around with the drinks trolley, before remembering that, after the humiliation of Saturday night, she had resolved to drink in moderation for the duration of the trip. She pulled a plastic bottle of water out of her handbag and took a sip, staring out of the aircraft's tiny window at the baggage handlers loading suitcases into the hold, and trying not to think about how much she longed for a vodka and tonic to steady her pre-flight nerves.

Three hours later, Bo stood shivering on the frosty runway of Aalborg airport, pulling her knitted bobble hat down over her ears against the freezing air. She had never felt cold like this before. Her lungs hurt with every breath, her cheeks felt raw, and the wind seemed to blow straight through her ineffectual coat. It was barely three o'clock but dusk was already falling. She grabbed her suitcase and followed the other passengers across the glistening tarmac to the tiny airport up ahead, which consisted of a small, single-storey building, illuminated in the lowering darkness.

Inside, she was struck first by the blissful warmth, and then by the atmosphere of calm and comfort. This was nothing like any airport she had been to in Britain: it felt almost cosy, with polished wooden floors and tasteful lighting.

Everywhere exuded good design, from the rows of leather-backed seats to the sleekly ergonomic luggage trolleys. The Danes all seemed to possess an air of serenity that was nothing like the fraught tension that emanated from the passengers at Gatwick. They seemed less hurried, less stressed – relaxed, even. They were also, almost without exception, unnervingly tall. Bo felt acutely conscious of her five foot five frame, being towered over by both men and women and even, she noticed with alarm, some children.

A shuttle bus took her from the airport to the train station, where her connecting train to Skagen (sleek and silver on the outside, comfortable and spacious on the inside) was waiting at the platform. Inside, the carriage was already filling up with passengers sliding their cases onto the luggage racks and removing their coats. As Bo made her way along the carpeted aisle in search of a seat, her wheeled case brushed against a laptop which had been placed precariously on a table, whilst its owner shoved his jacket onto the overhead rails.

'Oh, I'm sorry,' Bo exclaimed, reaching down to steady the laptop before it toppled onto the floor. The owner of the laptop, a young, intense-looking man in a beanie hat, turned and scowled at her.

'It's fine,' he said gruffly, in an English accent, sliding the laptop away from the edge of the table.

'Sorry,' Bo repeated.

Mildly annoyed with herself for apologising when, surely, it was not her fault that the laptop had been protruding from the table, Bo continued down the carriage and found her seat. At exactly its scheduled departure time, the train pulled away and Bo leaned back to watch the dusky scrubland of Northern Jutland flash past the window.

About half an hour into the journey, Bo realised that she had forgotten to switch on her phone after landing. It immediately began to beep with text messages from her mother, of increasing urgency: *Have you landed? Are you there yet? Bo, PLEASE text me.*

Flight was fine, on train now. Nearly there, she tapped out.

Almost instantly, a reply appeared: *Great. I'll call you later.*

She dozed off with her head against the glass and when she woke it was dark outside and horizontal streaks of rainwater flecked the windows. She peered at her reflection in the black glass, wiping away the smudges of mascara under her eyes with her fingertips. The train had made several stops while she had slept, and the carriage was almost empty. By the time the train began to slow down for its approach into the terminus at Skagen, there were only three other passengers remaining: a benign-looking elderly couple and the man in the beanie, who was typing on his laptop with a look of fierce concentration. Seeing the elderly couple gather their things, she did likewise, putting on her coat and pulling her hat down over her ears in anticipation of the freezing temperature she knew awaited her outside.

Sure enough, the air was even colder and thinner here than it had been at the airport. The northerly wind blowing in from the sea was biting, and fat drops of icy rain quickly soaked through her woolly gloves and hat. She ran across the forecourt in front of the station, a pretty building with balconies and a yellow-plastered façade, and climbed gratefully into a taxi. She showed the driver the summerhouse address, pulled off her damp hat, then sat back and listened to the tinny, slightly incongruous sound of Bruno Mars singing 'Uptown Funk' on the radio, as the taxi rolled through the dark cobbled streets.

Almost eight hours after setting off from her flat, Bo finally arrived at the summerhouse. Lights flickered invitingly behind its lowered blinds and its yellow walls and steeply pitched red roof made Bo think of fairy-tale cottages and gingerbread houses. The neat front lawn was enclosed by a white picket fence and boasted its own wooden flagpole, the red and white Danish flag snapping in the wind.

Bo rang the doorbell. She heard movement inside but a noise behind her made her turn round. Another taxi had pulled into the space just vacated by hers, and the driver had got out and was removing a suitcase from the boot.

The front door swung open and Bo turned back to see a pretty young woman smiling at her from the doorway.

She looked around thirty, with lively blue eyes, a slightly upturned nose, and blonde hair which had been cut in a funky, asymmetric style, shaved close around the ear on one side but falling in a sharply angled bob on the other. She wore a Breton-style striped cotton top with faded black jeans ripped at the knees.

'Hi.'

The sound of trundling wheels made Bo glance over her shoulder again, to see the man from the train wheeling his suitcase up the garden path towards the house. The young woman stood in the doorway with her arms wrapped around the front of her body, visibly shivering.

'Hello,' the man said, coming to a halt beside Bo on the doorstep. 'I'm Simon. I—'

'Can we do this inside, please?' the woman cut in, through chattering teeth. 'I'm freezing my tits off out here.'

Bo and Simon stepped inside, the front door emitting a satisfying *shtoom* sound as it sealed shut behind them, like the door on a safe.

Chapter 11

The blonde woman stepped forwards and held out her hand. 'I'm Florence,' she said brightly.

'I'm Bo,' replied Bo, inwardly acknowledging just how far off the mark her mental image of Florence had been.

'Simon,' said the man from the train carriage, giving Florence's hand a brisk shake.

They were standing in an airy kitchen-cum-dining room, with bleached wood floors and white walls. Compared to the arctic conditions outdoors, the room felt positively tropical, and Bo could feel sweat prickle at the back of her neck and under her arms. She began to peel off her outer layers and beside her Simon did the same, unzipping his coat and removing his hat and boots in silence. Bo noted that he was an attractive thirty-something, with a touch of grey at his temples and brown eyes beneath heavy brows which seemed inclined to furrow.

'I expect you're both dying for a cuppa?' Florence asked.

'Yes, please,' Bo replied gratefully. She could feel the warmth of the underfloor heating through her socks as she followed Florence over to the wooden dining table. Bo and Simon each took one of the architectural dining chairs beneath a pair of low-hanging pendant lights which cast two pools of yellow light onto the table. Florence went into the kitchen area, which was comprised of gleaming white, minimalist units and pale-wood worktops. She flicked on the kettle then leaned back against the counter and smiled at them. She had an open, friendly demeanour which made Bo instinctively warm to her.

'It'll be nice to have some company at last,' Florence said cheerfully. 'I've been rattling around in here on my own for days.'

'You're an artist, right?' Bo asked.

Florence nodded. 'Ceramics, mostly. But I love coming here to sketch the landscape. The beaches here are incredible, even in winter.'

Bo's eyes flickered across the table to Simon, but he had taken out his phone and was scrolling across its screen, seemingly oblivious to the conversation around him.

'Pernille said Kirsten's coming too,' Florence continued, seemingly unfazed by Simon's silence. 'You're friends of hers, I gather?' she asked, looking from Bo to Simon expectantly.

At this, Simon looked up abruptly from his phone. He and Bo exchanged a look in which his dawning realisation and embarrassment mirrored her own: Florence had assumed they were a couple.

'Oh, um,' Bo stuttered, feeling a blush rise in her cheeks. 'I am, yes, Kirsten's my flatmate,' she said. 'I don't know about—' She glanced at Simon. 'We don't – what I mean is—' Florence was staring at her with the benign but impatient look a teacher might give a struggling pupil.

'We're not together,' Simon said bluntly. Bo smiled and winced at the same time.

'We just met. On the doorstep. Just now,' she added, somewhat redundantly. Then, in an effort to relieve the awkwardness in the room, she turned to Simon and said, 'Although I think, actually, we might have been on the same plane. Or the same train at least. From the airport. You had a laptop?' Simon was staring at her as if he had doubts about her mental well-being.

'Oh? I hadn't noticed . . .' he answered vaguely, and Bo felt her cheeks start to burn. As introductions went, this one was going from bad to worse.

She was saved from further embarrassment by Florence placing three mugs of tea on the table and taking the chair at the head. 'Well, you've arrived just in time,' she said. 'There's a storm coming in.'

'Oh, right.' Bo gave a nervous giggle, but Simon's

sombre demeanour made her immediately regret her childishness. 'It's not going to be ... dangerous, is it?' she asked anxiously.

Florence shook her head and swallowed a mouthful of tea. 'No, babe, nothing like that,' she said. 'It just means we might be housebound for a few days. It's lucky your flight got in when it did. When the wind gets really bad they have to close the airport.'

They all sipped their tea in silence for a moment, listening to the rain which had begun to pound at the windows, until Florence said, 'So what about you, Simon? Do you know Kirsten too?'

Simon shook his head. 'Pernille is a friend of my mother,' he said. Bo and Florence looked at Simon expectantly but he showed no inclination to elaborate.

'Pernille was one of my tutors at art college,' Florence volunteered.

'I've never met Pernille,' Simon stated flatly.

Florence nodded slowly, then returned to her mug of tea. Bo sensed that she, too, was finding Simon hard work, and felt a rush of relief that she didn't have to deal with Simon's humourlessness alone.

'So, what brings you both to Skagen?' Florence asked convivially.

'I'm just here for a holiday, really,' Bo said. 'Kirsten suggested it. She had some annual leave left over, and I've just

134

been made redundant, so ...' She trailed off, feeling suddenly downcast at the reminder of her reasons for coming to Denmark.

'So you thought you'd come to Skagen and blow the cobwebs away?' Florence suggested.

'Something like that,' answered Bo. Across the table, Simon had raised his hand to his mouth to stifle a yawn.

'What about you, Simon? Are you here for a holiday too?'

Simon rubbed the back of his head. 'No, I'm here to work. I'm a writer.'

Bo and Florence both looked at him expectantly but Simon had become distracted by his phone.

They continued to drink their tea in silence until Florence placed her palms on the table, pushed her chair back, and said, 'Well, I guess I should show you around.'

She led them past the staircase through a pair of double doors into a living room, which combined pared-down simplicity with comfort in a way that Bo was beginning to recognise as typically Danish. Framed abstract prints hung in clusters around the white walls. A wooden coffee table painted in distressed, chalky paint stood on a bleached-wood floor between two stylish armchairs and a leather sofa. In the corner, a fire glowed invitingly in a cylindrical cast-iron stove.

'It really comes into its own in the summer, this place. The light here is incredible,' Florence said, walking across the room to lower the roller blind at the window, through which Bo had glimpsed a set of forlorn-looking garden furniture dripping with rain. 'But it's surprisingly cosy in the winter. Shall I show you upstairs?'

They collected their suitcases from the front door and followed Florence up the staircase to a wood-panelled landing.

'The bathroom's at the end,' Florence said, pointing to a door at the far end of the hallway. 'This room's mine,' she said, half-opening the first door on their left, affording Bo a fleeting glimpse of a room with clothes strewn messily across the bed, and a large black portfolio leaning against the wall.

'Bo, why don't you take this one,' she pointed to the room opposite hers, 'and, Simon, you can have the one next to mine. I'll leave you to unpack, then we can have something to eat.'

Bo pushed open the door and wheeled her suitcase inside. The bedroom was small and functional, painted white, in keeping with the rest of the house, with a single bed, a small chest of drawers and a simple desk and chair. Bo pushed her suitcase against the bed and walked over to the window, where she sank down gratefully onto the folded fluffy blanket and peered out through the rain-spattered glass at the neighbouring rooftops.

Bo looked at her watch, and her thoughts inevitably slid to Ben. It would be coming up to six o'clock in London now, the end of Aspect's working day. Perhaps Ben and his team would be heading out for a drink to mark the first day of his new job. Or maybe he and Charlotte would be heading out for a more private celebration, meeting in secret at the Crossrail hoardings, scurrying into Soho for dinner. *For God's sake, Bo, don't do it to yourself*, she berated herself, pinching the bridge of her nose tightly between her finger and thumb.

She sniffed, stood up purposefully, and set about unpacking her clothes into the chest of drawers. Then she checked her appearance in the mirror, did her best to smooth her wayward hair and dabbed some concealer under her eyes before padding back downstairs. She found Florence in the kitchen, unloading the dishwasher. Simon was nowhere to be seen, presumably still unpacking in his room.

'All right, babe? You hungry?' Florence asked.

'Starving,' Bo admitted, wandering over to help Florence stack the clean crockery and glasses in the cabinets. She couldn't help but notice how clean and uncluttered the kitchen was, and that none of the surfaces were coated in a layer of sticky, greasy dust like those in her flat.

Florence pulled open the fridge. 'I've got some cold meats and cheese, and some bread, but that's all, I'm afraid,' she said apologetically. 'I meant to go to the supermarket today but the weather's been *shit*.'

'Sounds perfect,' Bo said gratefully.

'There's not much booze either,' Florence went on.

'Alcohol costs a bloody *fortune* over here. There are a couple of beers in here, and there might be an old bottle of *glögg* in the cupboard if you're desperate.' Bo smiled. She and Kirsten had once had a memorable evening drinking *glögg* in the flat, served warm with almonds and raisins. Her hangover the next day had been particularly vicious.

They heard Simon's footsteps descending the stairs. 'Good timing,' Florence said chirpily as he appeared. 'We're just about to eat.'

They sat around the table, helping themselves to cold meats, cheese and salad.

'So, Simon, what kind of book are you writing?' Bo began, wondering whether Simon would be any more amenable now that he had settled in.

'A novel.'

A pause followed, during which Bo and Florence looked at him receptively. 'Is it set in Denmark?' Florence asked, buttering a slice of rye bread.

Simon exhaled through his nose. 'Yes. Partly.' He took a bite of bread, seemingly reluctant to provide any further detail.

'Right. Well ...' Bo trailed off. She decided to try a different tack. 'Do you think it's true what they say, that everyone has one novel in them?' Simon swallowed his mouthful.

'No,' he said flatly, 'I don't.'

Bo returned to her food, flummoxed. In her experience, men usually loved talking about work – during her Tinder dating phase she had spent many evenings bored senseless by men bragging about their jobs. Simon, however, seemed almost wilfully unforthcoming on the subject of his writing. But then, Bo reminded herself, she had never met a writer before, so she had no point of comparison. Perhaps sullen and unforthcoming was just what writers were like.

In tacit agreement to leave the subject of Simon's novel, the three of them made polite small-talk about the house and the weather until Bo decided enough time had passed for her to plead exhaustion and retire to her bedroom without appearing rude.

She closed the bedroom door softly behind her and stood for a moment, savouring the silence until a muffled buzz caused her to dart forwards and grab her handbag from the bed. She rummaged among the coffee shop napkins, folded boarding pass and empty sweet wrappers until she found her phone.

MUM calling, her screen announced.

'Hi, Mum,' Bo sighed, wandering over to sit in the window nook.

A fractional delay, then, 'Hello, darling. How's Denmark?' Her mother's voice had a tinny, distant quality and Bo imagined the satellite, somewhere in the sky above the North Sea, bouncing their conversation from her parents' executive estate in Buckinghamshire to the windswept northern tip of Denmark.

'Cold. Dark. And raining at the moment,' Bo replied, staring at her reflection in the black glass. She looked wan, exhausted.

'Oh dear. I hope you've packed enough layers,' her mother clucked, and Bo could picture her mother's concerned look as clearly as if she were in the room.

'I'll be fine, Mum,' she sighed.

'Is Kirsten there yet?'

Bo swung her legs up onto the folded blanket and turned sideways, pressing her feet against the side panel. 'Not yet,' she said, wearily. 'I told you, Mum, she's visiting her grandfather. But she'll be flying over in a day or so.' Bo had assumed the unnaturally upbeat tone she always used when trying to reassure her mother. 'I'm not in the house on my own,' she added. 'Two of Kirsten's mum's friends are here too.'

'Oh, right,' Barbara said in a tight voice. Barbara had met Pernille once, at Bo and Kirsten's graduation day. Barbara, elegant and understated in beige cashmere, had regarded Pernille's clunky jewellery and vibrant red hair with thin-lipped dismay, and in the car on the way home had conveyed her disdain with the observation, 'She's very *flamboyant*, isn't she?'

'What are they like, the friends?' Barbara asked warily.

'*Arty types*, I expect?' Bo's parents harboured an innate distrust of 'arty types', as if people who made a living from their creativity were somehow playing the system, dodging the responsibilities that other, *normal* people had.

'Sort of. Well, one's a ceramic artist. She used to be a student of Pernille's. The other's a writer.' Another pause followed. Bo was fairly certain that writers would fall into the same category as artists for her mother.

'It's all right, Mum,' she said, sensing Barbara's ambivalence. 'They're perfectly nice.' Not wanting to alarm her mother, Bo had decided not to mention that Simon seemed taciturn to the point of rudeness.

'Oh,' Barbara replied, managing to sound at once relieved and disappointed. 'Have they given you anything to eat?'

'They're not meant to be catering for me, Mum,' Bo sighed. 'They're guests here too. But, yes, we've just had dinner.'

Reassured that Bo was not in any imminent danger from either starvation or exposure-to-arty-types, Barbara proceeded to update Bo about the state of her father's bunions, the fence panels which had collapsed in a recent storm, and Lauren's husband's possible promotion at work. As she was bidding her daughter farewell, she implored, 'Keep me updated, won't you? And make sure you wrap up warm.'

'Will do, Mum,' Bo replied. 'Thanks. Bye.' The line went dead. Bo yawned and gazed blankly out of the window for a few moments. Then she picked up her phone again and sent Kirsten a text:

I've arrived. Florence is here (v nice!) and someone called Simon. (A writer – doesn't say much. Suspect he thinks I'm an idiot.) Wish you were here x

Then she stood up, took her toiletries bag from the bed, and padded along the hallway to the bathroom.

Twenty minutes later, Bo pulled the duvet back and climbed into bed. She turned off the lamp then lay in the pitch blackness, savouring the absence of sirens and traffic noise outside. The only sound was the rain. It was different from the rain in London; it was uncompromising and relentless. Yet there was something oddly comforting about hearing it pound against the roof and batter the windowpane from inside the well-insulated summerhouse. Bo thought of the draughty flat in Holloway, with its rotting wooden window frames and patch of damp on the hallway ceiling. The Danes, she thought admiringly, certainly knew how to protect their homes against the elements.

By the time Kirsten's reply arrived a few minutes later (*Great! Can't wait to join you. Never met Simon. Sounds like he's got you sussed though*) Bo had fallen fast asleep.

Chapter 12

When Bo woke from a deep sleep the following morning, raindrops were still bouncing exuberantly on the windowsill. She swung her legs over the side of the mattress, rubbed her face groggily, then went over to the window. It was nine o'clock, but the November dawn appeared still to be breaking, grey and half-hearted, with enough lingering darkness for the street lamps to remain lit. In the distance, between the red-tiled roofs of the neighbouring houses, she could just make out a triangular wedge of blue-grey sea, almost indistinguishable from the steely sky.

Bo pulled on her dressing gown, smoothed her hair back into a loose ponytail, and made her way downstairs. Simon was at the kitchen counter in a grey T-shirt and faded pyjama bottoms, cutting a slice of rye bread from what was left of yesterday's loaf.

'Morning,' she murmured, tying the cord of her dressing gown in front of her waist.

'All right?' he replied with a cursory nod. A tuft of brown hair was sticking up at the back of his head, lending his appearance a boyish quality which seemed at odds with his aloof manner.

'Morning, babe, sleep well?' Florence asked. She was seated at the dining table sipping from a cup of coffee, a sketchpad and tin of pencils spread out in front of her.

'Like a baby,' Bo replied, pouring herself a coffee. On her way to the table she peered over Florence's shoulder to look at the drawing on her pad. It was a pencil sketch of a seashell, its intricate spirals rendered in exquisite detail.

'Wow, that's amazing,' Bo murmured admiringly.

'Thanks,' Florence replied, visibly gratified. 'I'd hoped to get out and do some sketching today, but the weather's put paid to that.'

The rain continued to batter the outside of the summerhouse all morning, and it didn't take long for an air of frustration to descend on the group. Florence tinkered with her sketches and Simon set up his laptop at the opposite end of the table and was quickly engrossed in his work, pounding at his keyboard with two fingers. Not wanting to get in their way, Bo wandered through the double doors to the living room. She lit the fire in the stove, sank into an armchair and photographed her socked feet in front of the dancing orange flames then, for want of anything else to do, posted the pictures to Instagram with the hashtags #cosy and #Denmark.

At lunchtime, they helped themselves to the dwindling supplies from the fridge. (Simon had finished the bread at breakfast, so they had no choice but to eat crackers with their cold meats and cheese.) The atmosphere was strained, in a way that befitted three strangers living at close quarters in an unfamiliar house. Simon was just as unforthcoming and uncommunicative as ever, and even Florence seemed slightly dejected. Whether it was the rain that had lowered her spirits, or Simon's surliness, Bo wasn't sure.

After lunch, Bo peered out through the window. The terrace was slick with rainwater and the sky overhead was battleship-grey but, for now at least, the rain had stopped. It was not exactly inviting out there, but Bo was beginning to find the atmosphere in the summerhouse claustrophobic. Behind her at the table, Simon had opened his laptop and looked like he was settling down for an afternoon of typing and frowning.

'I think I might head into town to explore. I can pick up a few supplies for dinner. Anyone want to come with me?' Bo asked, turning to face the room. She saw Simon's jaw clench.

'I've got work to do here, thanks,' he said, not taking his eyes off the screen.

Florence sighed and closed the lid of her pencil tin. 'Yes, I think I need a change of scene too,' she replied, her gaze sliding pointedly back in Simon's direction. He had begun his relentless, two-fingered typing again, oblivious to the effect his mood was having on the girls. 'There's a little supermarket in the centre of town,' Florence said. After a pause, she grinned. 'And we can stop for a pastry at the harbour on our way back.'

It took Bo twenty minutes to get ready for the freezing temperatures she knew awaited her beyond the front door. She put on as many layers as she could: a thermal vest and leggings, followed by a knitted jumper and a thick fleece on top, with jeans and two pairs of socks. She forced her arms into her coat, feeling the seams give as the fabric strained to accommodate her extra bulk. Then she pulled her woolly hat on as low as it would go and wound her scarf around her face and neck, leaving only her eyes exposed. Catching sight of herself in a mirror, she thought she resembled a comically inept bank robber.

She eyed Florence's knee-length goose-down coat enviously when, at last, they were ready to set off. With their heads bowed against the biting wind, they picked their way between the puddles towards the town centre. Skagen's main shopping street was a cobbled thoroughfare lined with pretty buildings, in the town's typical yellow and red colours. The picturesque, colourful scene brought to mind a toy-town, almost as if the whole place were made of Lego, but most of the boutiques, craft shops and cafés which lined the street were shut, their window displays dark and doors locked, giving the place a mournful, out-of-season feel.

'Where is everyone?' Bo asked, fighting to hold her hood up against the wind.

'A lot of these places only open for the summer,' Florence answered, peeling away a strand of blonde hair that had blown into her mouth. They walked on, concentrating on maintaining their footing on the slippery cobbles, until Florence raised a gloved hand to indicate a side street, where Bo could see the brightly lit frontage of a Netto supermarket standing out amidst the darkened windows of the empty shops either side.

A blast of warm air from a heating vent hit them as soon as they stepped through the sliding doors, making the tips of Bo's ears and nose tingle. Florence seemed to know her way around, methodically filling their basket with enough essentials to see them through the next couple of days. Bo meandered after her, enjoying the novelty of browsing shelves full of mysterious foreign products.

Afterwards they carried their shopping bags to the harbour, in search of coffee and pastries as a reward for their efforts. They passed a huge industrial dock full of fishing trawlers and warehouses, then carried on to the adjacent marina, where a few forlorn fishing boats bobbed in the wind and seagulls cried, wheeling overhead. The marina's curved concourse was lined with cute red buildings beneath gabled rooftops. Bo tried to imagine the place in the summer, with yachts and pleasure boats moored at the water's edge, and crowds of holidaymakers thronging outside the bars and restaurants, but in the depths of winter the walkway was deserted and the picnic benches stood empty.

Their destination was the last building in the row. Bo pushed open the door and looked around the bustling café, savouring the tantalising aroma of warm pastry and coffee.

'What do you fancy?' Florence asked at the serving counter. Bo stared at the mouth-watering display of pastries and cakes presented in neat rows behind the glass, momentarily paralysed by the vast choice before her. She eventually pointed to a cinnamon-dusted pastry coiled like a snail's shell.

'A *snegle*. Good choice,' Florence said, and she indicated to the Nordic-looking blonde behind the counter that they wanted two.

Balancing their pastries and coffees on wooden trays, they weaved a path between the seated customers to an unoccupied table by the window.

'This is lovely,' Bo murmured, unzipping her coat, taking in the simple elegance of the décor and the flickering candle on the table.

'Bit nicer than Greggs, isn't it?' Florence said with a grin.

Bo sank her teeth into the *snegle*, which managed to be at once deliciously crisp yet gooey. 'Mmmohmygod, that's good,' she murmured, licking cinnamon sugar from her fingertips.

'The pastries over here are the dog's bollocks,' Florence agreed, taking a sip of coffee.

The cosy ambience of the café was a relief after the tense morning at the summerhouse. The background hum of chatter, clinking spoons and the hiss of the coffee machine was far more conducive to relaxed conversation than the intermittent clicking of Simon's typing.

In between sips of coffee and mouthfuls of pastry, Bo discovered that Florence was twenty-nine, lived alone in a flat in Hove, and that she sold her drawings and ceramics primarily at local markets, as well as in a little gallery in Brighton.

'I do a bit of teaching on the side, too, to make ends meet. Landscape classes on the beach, that kind of thing.'

'It sounds idyllic,' Bo commented enviously, thinking of the life she had left behind, the daily commute into central London and hours spent in an airless, corporate office.

Florence took a bite of her pastry, a slight frown forming between her brows. 'Dunno about idyllic,' she said matter-of-factly, 'but it suits me.'

The conversation had brought Bo's own lack of employment to mind, and she gave a downcast sigh.

'You all right, babe?' Florence asked, her blue eyes round with concern.

'I'm fine, really,' Bo insisted with a forced smile. 'I just remembered that I'm unemployed, that's all.' She gave a mirthless laugh.

'I'm sure something else will turn up soon,' Florence said encouragingly. Bo stared out of the window at the grey, wintry harbour, and watched the seagulls dive and soar above the choppy waters.

'Mmm, maybe,' she said thoughtfully. 'It's not like working in marketing for an IT company was ever my life's ambition,' Bo went on. 'It just, sort of, happened. And then it always felt like too much of a risk to chuck it in.'

Florence gave an understanding nod and the two of them sat in contemplative silence for a few moments.

'Did you always know you wanted to be an artist?' Bo asked, finally.

Florence's nose wrinkled. 'I guess from about the age of sixteen, I did,' she replied. 'But if it makes you feel any better, I've had my fair share of shitty jobs, too.' Bo raised a quizzical eyebrow. 'Let's see . . .' Florence said, screwing up her eyes in concentration. 'While I was at art college I worked in the kitchen of a greasy spoon in Camberwell. Spent every weekend up to my elbows in cooking oil. Then there was six months of telesales for an office stationery supplier in Worthing, trying to flog punched pockets and window envelopes to bored secretaries.'

Bo's face hovered somewhere between amusement and pity, but Florence wasn't done yet. 'After that I did a summer dressed as Wonder Woman, carrying a placard for an all-you-can-eat Tex-Mex buffet at a junction on the A23.'

Bo grimaced. 'You're a woman of many talents, clearly.'

'Aren't I just?' Florence said sardonically. 'And I can tell you something for nothing, babe. Don't ever wear a polyester cape with bustier and hot-pants. It will only end in tears. The static!' she gasped in a horrified stage whisper.

'I'll try and remember that, next time I'm choosing my cosplay outfits,' Bo giggled. 'Natural fibres only.' Florence nodded solemnly.

'But, the truth is, you just do what you have to do to scrape by, don't you?' Florence said philosophically. 'All those shitty jobs just made me even more determined to make a living as an artist. If it wasn't for the ceramics, I'd probably still be standing at those traffic lights plucking star-spangled wedgies out of my bum-crack.'

Bo snorted. 'Well, from what I've seen of your sketches, I'd say the A23's loss is the art world's gain.'

'Too kind, too kind,' Florence intoned grandly, clutching one hand to her chest.

'It must be nice to have a talent, though,' Bo commented wistfully, allowing her gaze to slide back out towards the sea. 'Something you're really passionate about.'

'Everyone's got a talent, babe,' Florence countered. 'Maybe yours is ... marketing for an IT company.'

Bo laughed. 'God help me if it is!' she whispered,

appalled. They were silent for a few moments. 'You know, when I was younger, I always dreamed of ... doing something with food,' Bo said quietly, as if she was making a slightly shameful confession.

'Oh, right?' Florence answered, intrigued. 'What kind of thing?'

'Well, something like this, I guess,' she said, holding up the last chunk of her cinnamon *snegle*. 'I've always loved baking. Making cakes for parties, or weddings perhaps. I'm not exactly sure.'

A memory came unbidden into Bo's mind, of the first (and only) time she had broached the subject of her culinary ambitions with her parents. It had been a balmy evening during the summer between her sixth form years, and they had just eaten dinner on the shade-dappled patio of the back garden in Buckinghamshire. Bo mentioned that she had found a pastry chef course at a catering college that she liked the look of. Her father's face had clouded, and he had muttered something about how *someone of her abilities* could *aim higher than that*. Her mother had strenuously agreed, reminding Bo that her education and upbringing meant that *the world was her oyster,* and that she knew something about the subject, as her cousin Jeanette had worked in catering.

'Catering is not a family-friendly profession. Very anti-social hours,' Barbara had said in a voice heavy with warning. 'You'd have to work evenings and weekends ...' She had trailed off with a pained look, knowing that the argument would carry a lot of force with a sociable seventeen-year-old for whom evenings and weekends were sacrosanct.

Sensing the opposition she would face, Bo had chosen to let the subject of catering college drop. Perhaps her parents were right and it was just a passing phase, an adolescent equivalent of her childhood dream of becoming a prima ballerina for the Royal Ballet (cruelly crushed at the age of eight by a sharp-faced ballet teacher who had told her that she would *never dance en pointe*). Better to play it safe and follow her parents' and teachers' advice, work hard on her A levels and apply to university.

With a disconsolate sigh, Bo dabbed the last crumbs of pastry from her plate with the tip of her thumb. 'Sometimes, life just . . . gets in the way, doesn't it?' she said wistfully. 'I took the first job I was offered when I graduated from uni. Which just so happened to be in marketing. And now here I am . . .' Her voice trailed away. 'Twenty-six and unemployed,' she concluded bluntly.

Florence drained her coffee then said breezily, 'Well, babe, just say the word if you want me to dig out the number for the Tex-Mex buffet. They're always recruiting for new Wonder Women.'

Bo smiled into her coffee cup. 'Thanks, I'll bear it in mind.'

Outside the window, the heavy sky threatened rain and the boats in the harbour were bobbing vigorously.

'We should head back. Looks like it's about to start pissing down again,' Florence said glumly.

'What do you think of Simon?' Bo asked, as they gathered their things. She had been dying to ask Florence about their housemate, and their conversation seemed to have established enough of a sisterly rapport for her to do so.

'Silent Simon?' Florence quipped with a mischievous grin, fastening her hood snugly beneath her chin.

'He's a bit intense, isn't he?' Bo mused. 'Grumpy, even. Or is that just me?'

Florence shook her head. '*Definitely* not just you, babe!' she grinned, with a roll of her eyes.

'I'm dying to know what he's writing, though,' Bo said, wrapping her scarf around her neck. 'Scandi noir, I reckon. Surly detectives, bleak landscapes, ruthless serial killers.'

'Maybe it's a gory account of how he would kill us both and hide the bodies,' Florence said blithely.

'Chop us up and burn us in the stove,' Bo said with a grin.

'Or dump us at sea,' replied Florence, staring at the grey waves in the distance.

'I don't think he likes us very much, do you?' Bo asked.

Florence shrugged. 'But, you know what, babe?' she said with a sly grin. 'When it comes to men, I've always liked a challenge.'

Bo gave a slow, knowing nod as she zipped up her coat, then together they headed back out into the dusky harbour.

Chapter 13

When they got back to the summerhouse, Simon was at the dining table, typing in the blue glow of his laptop. At the sound of the front door opening, he looked round sharply, as if irritated by the interruption.

'Hi,' Florence said, flicking on the light switch. 'How's the writing going?'

Simon blinked, startled by the light.

'Slowly,' he replied, turning back to his screen and rubbing his stubbled jaw.

Bo and Florence exchanged a comradely look and walked past him to the kitchen counter.

'Cuppa, anyone?' Florence asked, as Bo set about unpacking the shopping.

'Please,' Bo murmured, unloading the ingredients for their evening meal into the fridge. Simon seemed not to have heard her.

Clara Christensen

'Simon?' Florence repeated, a hint of a challenge in her voice.

'Hmm, sorry, what?' Simon mumbled, reluctantly tearing his eyes away from his laptop.

Florence fixed him with a steely look. 'I said, would you like a cup of tea?'

'Oh, okay. Thank you,' he answered with a martyred sigh, as if the burden of being offered tea was a heavy one.

Bo continued to empty the shopping bags in silence while Florence, her lips pursed, made tea.

'There you go,' Florence said crisply a few minutes later, as she placed a mug on the table next to Simon's laptop.

Bo wandered through the double doors to the living room, grabbed a magazine from the coffee table, and lowered herself into one of the stylishly ergonomic armchairs. The magazine offered a frothy mix of celebrity gossip and fashion, a combination which Bo usually found irresistible but, on this occasion, nothing in its pages held her attention. She found it impossible to muster any enthusiasm for an interview with a reality TV star who had recently split from her love-rat boyfriend, and a feature on *Hot Looks for the Office Christmas Party* merely reminded her that she would not have an office party to attend this Christmas.

Bo tossed the magazine back onto the coffee table and picked up her phone, to find an unread message from Kirsten.

Trying to book a ticket – no seats! Flights cancelled due to storm at Aalborg!

Bo's eyes flickered to the window. It was dark outside but she could hear rain billowing past in gales.

Oh dear. It is a bit stormy here. Hope you can get something soon x

Bo tried to fight a sinking feeling at the realisation that Kirsten would not be flying out imminently. She longed for her friend to arrive, not least to help ease the tension that was brewing between Florence and Simon.

At a loss for what else to do, Bo composed another message.

Hi Hayley. Missing you all. What's new in the office?

Her thumb hovered over the send button. She was certain that, with her appetite for high drama, Hayley would welcome the chance to furnish Bo with the latest Aspect gossip. But if the gossip was about Ben and Charlotte, would Bo want to hear it? The grown-up thing to do, unquestionably, would be to delete the message and try to put thoughts of Ben from her mind. That was, after all, part of the reason for her coming to Denmark in the first place. But, as Bo had discovered on many occasions, doing the grown-up thing did not always come easily to her. With a pulse of dread mingled with excitement, she pressed send.

Next, she opened her email to see if any of the recruitment agencies had been in touch. They hadn't, and her email inbox boasted nothing more than a string of sales mailshots exhorting her to take advantage of their *limited time only* offers. She had only once succumbed to such an offer, signing up for a course of eight stand-up tanning sessions for the price of six at her local beauty spa. She had convinced herself she was getting a bargain, although in reality she had only turned up for one session, having found the experience of stripping to her knickers to stand in a neon-lit cubicle blaring out dance music thoroughly demoralising from start to finish.

She deleted the emails from her inbox without opening them. Whatever they were offering would be of little interest to her here, in this remote, rain-soaked seaside resort.

She was about to check Facebook when a text from Hayley flashed up.

Hi Bo, good to hear from you. It's all kicked off since you left – are you sitting down?

Bo felt a lurch of apprehension. She could hear the glee behind Hayley's words, and had a sudden vision of the view from her old desk, of Hayley grinning eagerly at her across the blue divider, about to impart her latest snippet of gossip.

As a matter of fact, I am. What's happened? Bo replied.

Bo stared at the crackling orange logs in the stove, trying to steady the fluttering sensation in her stomach, until a swooshing sound from her phone heralded the arrival of Hayley's reply.

Matt's resigned, and been replaced by Ben. Didn't see that coming!

'Nope, nor did I,' Bo muttered under her breath.

Turns out I was wrong about Charlotte getting the chop, too. She's taken over Ben's accounts.

Bo sighed and scrolled down the message with her thumb, wondering if Hayley was simply going to repeat the same news she had already heard from Ben, but her peripheral vision had glimpsed something further down the screen which made her stomach drop.

AND, guess what? Hayley went on, the use of caps-lock eloquently conveying her excitement. *THIS IS TOP SECRET! It wasn't Ben who made a move on Charlotte in Milton Keynes, it was Matt!*

Bo stared at her screen in disbelief.

No way! Bo typed. *Who told you?* she added, needing to hear corroboration before she could believe what she had read. 'Come on, Hayley,' Bo muttered under her breath, impatiently watching the three flashing dots on her screen while Hayley typed.

Her phone swooshed.

Charlotte told me herself! We went for lunch yesterday and she fessed up. The three of them were summoned to MK at short notice. Client throwing his toys out of the pram. They ended up getting pissed in the hotel bar. Ben went to get drinks and next thing Charlotte knew, Matt grabbed her leg under the table and tried to shove his tongue down her throat! Ben practically had to peel Matt off her! Talk about #awks.

Bo curled her legs up onto the leather-cushion and hugged her knees. Her heart was racing.

Cringe! Poor Charlotte, she typed, feeling a flicker of sisterly compassion for her former colleague. There was so much she wanted to ask Hayley, but couldn't risk typing something that might reveal the extent of her own involvement in this particular office drama. She needed time to process what she had read so, rather than fish for more details, she signed off the text with a bland *Gotta go. Missing you all x*

She placed the phone on the arm of the sofa and stared blankly at the flickering fire, vaguely aware of the sound of Simon's typing drifting through the double doors. Why had Ben not told her the truth about what had happened in Milton Keynes when she confronted him about it? Had he been adhering to some blokeish code of honour which required him not to expose his boss as an office lothario? Whatever his reasons had been, she felt cross with Ben for allowing her to blunder into a mire of recrimination rather than tell her the truth. But none of that changed the fact she had wrongly accused him of cheating. On that score, she was undeniably in the wrong.

With a long exhalation, Bo picked up her phone and composed a message to Ben, typing, deleting and retyping, before eventually settling on, *I think I owe you an apology.*

*

That evening, when the three of them were eating meat-balls and spaghetti in the encircling glow of the pendant lamps, Florence made a renewed attempt to engage Simon in conversation.

'So, Simon, I'd be happy to read whatever you're working on, if you'd like a second opinion,' she offered.

Simon's face twisted uncomfortably. 'Thanks, but I don't think so,' he replied. Bo noticed the flicker of disappointment in Florence's eyes, but Simon seemed oblivious.

'So, do you live in London, Simon?' Florence persevered. Simon blinked at her.

'Yes. Streatham,' he answered, twirling his fork in his spaghetti. There was a short pause, after which it seemed to occur to Simon that he ought to reciprocate. 'How about you?'

'Hove,' Florence replied. 'I grew up in Sheen, but moved down to Sussex after art college and have been there ever since.' Then, with a slightly forced casualness, Florence said, 'So, do you live on your own, Simon? Or with a—' She was cut off by a sudden blast of freezing air which made the pendant lights sway and the blinds rattle against the windows.

Bo looked over her shoulder to see a man closing the front door behind him. He looked around thirty. Fair-haired, wearing a goose-down jacket, skinny jeans and metal-framed glasses, his appearance exhaled Danishness.

'Hi, hi,' he said deferentially, upon seeing three surprised faces staring at him from the dining table. 'I'm Emil. I'm sorry to interrupt your meal,' he apologised, in barely accented English.

'No worries, babe. I'm Florence. Pleased to meet you,' Florence said convivially, pushing back her chair and walking over to shake his hand. 'You've come to stay, I take it?' she asked, glancing at the small suitcase at his feet.

'Yes, for a few days,' Emil replied. 'Pernille said it would be okay. Did she . . . er . . . tell you I was coming?' he asked anxiously, stamping his wet boots on the doormat. There was something endearing, Bo thought, about his courteousness, and his eagerness not to intrude.

'She didn't mention it to me, but don't worry,' Florence reassured him. 'The more the merrier, eh?' she said chirpily, with a sidelong glance at Simon, whose demeanour was far from merry.

Bo stood up and went over to the door, doing a mental inventory of the bedrooms along the upstairs landing, wondering with faint alarm if there were enough to accommodate another guest. She could imagine Simon's appalled response if Florence broke the news that he and the new arrival would have to share.

'Hi, I'm Bo,' she said, offering her hand to the stranger.

'Bo – that's a Danish name, no?' Emil said, turning to her with a smile, and she couldn't help but notice he was rather attractive, in a typically Scandinavian way: his blond hair was cut short at the sides but longer on top, he had pale blue eyes and a light stubble across his jaw. His hand hadn't yet adjusted to the warmth of the house and, when he took her hand, his skin felt cool to the touch.

'No, I don't think so,' she replied, noticing a glimmer of disappointment in his eyes. 'It's short for Boughay,' she explained, as if that might somehow compensate for its lack of Danishness.

'Nice to meet you, Boughay,' Emil said, his blue eyes creasing at the corners. She smiled coyly and reflexively raised her free hand to smooth her hair.

Aware that Simon had come over and was hovering behind her, Bo dropped Emil's gaze and stepped sideways.

'I'm Simon,' Simon said gruffly, giving Emil's hand a brisk shake.

'Would you like something to eat, Emil?' Florence asked, making for the kitchen counter. 'There's some spaghetti if you're hungry.'

Emil unzipped his puffy jacket and hung it on the bulging coat rack. 'Thank you, it smells delicious,' he said politely. It was only the rhythm of his speech, the inflection in slightly unexpected places, that gave away that English was not his mother tongue. Bo returned to her seat but watched out of the corner of her eye as he bent down to unlace his boots. He had the slim, long-limbed physique which, she had noted enviously, many Danes seemed blessed with.

Relieved of his outer layers, Emil followed the others to the table. As he took the seat next to Simon, Bo noticed a subtle shift in Simon's body language; he leaned back in his chair, folding his hands behind his head. Bo had seen Ben assume the same pose many times, when he was trying to assert his superiority over male colleagues. Did Simon feel threatened by the appearance of a rival male? she wondered.

'So, what brings you to Skagen, Emil?' Bo asked, twirling her fork in her spaghetti. 'Are you here to visit family?'

'No, not exactly,' Emil answered. 'My mother died, two months ago.' Bo's fork froze on its way to her mouth.

'Oh,' she whispered, appalled.

'She wanted to . . . I've brought her back to . . . um . . .'

Bo felt paralysed with awkwardness, terrified Emil was about to tell them his mother's coffin was outside. Out of the corner of her eye, Bo glimpsed Florence at the kitchen counter: she had been spooning meatballs into a bowl for Emil but seemed to have halted in mid-scoop. Even Simon looked aghast.

Florence was the first to regain her composure. 'Are you here to scatter her ashes?' she volunteered, gently placing the bowl of spaghetti on the table in front of him.

'Yes, that's right,' Emil said, to everyone's palpable relief.

If ever there was a conversation killer, Bo discovered, it was finding out that your new houseguest had his mother's ashes stored in his luggage. Simon fiddled with the cutlery on his empty bowl, while the others concentrated hard on their food, relieved at having a pretext for not talking.

'My family used to come to Skagen every summer, when I was a child,' Emil explained, as if sensing their discomfort. 'My parents rented a summerhouse like this one. Do you know Grenen?' he asked, looking around the table.

Simon and Bo looked at him blankly but Florence's face flickered with recognition. 'Just north of here, right?' she asked.

'Yes, that's right,' Emil said. 'It's well known in Denmark.'

He described a strip of sand protruding from the northernmost tip of the country, where waves from the North Sea and the Baltic collide.

'I've sketched the view there many times,' Florence chipped in. 'It's beautiful.'

Emil nodded. 'That is where my mum wanted to have her ashes scattered. I might wait for the rain to stop first, though. Mum always hated rain.'

He caught Bo's eye across the table and smiled shyly. Bo smiled back, racking her brain for something appropriate to say, something that would sound tactful and supportive and . . . grown-up. But nothing came to mind. Bo had never known anyone of her age who had experienced the loss of a parent, let alone a quietly attractive Danish man whom she had only met five minutes earlier.

The rest of them had all finished eating, and the conversation seemed to have petered to a halt.

Eventually, Emil stood up and went over to the rucksack which he had propped against the door. They all watched as he unzipped the bag and started rooting around inside. *Oh please,* thought Bo, *please don't show us your mother's ashes.* But, instead of a casket, Emil drew out a glass bottle full of bright yellow liquid.

'Would anyone like some schnapps?' he asked.

At the table, there was an almost audible collective sigh of relief.

'Now you're talking, Emil,' Florence said, rising from the table and moving across the kitchen to retrieve four shot glasses from a cupboard, while Bo and Simon cleared away the dirty plates. Emil removed the stopper from the bottle and placed it in the middle of the table.

'It's home-made, with juniper berries—' he began.

'Emil, babe, you had me at schnapps,' Florence deadpanned, placing a hand on his shoulder as she set a shot glass down in front of him. Bo thought she saw Simon register the gesture with a peeved look.

Emil filled the tiny shot glasses. '*Skål*,' Emil toasted genially, holding his glass out to clink against the others'.

'*Skål*,' they repeated. Bo raised the glass to her lips. It smelt of pine but tasted pleasantly spicy and sweet, warming her throat as she swallowed it.

'So what do you do, Emil?' Florence asked genially, returning her glass to the table.

'I'm a chef. In Copenhagen.'

'Well, *why* didn't you say?' she admonished him, with an exaggerated eye roll which belied the disinhibiting effect of the schnapps. 'We'd have let you cook dinner, if we'd known.'

Emil raised his hands in a gesture of humble apology. 'I would be happy to. Tomorrow, perhaps?'

Across the table, Bo noticed Simon's eyes darting between Florence and Emil, and the thought flashed across her mind that he seemed a little put out by the way Emil had become the focus of Florence's attention. Perhaps Simon cared more about what Florence thought of him than he had let on.

'Simon's writing a novel set in Denmark,' Bo said mischievously, curious to hear whether Simon would offer any more detail about his work, under the influence of the schnapps.

'Is that right?' answered Emil, facing Simon with a look of curiosity.

'Oh, he won't tell you anything about it; it's a *secret*,' Florence drawled sarcastically, swigging the last of her schnapps. 'It must be really *shocking*,' she teased. 'Full of sexual violence and torture.'

Simon frowned and shook his head, but seemed caught between annoyance and amusement. 'It's not like that at all,' he said quietly, the merest trace of a smile hovering around his lips. Bo suspected he was secretly enjoying the attention.

'Well then, why won't you tell us anything about it?' Florence persisted. 'Unless—' She gasped dramatically, her eyes widening. 'Unless, you're not really writing anything at all, just pretending to. Typing out the same phrase over and over, like Jack Nicholson in that film – what's that – what's it . . .' Florence clicked her fingers woozily.

'*The Shining?*' Bo suggested, watching Emil top up Florence's glass.

'That's the one!' Florence shrieked. 'He pretends to be writing a book then goes crazy and tries to murder his wife.'

Simon eyed her levelly across the table. 'I am *not* like Jack Nicholson in *The Shining*. And I *am* writing a book.' He fixed Florence with an intense stare. 'But if I do decide to murder anyone,' he said darkly, raising the glass to his lips, 'you'll be the first to know.'

Florence narrowed her eyes, as if she had taken the comment as a gauntlet being thrown down. 'I'm going to make it my mission,' she intoned sombrely, 'to make sure Simon does not spend *all* his time in Skagen working.' Simon rolled his eyes and sipped his schnapps. 'No complaints, Simon. It's for your own good. In fact, I think we should start now. Who wants to play a game?' she asked, looking around the table, her eyes twinkling.

'I think a game is an excellent idea,' Emil said convivially.

Simon looked sceptical, as if he was wary of Florence's motives. 'It's not Spin the Bottle, is it?' he asked suspiciously.

Bo giggled, but Florence gave him a prim look. 'Of course not, Simon. What are we, fourteen? And before you ask, it's not Truth or Dare either.' Florence levered herself up from the table and walked a little unsteadily to the cupboard under the stairs.

'Don't worry, I'll find something *wholesome* and *educational* for us, Simon. I know you don't approve of *fun*.' Simon's jaw was clenched but Bo thought she saw amusement in his eyes.

Florence flung open the door to the cupboard beneath the stairs and began to rummage noisily through its contents. 'It's like a treasure trove of outdoor pursuits in here!' she called from inside. A kite, cricket stumps and a tube of shuttlecocks flew out from behind the door and landed with a clatter on the floorboards. 'Not much use for these in the pissing rain in November!' she complained. More scraping and a muffled crash as something toppled over inside the cupboard. 'Bollocks!' Florence muttered.

'Aha!' she shouted at last. 'This is just the thing.' She shuffled out of the cupboard on her knees, a rectangular cardboard box tucked under her elbow. 'The perfect game for being locked in a house with a writer who may or may not be a psychopath,' she announced, getting to her feet unsteadily. 'Scrabble!'

Bo's heart sank. In her experience, Scrabble was a game which inevitably outlasted the players' enthusiasm by several hours, besides which she lacked both the mental dexterity and the patience to come up with high-scoring words.

While Florence spread the board out in the middle of the dining table, Bo plugged her iPod into the speaker dock on the kitchen counter in the hope that background music might make the ordeal more bearable.

When she returned to her seat, Emil passed her the green cloth bag of letter tiles and she took seven and placed them on her little plastic shelf. She frowned. This was the Danish edition of the game, and she had selected an H, an L, and a hopeless selection of random vowels with mysterious accents, including three variations on the letter A.

She watched as the others placed the first round of words, hoping in vain that inspiration would strike while she waited. It didn't, and so, when it came to her turn, she reluctantly placed *æro* on the board.

'That's seven points, I think,' she mumbled, disappointedly. Simon, however, looked troubled. He leaned forwards and tapped his lip with the tip of his index finger. Bo noted his furrowed brow, and braced herself for an objection.

'*Aero*?' he asked in a nit-picking voice.

Bo nodded. 'I figured this' – she pointed to the Æ tile – 'would double as an *A* and an *E*. Given that it's not a letter we have in English.'

Emil gave her a supportive smile. 'That sounds fair,' he said.

Simon grunted. 'That's not my issue. *Aero* is not a word.' The others looked at him blankly.

'It is a word,' Bo protested, trying to keep the childish indignance out of her voice.

Simon shook his head. 'It's used in the formation of compound words. Aeronautics. Aerospace. But it's not a word in its own right.'

'It is a word, Simon,' Florence chipped in, her eyes blazing defiantly. 'It's a noun. An Aero's a chocolate bar, isn't it?'

Bo's face brightened. 'Good point,' she said, rallying, but Simon's lips remained pursed.

'Brand names are not accepted in Scrabble,' he stated quietly. Bo's shoulders sank.

'I think we should take a vote,' Florence said brightly. 'All those who think *Aero* is a word, raise a hand.' Florence's arm shot up, and Bo was touched to see Emil lift his right hand. Involuntarily she smiled at him, and he held her gaze for a fraction longer than was necessary. Feeling a blush rising, she lifted her own hand. 'There we have it,' Florence said briskly. 'Sorry, Simon, you're outvoted. *Aero is* a word.'

Thwarted, Simon let it pass, and made a note of Bo's modest score on the marking sheet.

'No need to look like you're sucking a lemon, Simon. You're still in the lead,' Florence teased. When it came to Simon's turn, he stared at his row of little plastic tiles, face twisted in agonised indecision. 'Come on, Simon,' Florence chided. 'It's one word, not a fucking novel. How hard can it be?'

Eventually he leaned forwards and placed *zygote* on a triple word score. Florence groaned and rolled her eyes, while Simon totted up his score. 'I think, including the double letter score on the Z, that makes ... eighty-four points.' Bo sank forward, her elbows on the table, her chin resting on her hands. This was going to be a long evening.

In the background, a Sugababes track segued into Girls Aloud on the speaker dock. 'Bo, is there anything on your iPod other than girl groups of the Noughties?' Simon asked, deadpan, as he restocked his letter tiles.

Bo looked up, hurt. 'There's nothing wrong with Girls Aloud,' she said, affronted, but she noticed Florence seemed to be stifling a laugh, and Emil stared hard at the board, keeping a diplomatic silence. She caught Florence's eye and gave her a hurt look.

'Sorry, babe,' Florence said earnestly. 'It's just ... have you added any music to your collection since 2004?'

'Actually, I have,' Bo countered defensively. 'There's some Taylor Swift on there as well.' A derisive snort issued from Simon's direction. 'It's the music I grew up with. Sorry if it isn't *cool* enough for you,' Bo said peevishly.

Bo's music preferences had long been subject to the teasing of her peers, being firmly at the mainstream end of the pop spectrum. Flicking through the playlist on her iPod once, Ben had laughingly dismissed her as having 'the musical taste of a nine-year-old girl'. Even during her teenage years, Bo had never had any inclination to seek out the edgier, more alternative groups that the cooler girls were into. As far as she was concerned, if a song had a catchy melody and a beat she could dance to if she felt so inclined, where was the shame in that?

The game wore on. Simon's victory was never in doubt, but, perhaps due to the schnapps, he became less doggedly pedantic as the evening went on. When Florence placed the word *psycho* with a barely concealed smirk, he made a note of her score without mentioning compound words once.

As Bo climbed the stairs to bed that evening it occurred to her that, for the first time since she had arrived in Skagen, she felt properly relaxed. She wasn't sure if it was the arrival of Emil, the effect of the schnapps on everyone's mood, or even the Scrabble, but she had not thought about Ben, or Charlotte, or her redundancy all evening. Closing the bedroom door softly behind her, she switched on the desk lamp and padded over to the window nook and fished her phone out of her bag.

Her feeling of bonhomie immediately drained away upon discovering a text from Ben: *An apology for what?*

Chapter 14

'Hey, Blu-ray.' Ben's pixelated image appeared on her phone via Skype. He was lying on the sofa in his flat, still wearing his work clothes.

'Hi. How are you?' she replied, curling herself into the cosy window nook and propping a cushion behind her head.

'Knackered,' he answered, shielding a yawn behind the back of his hand. He looked it: grey shadows circled his eyes, his complexion was pallid and his wavy hair looked messy and unkempt. Bo could hear the tinny babble of his TV in the background, and behind the sofa she could see the remains of a takeaway on the dining table: a crumpled brown paper bag, sauce-spattered foil trays and a single dirty plate.

'How's the new job going?' Bo asked dutifully. Ben's brow furrowed and he took a long gulp from a bottle of Cobra. She watched his Adam's apple rise and fall as he swallowed; there were shaving cuts and an angry rash on his neck.

'Stressful,' he said, wiping his mouth with the side of his hand. 'Being accounts director means the whole department's shit ends up as my shit.' He sounded bitter. 'I'm basically the whipping boy for any client with an axe to grind.'

She heard the angry honk of a car horn close outside his window; it made her jump but Ben didn't even notice. The soundtrack of urban life seemed jarring and discordant in contrast to the elemental quiet of Skagen. 'Oh dear. I'm sure it'll settle down soon. It's only been two days,' Bo soothed blandly.

Ben sneered. 'Yeah, we'll see about that.' He took another swig of beer and looked down the lens at her. 'So, I got your text,' he said guardedly. 'Apologise for what?'

She inhaled deeply through her nose. 'For what I said about Charlotte,' she replied expressionlessly. 'About Milton Keynes. Hayley got the wrong end of the stick, and when I saw that photo on Facebook, I just assumed . . .' On her phone screen, Ben's face twisted.

'Yeah well, I tried to tell you nothing happened, didn't I? And we were all pissed in that photo. You of all people should understand that drink can make you do stupid things.' His speech was slightly slurred, and she wondered how many Cobras he had consumed.

'I know. I'm sorry,' she said contritely. 'I just jumped to conclusions. I—'

'Forget about it,' he said, rubbing his eyes. 'It's no big deal.'

'But it is a big deal. I accused you of cheating. Aren't you pissed off with me?' In the corner of Bo's phone screen was a thumbnail-sized image of her perplexed face, her mouth forming a pout.

'To be honest, Blu-ray, I've got enough work shit pissing me off at the moment.' He gave a mirthless smile. 'I really haven't got the energy to be pissed off with you too.' Bo wasn't sure how she felt about this remark, so she said nothing.

'How's Denmark, anyway?' he asked, in a changing-the-subject voice, and raised his beer bottle to his lips once more.

She glanced out of the rain-speckled window beside her, into the blackness of the night. 'Cold, dark, wet,' she said frankly. 'But kind of invigorating.'

'Sounds ... Scandinavian,' he replied, bemused. 'Done anything exciting since you arrived?'

She considered the question for a moment. 'Um, not a lot. I walked to the marina this afternoon for a pastry. Tonight, we played Scrabble.'

'You and Kirsten *really* know how to have a good time, don't you?' he teased, but there was affection rather than malice in his voice.

'Oh, Kirsten's not here yet,' Bo said quickly. 'Her grand-father had a stroke on Saturday. She's planning to fly out as soon as the weather improves.'

'Oh,' he replied, raising a faintly quizzical eyebrow. 'So, who did you play Scrabble with?'

She hesitated. 'One of Kirsten's mum's friends is staying here too. She's called Florence,' she said in a light, incidental tone.

'Oh, right.' Ben's eyes glazed over and he gave another wide yawn. They talked for a little longer, with Bo asking innocuous questions about Ben's new job which led into another diatribe about his frustrations with work. Bo listened patiently, aware of a tightening sensation in her chest and a gnawing in her stomach, as if she was physically absorbing his stress. 'They're all fuckwits,' he concluded contemptuously, shaking his empty bottle by the neck before tossing it into a wastepaper bin next to the sofa.

'I'm sorry,' she murmured.

He pushed his hair out of his eyes and smiled at her. 'It's good to see you again, Blu-ray,' he said. 'The office isn't the same without you.'

A little later, lying in her single bed in the pitch darkness, Bo replayed their conversation in her mind. It had not gone at all as she had anticipated. She had anticipated sarcasm and sly remarks about how she had believed office tittle-tattle and jumped to conclusions. But instead, Ben had told her that he couldn't be bothered to be angry with her. She knew she ought to feel grateful, but in fact she felt obscurely short-changed.

She took a deep breath, inhaling the pine scent of the duvet, then exhaled slowly, trying to expel the agitation which she had absorbed from Ben. His casual dismissal of how she was spending her time in Denmark had stung, but hadn't surprised her. Ben would go out of his mind with boredom in a place like Skagen, without the buzz and bustle of city life, of restaurants and bars and parties and casual flirtations with attractive women. How would he cope being cooped up in the summerhouse with nothing but Scrabble for entertainment? She imagined his reaction: 'Fuck me, this is tedious,' he would mutter, pacing back and forth, staring out of the window at the rain. Then he would make some joke about this being why there were so many serial killers in Scandinavia, because at least murdering someone would give you something to do. The thought made her smile.

Before long, her mind started to wander and she knew that sleep would soon arrive, bringing respite from her confusion, temporarily at least. The last conscious thought to dart through her mind was to wonder why she had not mentioned that Simon and Emil were also staying at the house. What was behind the omission? she asked herself drowsily. It was not like she had anything to hide, after all. But before she could come up with an answer, her thoughts scattered and she drifted into the oblivion of sleep.

*

When Bo padded downstairs the following morning, she found all the others seated around the dining table. Simon was working at his laptop, Florence was sharpening pencils, and Emil was sipping coffee and flicking through a newspaper. He glanced up at her as she walked in.

'Good morning, Boughay,' he smiled. Something about being addressed by her full name made Bo feel unaccountably bashful. It struck her as endearingly polite and old-fashioned and, she had to admit, it felt so much nicer than being called Blu-ray.

'Morning,' she mumbled in his general direction, without meeting his eyes. Her conversation with Ben the previous evening had left her feeling even more preoccupied and troubled than before, and she had a vague notion that Emil's presence was adding to her confusion.

She made herself a coffee and sat down in the empty chair opposite Emil. Simon's look of pained concentration had the effect of making the others feel they ought not to talk so, for want of something to do, she checked her emails on her phone. She felt a tiny flurry of excitement when she saw she had a message from a recruitment agency informing her of a job opportunity that had come through. But upon closer inspection it turned out the job was a junior marketing position at a company in Staines, offering a salary significantly lower than the one she had been on at Aspect. She sent a polite reply declining to apply for the job. She set the phone back on the table with a disappointed sigh.

The weather worsened as the morning went on, the rain turning to sleet and, at times, snow. The tap of Simon's typing and the occasional gentle ting as Florence dropped a sharpened pencil into the tin box were the only sounds in the room.

'Does it ever get you down, Emil, the Danish weather?' Florence asked, when they all gathered to prepare lunch.

Emil looked out at the rain billowing past the window. 'In Denmark we have a saying: there is no such thing as bad weather, only bad clothing.'

'I can vouch for that,' Bo said ruefully, thinking of her woefully inadequate wool coat which was still drying out after her last foray into the Danish weather. She was leaning over the table, lighting a row of tealights in an effort to counteract the gloom.

'But even with the right clothing, there's only so much you can *do* in weather like this,' Simon observed, slicing a loaf of bread at the worktop.

Emil nodded. 'Yes, of course. That's why we have hue-gah.' From their various positions around the room the others looked up with puzzled, uncomprehending expressions.

'Hoo-what?' Florence repeated. Emil scribbled on a pad of Post-it notes then held it up for the others to read: *HYGGE.*

'Higger?' Florence said, squinting.

'Pronounced hue-gah,' Emil explained. 'It's what the Danes do in winter. We spend time in our homes, getting cosy, being with friends and family. And avoiding the weather,' he quipped, pressing the Post-it lightly onto the fridge door.

'That's all I've done since I got here – I'm *great* at *hygge*,' Bo joked, shaking the match to extinguish the flame.

'Maybe you are part-Danish after all,' Emil said approvingly, and she found herself, unaccountably, blushing.

'So, in other words,' Simon clarified, assuming the supercilious expression which Bo had privately begun to think of as his Scrabble face, 'if you're going to be stuck indoors for weeks on end, you might as well make yourself cosy.'

'Exactly,' Emil replied cheerfully.

'Well, come on then, Emil,' Florence said, placing a plate of cold meats on the table and sitting down. 'What should we all be doing, while we wait for the weather to improve? How can we get some *hygge*?'

Emil sniffed and looked around thoughtfully. 'We have the perfect *hyggeligt* environment,' he said. 'A cosy house, a fire in the stove, candles . . .'

'So, what you're saying is that *hygge*, basically, is all about soft furnishings?' Simon said archly. There it was again, the Scrabble face.

'I think you're missing the point, Simon,' Florence tutted, shooting him a stern look.

'Not just soft furnishings,' Emil answered patiently. '*Hygge* is a feeling of well-being, of togetherness, of enjoying what you are doing, and who you are with.' Bo glanced at Simon, half expecting him to make some quip about how *hygge* would be out of the question, if it required him to enjoy their company. But if he was thinking it, he didn't say it.

Sensing their scepticism, Emil went on, 'Last night, we played a game. That was very *hyggeligt*. Today, we could cook together.'

'Cook? Together?' Simon repeated, dubiously. 'All of us?'

'Why not?' answered Emil. 'To be *hyggeligt* we must do it together. *Hygge* is about the shared experience, not the end result.'

'I think it's a great idea,' Florence said decisively. 'It sounds like fun. And besides,' she added, with a sly grin at Simon, 'your Scandi–slasher–thriller can wait for a few hours.' Simon glared at her indignantly, but let the comment pass.

'What do you suggest we cook, Emil?' Bo asked, feeling a flutter of childlike excitement at the prospect of having a project for the afternoon.

Emil pondered for a moment. 'To be *hyggeligt*, it should be something slow and simple. You can't rush *hygge*. How about braised pork, perhaps with a celeriac and potato mash?'

'Sounds good to me,' Bo said enthusiastically.

'And to me,' Florence concurred. 'I've been living off cheese and rye bread for the last few days. Simon, how does braised pork grab you?'

Simon was cultivating the resentful air of a teenager being corralled into some sort of family activity against his will. He chewed on a mouthful of sandwich and shrugged to suggest that, when it came to braised pork, he held no opinion either way.

'But before we can cook, we need to shop for ingredients,' Emil said. As one, they all turned to look at the rain which was pounding the windows with renewed vigour.

'I think we should all go. That's fair, isn't it?' Bo said eventually. Emil nodded. Simon glowered.

'Come on, Simon,' Florence insisted, blowing out the candles and rising from the table. 'You haven't left the house since you got here. You need some fresh air. It won't take long and, besides, it'll be fun,' she insisted brightly. As the others gathered on the doormat waiting for him, Simon had no choice but to finish his sandwich and do as he was told.

The walk to the large supermarket on the outskirts of town was a freezing, windswept affair, during which they were alternately assailed by rain, sleet, and even a brief snow shower. Simon kept up his surly demeanour inside the supermarket, trailing three paces behind the others to signal his resentment at being made to forgo writing time for *this*.

Emil located the ingredients for his dish quickly, they paid at the till, and within an hour they were back at the house, laden with carrier bags.

'See, that wasn't so bad, was it, Simon?' Florence teased, stamping her wet boots on the doormat. Bo's woolly gloves were soaked through and her work coat, she noticed with mild alarm as she peeled it off, was acquiring the odour of mildew.

In the kitchen, Emil fastened an apron behind his back and briefed the others. 'To cook the Danish way means we share responsibility. This is about working together.' He placed the bag of vegetables on the table.

'Yes, boss,' Florence joked, rifling through the cutlery drawer.

'No, not boss,' Emil corrected her.

Florence looked chastened. 'All I'm saying is, you're the one who's the actual professional chef. Which, whether you like it or not, kind of makes you the boss. Not that I'm underestimating the importance of my contribution as peeler-in-chief,' she added, pulling the peeler out of the drawer and slamming the drawer shut with her hip.

Florence and Simon sat either side of the dining table, peeling and chopping vegetables, while Emil browned the pork cheeks on the hob. Bo, on a whim, had added the ingredients for chocolate muffins to their shopping basket, and she stood at the worktop whisking eggs and sugar in a large bowl.

'What do you think, Emil?' Florence said, holding up a peeled celeriac for his approval. 'Would you give me a job at your restaurant?'

Emil smiled. 'Well, first of all, it's not *my* restaurant,' he pointed out. 'I'm a sous-chef. But I think your peeling skills are . . . impressive.' Florence beamed.

'Is this the kind of food you make at the restaurant, Emil?' Bo asked, lifting the whisk to check the consistency of the pale, fluffy egg mixture.

Emil shook his head. 'No, the restaurant serves New Nordic cuisine.'

Simon's brow furrowed. 'New Nordic cuisine?' he repeated, with a glimmer of scepticism. 'Isn't that a fancy way of saying you serve weird stuff like live ants and moss?'

Emil's patient smile suggested this was not the first time he had been asked such a question. 'We have never served live ants, but the restaurant's ethos is to use native, seasonal ingredients in inventive ways. And yes, we sometimes serve moss in our dishes.'

Simon looked unconvinced, but Florence said, 'Well, I think it sounds amazing, babe. And if you'd cooked it I'd eat it, even if it was ants on a bed of moss.'

'Did you always want to be a chef, Emil?' Bo asked. She was stirring cocoa and melted butter into the bowl, watching as the mixture turned from opaque white to glossy brown.

'I've always loved to cook,' he answered. 'But, for me, I get most pleasure from cooking like this, for friends.'

'*Hygge*-cooking, you mean?' Florence piped up, looking pleased with herself.

'Exactly. In a restaurant, there are lines of command . . . even in Denmark,' he smiled. 'You work on your dish, but you don't know who is eating your food . . . For me, the pleasure is in the process. It is about cooking and talking, and then eating together afterwards.'

Bo listened thoughtfully, carefully folding in pieces of crushed Daim bar to the mixture. 'I think I know what you mean, Emil,' she commented. 'That's how I feel about baking, too. I want to see people's faces when they eat something I've baked. Otherwise, what's the point?'

She remembered, unexpectedly, the brownie she had taken into the office for Ben, on what had turned out to be the day she was made redundant. She had ended up throwing it in the bin beneath her desk, feeling that it was somehow to blame for everything that had gone wrong that day. This, she realised, was the first time she had baked since she made those chocolate brownies. She was lost in thought for a few moments, then glanced up to see Emil looking at her intently.

'Yes, that's it exactly,' he said softly.

Bo divided the mixture into muffin cases and slid them into the oven. Filling the sink with soapy water, she half-watched Emil at the hob, emptying a bottle of beer over the pork and vegetables, causing the hot pan to hiss and spit. Against her wishes, she found herself comparing him to Ben. The more she thought about it, the more diametrically opposed they seemed. It wasn't just the fact that Emil loved to cook, whereas Ben was proud of the fact that he struggled to boil an egg. It was something more fundamental than that. Emil seemed more at ease with himself as if he had nothing to prove; with Ben there was always an implicit competitiveness lurking beneath the surface, the sense that he was forever comparing himself to others, measuring his success against those around him. She realised how much it had put her on edge when they were together and made her feel that she continually had to prove herself worthy of him. It was only now that she was apart from him that she could see how exhausting it had been.

While the pork cheeks cooked, Simon made tea and they each chose a muffin, still warm from the oven, to take through to the living room. Bo sank into the armchair by the stove, curled her feet up under her and took her first bite. The muffin was gratifyingly soft and fluffy, and the nuggets of butterscotch from the Daim bar added a moreish crunch.

'Oh my God, Bo, that was amazing,' Florence said, scrunching up her empty muffin case and wiping crumbs from her lips. She was sitting on the sofa beside Simon and looked to him for confirmation.

He nodded. "'s good, Bo,' he agreed, through his mouthful.

For a few moments, the room was silent but for the tapping rain outside, the crackling logs in the fire, and the occasional slurp as they sipped their tea. The aroma of braising pork cheeks drifted through the double doors from the kitchen.

'You know what, I think there might be something in this *hygge* concept, Emil,' Bo said, snuggling luxuriantly into the padded curves of the armchair.

'Oh really?' he replied, and in the low light she could see the flickering flames inside the stove reflected in his glasses.

'Mmm. I mean, admittedly, the weather's still shit. And all I've really done since I arrived here is loll around in front of the fire. And sleep. And eat. But I have to admit, there's something quite cosy and relaxing about it.'

Bo stared into the fire, suddenly overcome by a profound weariness. She felt like five years of the relentless daily commute and frenetic lifestyle in London were giving way to an overwhelming need to slow down and just ... stop. But if she allowed herself to stop, Bo wondered, would she ever want to start again?

Across the room, Simon was stretched out on the sofa. Beside him, Florence had kicked her slippers off and turned sideways, her knees tucked under her chin, her bare feet resting on the leather cushion.

Florence scanned the room, a slight scowl on her brow. 'Honestly, look at us all. It's like an old people's home in here,' she joked.

'It's *hygge*, Florence,' Simon said sleepily, without lifting his head from the cushion he had propped under his neck. 'It's the Danish way. Don't try and fight it. When in Rome, and all that.'

Florence frowned and looked at her watch. 'Tell you what, we've got time for a game before the pork's ready. Who's up for it?' She looked around hopefully.

Bo let out a long, low groan. 'No more Scrabble, please,' she wailed.

'Fine. I'll go and see what else is in the cupboard,' Florence said, springing up from the sofa and walking through the double doors. The others listened as the door to the under-stairs cupboard creaked open.

'There's Monopoly,' Florence shouted. Bo winced. Monopoly, in her experience, was even worse than Scrabble for taking so long that it outlasted its enjoyability quotient by several hours. 'Cluedo? You might like that one, Simon. It could give you some ideas for your Scandi-murder-mystery.' Simon tutted and rolled his eyes.

Florence peered around the doorway and assumed a hokey accent: 'Eet was Herre Johansson, in dee billiards rumm, wid dee lead pipping.'

Bo giggled. 'Was that meant to be a Danish accent,

Florence?' she asked. 'It sounded kind of Italian. With a touch of Afrikaans thrown in.'

Simon had covered his face with his hands in embarrassment. 'Someone stop her!' he pleaded.

Florence disappeared back inside the cupboard. 'The only other game in here,' she called dubiously, 'is something called Daldøs. It's got some weird rectangular dice and a thing that looks like a toy boat full of holes.'

'You're really selling it to us,' Simon said archly.

Emil laughed. 'Yes, I know Daldøs. I used to play it all the time with my brother. Unfortunately, it is a game for two players only.'

'Thank goodness for that,' Florence said briskly, sliding the pieces back inside their cardboard box. 'Well, in that case, there's nothing else for it.' Florence slammed the cupboard door shut, and they watched her stride purposefully past the doorway towards the kitchen, reappearing a moment later brandishing a bunch of pens and the pad of Post-its.

'It'll have to be the Post-it game.' She waved the orange pad at them. Simon tutted and rolled his eyes.

'I'm up for that,' Bo said, sitting up in her chair. This was more her sort of game, something silly and fun, which didn't involve brainpower and waiting ages for other people to take their turn.

Florence handed out pens and Post-its and they each

scribbled a name, shielding their writing like schoolchildren guarding their answers during a test.

Florence turned to Simon. 'No peeking!' she warned, pressing the sticky note to his forehead. *Jack Nicholson in The Shining* it read, in her messy scrawl. Bo knelt up on the seat of her chair and leaned across to Emil, who had helpfully removed his glasses so that she could attach the Post-it to his head.

'Your turn,' Emil said, and she pulled her hair away from her face. She could feel the warmth of his fingertips through the paper and when she opened her eyes she saw he was smiling at her, but what could have been an intimate moment was rendered faintly comical by the fact that he had *Caitlyn Jenner* emblazoned across his forehead. Bo giggled and turned to Florence, who now had *Miss Marple* flapping against the bridge of her nose.

'Everyone ready?' Florence asked, clapping her hands together. 'I'll go first.'

'Oh, give it up, Simon, you're *such* a poor loser,' Florence chided. They were sitting around the table, eating the braised pork cheeks and mash and drinking wine. Bo had found more tea lights in a kitchen drawer and arranged them in a line, creating a column of dancing flames down the middle of the table.

'I am *not* a poor loser,' Simon said through a clenched jaw.

'I'm just pointing out that the rules of the Post-it game' – Florence opened her mouth to protest but he continued to speak over her – 'and yes, there *are* rules.' Florence closed her mouth and folded her arms, making a show of allowing him to finish.

'The rules state,' he went on pedantically, Scrabble face firmly in place, 'that you choose a name which is *either* a character from a film or TV show, *or* ...' He paused for emphasis. 'The name of a real person.' Florence stared at him defiantly. 'Jack Nicholson in *The Shining* combines both the actor and the character and is therefore, technically, in breach of the rules.'

'Oh, for God's sake, Simon, do shut up about your bloody rules,' Florence said tetchily. 'I couldn't remember his character's name in the film, that's all. And you got there in the end, didn't you? Admittedly it did take you about three times as many questions as the rest of us.' Simon shook his head despairingly. 'Besides,' Florence continued, 'your pity party is distracting attention from the rightful winner. Isn't that right, Taylor Swift?' Florence raised her glass in a toast to Bo, who nodded graciously.

They returned to their food, using chunks of rye bread to mop up the last of the sauce. There was a lull in the conversation, during which Bo noticed that the pattering rain, which had been continuous since she had woken up, had ceased. She looked up and stared into the middle distance.

'What's up, babe?' Florence asked, taking a sip of wine.

'I think the rain's stopped,' Bo said. She stood up and went over to the window, peering round the edge of the blind. 'Look at that!' she exclaimed, as excited as a little girl looking for Father Christmas. 'A clear sky!' A fat, silver moon hung in the inky sky, which was streaked with stars. She looked back over her shoulder excitedly. 'If it stays clear tomorrow, we might even get to see the sun.'

Later, as they were washing up in the kitchen, Bo turned to Emil. 'So how *hyggeligt* has today been, on a scale of one to ten?'

'Ten, definitely,' Emil replied.

Bo found herself inclined to agree.

Chapter 15

Bo balanced the tray of muffins precariously on the upturned fingertips of her left hand. In her other she clutched her phone. She was expecting an important call and kept glancing at the screen as she waited for the pedestrian lights to change. With the flashing green man, she started to walk, breaking into a run upon realising that she was going to be late for the meeting. She weaved between the sour-faced commuters on Oxford Street towards the Aspect office, doing her best to keep the muffins from falling from the tray onto the pavement. At the office she forced her way into the meeting room, to find Ben and Emil playing Scrabble at the table. 'Oh, hi, Blu-ray,' Ben said. 'You're late.'

'Shit,' Bo mumbled, waking from the dream with a start, disturbed by the lingering image of Ben and Emil playing Scrabble together. She flopped back onto her pillow and waited for her heart to stop racing. It took a few moments for her to register that sunlight was slanting into her room around the edges of the window blind. She clambered out of bed and staggered over to the window to yank open the blind.

'Wow,' she murmured, peering out through the glass. A bright blue sky filled the gaps between the rooftops and, in the distance, the sea sparkled.

Downstairs, sunshine poured in through the window onto the dining table where the others were eating breakfast. Conversation quickly turned to their plans for the day.

'Have you ever seen the Råbjerg Mile?' Emil asked. His question was greeted by blank looks. 'The Danish Desert,' he elaborated. 'It's an inland sand dune. You will want to see it. Trust me.' There was a general murmur of agreement.

'I'd like to see the sea, too, if there's time,' Bo said.

'We should be able to do both. Does Pernille still keep bikes here?' Emil asked.

'I think so,' Florence replied, rifling through one of the kitchen drawers and pulling out a bunch of keys. She stuffed her feet inside her boots, grabbed her coat and went out onto the terrace to open up the shed.

'I think I might take a look, too,' Simon announced authoritatively, rising from the table to follow her. 'I know a bit about bikes.'

The back door slammed shut behind Simon, and Bo found herself alone with Emil.

'Would you like a tea?' Bo asked, staring at the kettle self-consciously, irrationally concerned that her face might reveal to Emil that she had been dreaming about him.

'Thank you, that would be nice,' he replied, the corners of his blue eyes crinkling.

She made two teas and carried one over to where he was sitting at the table. As he took it from her, his hand brushed against hers and she turned away to hide the blush she knew was rising in her cheeks. *For God's sake Bo, get a grip,* she thought, inwardly cursing the dream which seemed to have rendered her as bashful as a schoolgirl. To spare herself further mortification she walked over to the window. On the terrace, Simon was hunched over one of the upturned bikes, fiddling with its chain. Florence was standing beside him, arms folded, wearing a look of impatience.

'They're getting like an old married couple, those two,' Bo observed wryly. Emil rose from his chair and came over to look, standing close behind Bo, so that she could almost feel his breath on the back of her neck. Simon squeezed the bike's tyres then turned it the right way up, before methodically moving on to the next. With an exasperated shake of her head, Florence turned and stomped back towards the house.

The back door swung open and Florence came inside, pink-cheeked and shivering. 'Simon's checking the bikes for *roadworthiness,*' she muttered.

Once Simon was satisfied that the bikes were up to par,

they put on their coats and boots and packed some food in a rucksack. Pulling her woolly gloves out of her coat pocket, Bo discovered she had forgotten to dry them out after their walk to the supermarket, and they were bunched up together in a mildewy ball.

'Urgh,' she groaned, pulling them apart to sniff the slightly sheepy odour of the damp wool.

'Hang on a minute,' Emil said. He bounded upstairs and she heard his footsteps through the ceiling as he ran down the hallway and into his room. A couple of minutes later he reappeared at the bottom of the stairs. 'You can borrow these, if you like. They're spares,' he said, handing her a pair of waterproof, insulated gloves.

They wheeled the bikes down the garden path, climbed onto their saddles then cycled in convoy through the quiet residential streets to pick up the main road heading south. Bo had not ridden a bike since she had moved to London. Cycling on the capital's fume-filled roads, at the mercy of impatient taxi drivers and diesel-belching buses, had never tempted her. But the flat, empty roads of Northern Jutland seemed purpose-built for cycling and, pedalling along behind Emil, her heart pumping, Bo felt a childlike sense of exhilaration.

About a mile out of town, a wall of white sand about forty feet high rose dramatically out of the flat, grassy scrubland. Emil pulled over at the side of the road and dismounted.

'This is Råbjerg,' he said, with a hint of patriotic pride.

'Bloody hell,' said Florence, propping her bike against a bench. 'How could I not have noticed this before?'

'You need to see the view from the top,' Emil urged.

They left their bikes by the bench and began to scramble up the side of the dune. The fine white sand gave way underfoot so they held hands, like a crocodile of nursery children, to keep themselves from slipping down the steep bank. Bo was at the back, clutching Emil's gloved hand tightly, struggling to keep up as the sand seeped into her boots.

When they reached the crest of the dune, a gust of wind made Bo squeeze her eyes shut to keep out the sand that swirled through the air, settling on her lips and coating her skin like a layer of dust. Turning her back to the wind, she gingerly opened her eyes. They were on the highest point for miles around. In the distance were the red rooftops of Skagen, the warehouses and trawlers at the port, and the glistening blue-grey sea beyond. Several tributaries snaked across the grassy scrubland out to sea, and she counted five lighthouses along the coastline. Simon took a camera out of his pocket and began to photograph the view.

'This is amazing!' Florence shouted. 'It's like a beach that's been dumped in the wrong place.'

'That's exactly what it is,' Emil laughed. 'The dune has been blowing inland from the coast for hundreds of years, and it's still moving.' He pointed to a white stone structure with a stepped gable roof on a distant patch of scrubland. 'See that?' he asked and they all turned to follow his eyeline. 'That's *den Tilsandede Kirke* – the buried church. It was abandoned after it was buried by sand. Now all that remains is the top of the tower.'

They traipsed along the crest of the dune until their boots were so full of sand that it was almost impossible to walk, then they half ran, half slid back down the slope to the grassy bank by the road. It was like playing in a giant sandpit and Bo had a childlike urge to shriek and roll sideways down the hill to the bottom. Once back on solid ground, they shook the sand off their clothes and out of their hair then removed their boots, tipping them sideways to send white sand cascading onto the ground.

'What do you think, Simon?' Florence said, nudging his arm with her shoulder, as they ate their sandwiches on the bench. 'A moving desert. A buried church. Perfect setting for a murder mystery, don't you think?'

He gave her a withering look. 'Good idea. You should write it,' he said drily. Bo laughed and wiped her mouth on the back of her sleeve to remove the layer of salty sand which had settled on her lips.

'I saw you take all those photos,' Florence went on, teasingly. 'Don't try and tell me you're not plotting something in that brooding head of yours.'

Simon took a sip from his water bottle but permitted himself a trace of a smile. 'Just research, that's all,' he said.

After lunch, they climbed onto the bikes and doubled back towards Skagen, skirting around the town to the beach at Ålbæk Bay. The sun was already beginning its descent by the time they arrived and the beach was deserted apart from the odd dog walker. Simon opened his rucksack and pulled out the kite from the under-stairs cupboard.

'You brought the kite, Simon?' Florence asked, astounded.

'Yep,' he replied airily. 'You jealous?'

'No,' she said, 'just surprised. I would have thought flying a kite would be a bit . . . fun . . . for you.'

'I don't have a zero-fun policy,' he shot back, methodically unwinding the strings from the plastic hand-grip. He placed the kite gently on the sand and began to walk away, unfurling the strings behind him. 'If you're lucky I might let you have a go,' he said, turning to grin at Florence over his shoulder. He yanked on the handle to pull the strings taut and the kite fluttered into life, soaring upwards towards the sky. Beaming, Simon jogged away across the dune, the kite snapping and straining above him.

'I might take you up on that,' Florence shouted after him, before adding in a quieter, faintly lascivious voice, 'And when I've done that, I might have a go with the kite, too.'

Bo giggled. Oblivious, Simon ran at full pelt along the beach, yanking at the kite's cords to make it swoop and dive.

The others watched him for a few moments, till Florence sighed and said, 'Right, I've got work to do. The light will be going soon.' She unstrapped her folding stool from the back of her bike and grabbed the rucksack containing her art materials. 'I'm heading that way,' she said, gesturing to a sheltered spot further along the dune, in the shadow of a grassy bank. 'See you guys later.'

A freezing gust of wind from the sea made Bo shiver and wrap her arms across the front of her body.

'Shall we walk?' Emil asked.

The sinking sun cast long shadows beside them as they walked along the wet sand. The feeling of self-consciousness she had experienced that morning had returned, and Bo had the uncomfortable sensation of feeling like a gawky school-girl on a first date. She cast sideways glances at Emil as they walked, wondering if he felt awkward too, or whether he was just lost in thought.

'Did you use to come to this beach as a kid?' she asked eventually.

He nodded. 'Every year. It's a lot busier in the summer.'

'Yes, I bet it is.' Bo smiled.

They walked on, side by side but maintaining a chaste gap between them. Simon had stopped at the water's edge, his arms braced to maintain the tension on the kite-strings. Even from a distance Bo could make out the look of intense concentration on his face as he stared up at the kite. He yanked sharply on one of the strings, forcing the kite into a spin which turned into a sharp nosedive. It zoomed downwards, landing in a crumpled heap about thirty feet away from him. Simon's head dropped and he jogged forwards to rescue the forlorn kite, picking it out of the wet sand and dusting it down tenderly, like a wounded bird.

'Oh dear, poor Simon,' Bo murmured compassionately.

A gust of wind roared off the sea, temporarily halting Bo in her tracks and making her squeeze her eyes tight and purse her lips.

'Are you okay?' Emil asked. She opened her eyes to find Emil facing her with a concerned look.

'I'm fine, sorry,' she mumbled, feeling foolish. 'It's just – the wind goes right through me.'

Emil playfully tugged at the sleeve of her coat. 'Like I said, there is no such thing as bad weather—'

'Only bad clothing. You think I don't know that, now?' Bo interrupted, half laughing, half exasperated. 'The gloves are helping, though,' she said, raising her hands in the borrowed gloves and waggling her fingers. 'I'm snug as a bug in these,' she said.

Emil looked perplexed. 'Snug as a bug?' he repeated.

'I mean my hands are lovely and cosy,' she explained. 'Very *hyggeligt*, you could say. Can you have *hyggeligt* hands?'

Emil pulled a face that suggested he was struggling to find

a polite way to say no. 'Not really,' he said diplomatically. 'But I think I understand what you mean.'

He smiled at her and she smiled back, and when they started to walk again Bo felt her self-consciousness start to recede. Her stride fell into step with his and she was no longer worried about whether she was walking too close to him, or whether she ought to say something to fill the silence.

'It's amazing how much more you appreciate the sunlight when the days are so short,' Bo remarked.

'That *is* very *hyggeligt*,' Emil said approvingly, 'appreciating what you have, living in the moment, and being grateful.'

Bo looked across at him and, from nowhere, felt her eyes start to prickle. She was suddenly struck by the poignancy of Emil talking about being grateful, when he had so recently lost his mother. Not wanting him to see how moved she was, she looked out towards the sea.

'Well, Simon certainly seems to be living in the moment,' she laughed. After many failed attempts, Simon had finally succeeded in making the kite perform a loop-the-loop, and he punched the air in delight.

They walked on until they found a cluster of rocks sheltered from the wind by the edge of the dune. Bo perched on the largest rock and Emil came and sat beside her. Bo was acutely aware that Emil's leg was touching hers, but she made no attempt to move away, and neither did he. Behind them, the sun was sinking ever closer towards the horizon, turning the sky pink. They sat in comfortable silence, staring out at the crashing waves, lost in the moment.

'So, Emil, if you don't mind my asking, how come you're scattering your mum's ashes on your own?'

It was a question Bo had been pondering since Emil first explained the purpose of his trip, but she had felt it would be impertinent to ask. Her eyes flickered across to gauge his reaction, hoping he wouldn't find her question intrusive. But, if anything, he looked relieved.

'My brother lives in Germany. He took a lot of time off work while our mum was in hospital. He had to go home after the funeral.' He sounded sad, but there was no resentment in his voice.

'And, what about your dad?' Bo probed gently. 'Is he . . . still alive?'

Emil nodded. 'He lives in Aarhus. My parents divorced when I was young,' he explained matter-of-factly.

Bo felt a rush of compassion, a deep sadness for the loss Emil had suffered and for the way he had been left to say goodbye to his mother on his own. And yet she could not help but admire his quiet stoicism and the fact that, in spite of everything he had been through, he never sought her pity.

'That's me done.' Florence's voice seemed to come from nowhere, startling Bo out of her contemplation. As one, she and Emil turned to see Florence striding along the dusky beach, her sketchbook tucked under her elbow, her stool folded and hanging from its shoulder strap. 'It's too bloody cold out here for me to do any more. Where's Simon?'

Bo gestured towards the sea. 'Doing stunts with the kite,' she said.

Florence gazed out at the darkening waterline, just as Simon succeeded in weaving the kite into a figure-of-eight manoeuvre. 'Who knew he had it in him?' she remarked wryly.

As if he sensed he was being talked about, Simon wound the kite in and ran across the sand towards them, arriving at the cluster of rocks out of breath and exhilarated. His eyes glinted with boyish excitement and his cheeks were rosy. 'Nailed it,' he announced proudly, winding the kite-strings around the plastic handle. He glanced in Florence's direction. 'Did you see?'

'Course we did, babe,' Florence cooed.

'Is it time to head back?' Bo asked, reluctant to bring their day out to an end.

The others nodded. Bo stood up and dusted the sand off her trousers, while Simon packed the kite carefully back inside his rucksack. They walked along the beach beneath a violet sky, discussing what they wanted to eat for dinner and arguing over who should be first to have a shower when they got back.

'Hang on!' Bo shouted, as they neared the start of the dune path. 'Group selfie!'

They huddled together with their backs to the sea, wincing into the sunset. Bo held her phone in an outstretched hand and called, 'Say "*Hygge*" everyone!'

'*Hygge*!' they shouted in unison, and Bo's phone clicked.

They fell into pairs to walk through the dune to their bikes. Bo wasn't conscious of slowing her pace, but she became aware that the distance between them had stretched. Up ahead, Florence and Simon disappeared around a bend in the winding path, and Bo noticed Emil slowing to a halt beside her.

'Can I ask you something, Bo?' Emil said.

She stopped walking and turned to face him. 'Course you can,' she answered. For the first time, there was an unmistakable sadness in his pale blue eyes.

'Tomorrow, I'd like to go to Grenen to scatter my mother's ashes.' He paused for a moment, and Bo found herself fighting the urge to step closer to him and stroke his cheek. 'Would you come with me?'

Bo felt a swell of emotion which made her throat constrict. 'Of course, it would be an honour,' she replied. His eyes creased into a smile and for a moment they stood facing each other on the sandy path, both unsure what should happen next.

'Come on, you two!' Florence had reappeared in a gap

between the dune grasses some way ahead, and was waving at them impatiently.

'Coming,' Bo called. She glanced at Emil, he smiled shyly and, without thinking, she slipped her gloved hand inside his.

On their way back, Bo and Emil stopped at the harbour to pick up some fresh fish for dinner. It was dark by the time they arrived at the summerhouse. Frost was already beginning to glisten on the tarmac as they wheeled their bikes up the path.

The windows were unlit. 'Aren't they back yet?' Bo asked, twisting the key in the lock.

'Maybe they stopped for a coffee,' Emil replied with a shrug.

Inside, the house was dark and still.

Bo flicked on the lights. 'Their stuff's here,' she noted, seeing Florence's goose-down coat hanging from the rack and Simon's rucksack on the floor.

Emil removed his boots and jacket. 'I'll take a shower before dinner,' he said, and loped upstairs.

Bo placed the fish in the fridge, switched on the kettle and looked around the room. This was the first time she had ever been in here alone, without Simon typing on his laptop or Florence chatting at her sketchpad. She made herself a tea and lowered herself stiffly onto a dining chair.

The exertion of the day had caught up with her: the combination of cycling and scrambling up the sand dune had left her aching and sore. Sipping her tea, she heard the thrum of the shower pump through the ceiling. She found her thoughts returning to Emil, and what had happened at the beach. But what *had* happened? They had sat next to each other on a rock, and she had held his hand for a few minutes as they walked back to the bikes. In physical terms, it was childishly chaste. And yet he had also asked her to be with him when he scattered his mother's ashes which, surely, suggested a growing intimacy between them.

She yawned and rubbed her eyes, reluctant to dwell on an issue which seemed riven with complication and confusion. Instead, she picked up her tea and shuffled across the wooden floor to the double doors, reasoning that she might as well light the fire before dinner.

Some movement in the dark living room made her jump back and emit an involuntary 'Oh!' of surprise.

She instinctively reached for the nearest light switch, illuminating the floor lamp in the corner. A pool of yellow light was cast over the leather sofa to reveal Florence sitting astride Simon, her arms wrapped around his neck. Blinking in the light, Florence pulled away from Simon's face.

'Oh, hi, Bo.'

Bo felt frozen to the spot, torn between shock at what she

was witnessing, and mortification that she had found herself, unwittingly, in the role of voyeur.

'Oh my God, sorry!' she squeaked. At a loss for what else to do, she switched the lights off and took a backwards step towards the kitchen. Florence giggled in the darkness.

'It's all right, babe, you can put the lights on. We're fully dressed!' she said cheerfully.

Bo set her face into what she hoped was a look of blasé indifference, then flicked the light switch.

'Sorry,' she repeated sheepishly. 'I didn't realise you were in here.'

'No worries, babe,' Florence replied amiably, as if she had been interrupted doing a crossword puzzle. A pause followed, during which Bo scoured her mind for something to say, and settled on the most banal thing she could come up with.

'I've just made tea. Would either of you like one?'

'Nah, I'm good, thanks, babe,' answered Florence. 'Simon, do you want tea?' she said, as if he might not have heard Bo's question.

Simon twisted his head to look over the back of the sofa at Bo. 'No thanks, I'm fine.'

Bo stared at him, half expecting to see a look of embarrassment or even terror in his eyes. But Simon looked far from terrified. In fact, he looked, as Bo's mother would have put it, like *the cat who had got the cream*.

A moment passed, then Bo sniffed and said purposefully, 'Right, well, I think I'll just take my tea and . . . go upstairs. To my room. For a bit.' She reversed out of the room as non-chalantly as she could, making a point of closing the double doors firmly behind her. Then she stood for a moment, cradling her steaming mug of tea in both hands and staring into the middle distance for a few moments, before climbing the stairs to her bedroom.

A little later, after Bo had showered and washed the sand out of her hair and skin, she curled up on the window seat in her dressing gown and opened her phone's camera roll. The photo she had taken at Ålbæk Bay filled her screen. The four of them were all smiling widely, with rosy cheeks and windswept hair. Behind them, the sea glistened beneath a sky streaked with pink.

'We look so *happy*,' she said out loud. Feeling sentimental, she texted the photo to Kirsten: *It's stopped raining! Made it to the beach today! Wish you were here!*

She was blow-drying her hair when her phone buzzed with Kirsten's reply. *You all look like a bloody Boden catalogue! Is that Emil Jenssen? Haven't seen him for years!*

When Bo went downstairs she found Emil filleting fish at the kitchen worktop. She cast a surreptitious look through the double doors as she walked past, but the living room was empty.

'Have you seen the others?' she asked with a forced casualness.

'They went upstairs, I think,' he said, and his even tone suggested that he had no idea what had happened while he was in the shower. She poured herself a glass of water and leaned against the sink.

'Can I help?' she offered, taking a sip. 'It's not very *hyggeligt* for you to be cooking on your own.'

Emil's eyes flicked over to her and he smiled gratefully. 'You could slice some onions and potatoes if you like?'

'Yes, chef,' she quipped, touching her forehead in a pretend salute.

She placed the chopping board on the worktop next to him.

'Would you like to have your own restaurant, one day?' she asked, peeling the papery outer layers from the onions.

Emil straightened his back and looked thoughtful. 'Perhaps,' he said modestly. 'One day.'

'Did your mum ever get to eat in your restaurant?' She kept her eyes on her hands, hoping that the question would not upset him.

'Yes, a few times. She loved to cook too, before she got cancer ...' He trailed off, and a poignant silence filled the room.

'She must have been very proud of you,' Bo said softly, glancing sideways at him.

211

Emil's head was lowered, his fair hair falling forwards obscuring his eyes. 'Yes. I know she was,' he said quietly.

Bo felt an overwhelming sadness rising in her chest. The more she learned about Emil's situation, the sorrier she felt for him. But alongside her sadness, she felt humbled by the way he seemed to have accepted the hand he had been dealt, apparently without anger or bitterness. She thought of her own family circumstances, of Barbara and Clive and their comfortable house in Buckinghamshire. She had always taken their presence for granted, with the complacency that comes with a privileged upbringing, untouched by tragedy or loss. She felt a flicker of resolve to do things differently when she got home, to be more grateful, to make more of an effort to see Lauren, and try to have more patience with her parents. To be more grown-up. She stared at the chopping board, grateful that the raw onions gave her a pretext for her watering eyes.

She was layering sliced onions and potatoes in a dish when Florence appeared at the bottom of the stairs, fresh from the shower, damp-haired and fragrant-smelling. She wandered into the kitchen and nonchalantly took a bottle of wine from the fridge.

'Evening,' she said, beaming like a hostess at a cocktail party. 'Emil, babe, this looks amazing,' she cooed, touching him on the shoulder as she reached into the cupboard above his head for a glass. Bo caught Florence's eye as she poured the wine, and raised a quizzical eyebrow at her, but the sound of Simon's footsteps on the stairs prevented her from saying anything.

'All right, everyone?' Simon said in a voice that almost sounded cheerful.

Bo looked across, registering his relaxed manner and unfurrowed brow.

Florence took a sip of wine. 'Would anyone else like some?' she asked.

'Yes please,' answered Emil.

'Go on then, just a small one,' said Bo, accepting that her interrogation of Florence would have to wait.

Florence poured the wine and sat down opposite Simon at the table.

'Shall we put some music on?' Bo asked, wiping her hands with a tea towel and turning to face the table. 'It doesn't have to be *my* music,' she added pre-emptively, registering the sardonic look that passed between Florence and Simon.

'Thank God for that,' Simon teased, 'I don't think my nerves could stand the greatest hits of Atomic Kitten this evening.' Florence smirked into her wine glass.

'Fine by me, Simon,' Bo riposted. 'Let's listen to your music then, shall we? I can't wait to see what delights are on there. My money's on heavy metal. Something really angry. Slipknot, perhaps?'

In fact, Simon's music collection turned out to be a

pleasingly un-angry mix of rhythm and blues classics. While Emil fried the fish fillets in a garlic and herb butter, they all sang along to Aretha Franklin and Smokey Robinson.

They ate dinner and drank wine in the flickering candle-light, and after the plates had been cleared away Bo pulled her phone out of her pocket.

'Here, take a look at this,' she said, finding the group selfie they had taken at Ålbæk beach.

'My God, don't we look *wholesome*!' Florence cackled, taking the phone from Bo. 'It's like one of those pictures you see on the news.' Assuming the sombre tones of a crime reporter, Florence pulled a dour expression. 'Four young, attractive people ...' She paused, then corrected herself. 'Attractive-ish people, enjoying a fun day out at the beach. Little did they know the horror that was about to befall them ...'

Simon scowled. He knew what was coming '... that one of them was, in fact, a psychopathic serial killer intent on murder ...'

'Here we go,' he muttered under his breath. 'Are you ever going to give that up?'

'Not until you let us see your novel, Simon,' Florence replied in a schoolmistress voice, 'and prove that you're not secretly plotting how to kill us all.'

Simon rolled his eyes. 'You can see it when it's finished,' he said wearily. 'I'll send you a copy. All right?' Florence smirked into her wine glass.

Having been passed around the table so that everyone could admire the photo, Bo's phone was still in Emil's hands when it buzzed. His eyes flickered across the screen momentarily. 'You've got a message,' he said, passing the phone to her across the row of tea lights.

'Oh, thanks,' she answered, taking her phone with a tremor of apprehension.

It was a message from Ben. *You free for a chat? I could do with cheering up.*

Bo felt a jolt of discomfort, as if an icy draught had just invaded the room. She had, with some effort, succeeded in keeping Ben from her thoughts all day and she felt irrationally cross with him for interrupting her evening. She frowned at the screen, struggling with the contradictory feelings that raged inside her. There was an undeniable gratification in knowing that he wanted to talk to her, but the thought of having to listen to him complain about his job filled her with dread, and then there was the small matter of what had happened with Emil at the beach . . .

Bo stared at the text, sensing Emil's eyes on her. With a pang of guilt, she switched her phone off and placed it face down on the dining table.

Chapter 16

Bo lay in bed, staring at the shaft of morning light on her bedroom wall. She had left Ben's text unanswered, and her phone switched off overnight. She knew she ought to reply, but to decide what response to give felt beyond her at the moment, as if her mind had been filled by what was happening in Skagen and there was no room left for anything else.

In truth, she wasn't sure how she felt about the day ahead. She had agreed to cycle to a remote sand spit at the northernmost tip of the country, with a man she had only known for a couple of days, in order to scatter his mother's ashes. It sounded absurd, when she thought about it. What would she and Emil say to each other? What on earth would she do if he cried? What had seemed like a perfectly natural thing to agree to at the beach the day before now seemed to be ripe with potential awkwardness and embarrassment. She felt flattered that Emil had asked her to accompany him, but also anxious that, when the time came, she would feel like an intruder in what should have been a private moment.

When she eventually dragged herself out of bed and went downstairs, she found that Simon and Florence had gone out. Emil was filling the kettle at the sink and, although he greeted her with his habitual, 'Good morning, Boughay,' he seemed preoccupied. His pensiveness only added to her discomfort, and she kept shooting furtive glances at him as they padded around the kitchen preparing their breakfast in silence.

'How are you feeling?' she asked, when Emil sat down opposite her at the table.

'I'm okay,' he answered. 'I'm ready. It's the right time.'

She waited for a moment. 'And are you sure you want me to come with you? You wouldn't rather ... have some privacy?' she continued tentatively, in case he had changed his mind.

He smiled shyly. 'No – I mean yes – I mean, I'm sure I want you to come. I would prefer not to be alone.' Bo saw tears well up in Emil's eyes, and immediately felt her own eyes start to prickle in response.

'It's a beautiful day for it,' Bo observed, noting the vivid blue sky outside the window.

Emil looked thoughtful. 'I want to do it at sunset,' he said quietly. 'Let's set off after lunch.'

Bo glanced at the clock. It was nine-thirty, and the morning stretched before them. 'Do you want to go to the harbour first? We could get a coffee and a pastry,' Bo asked, in a purposefully upbeat tone.

Emil shook his head. 'I think I would rather stay here.' He looked sad, and Bo had a sudden longing to reach out and take his hand.

'We could bake something together if you like?' she suggested. 'That always helps take my mind off things.'

After a quick scan of the cupboards to see what ingredients were available, they spent the morning baking *saltkringler* – salt pretzels. They chatted while they baked, exchanging trivial information about their lives – their favourite books, earliest childhood memories, which TV shows they watched (Bo's fondness for Danish crime dramas gave them plenty of common ground) – in tacit agreement to avoid the subject of what lay ahead. For Bo, it was not just the thought of the trip to Grenen which loomed over her, but the question of what would happen afterwards. The sole purpose of Emil's trip to Skagen had been to scatter his mother's ashes. Once he had done so, there would be no reason for him to stay at the summerhouse.

She had avoided the subject of his departure and he did too. Eventually, though, leaning against the worktop while Emil slid the pretzels into the oven, Bo asked, 'So, when will you have to go back to Copenhagen?' She kept her

218

voice level and her eyes lowered, purposely avoiding his eyeline.

Emil exhaled heavily. 'I need to be at the restaurant for the weekend service,' he said sombrely, slamming the oven door shut and straightening up. 'I will have to go back tomorrow.' Bo nodded, trying to keep her expression neutral, but she could feel regret start to creep up on her, and with it a conviction that there was not enough time, and that she didn't want him to go yet.

After lunch, they wheeled their bikes down the path and picked up the cycle route that headed north. The pale sun hung low, casting long, slanting shadows of their bikes onto the asphalt, and soon the sea appeared on the horizon, shimmering beneath a vast sky.

The car park at Grenen was enormous, designed to accommodate the summer hoards, but only a handful of cars dotted the tarmac today. They propped their bikes against the perimeter fence and joined the path through the dunes, which opened out onto a seemingly endless expanse of sand.

'It's huge,' Bo exclaimed, looking around in awe.

'In summer, there is a tractor bus to take people to the tip,' Emil explained, faintly apologetic. 'In winter, I'm afraid we must walk.'

Bo wound her scarf around her neck and hooked her arm purposefully through his. 'Okay then,' she said. 'You ready?'

He nodded, adjusted his backpack on his shoulders, and they set off across the empty beach.

As they walked, the beach gradually began to taper, funnelling them towards the waterline. In the distant waters Bo could see the bobbing heads of seals, and seagulls wheeled and dived overhead. They kept walking until the wide beach was behind them and all that remained was a crescent of white sand about thirty feet long, protruding into the water, curved like the handle of a hunting knife. Waves crashed insistently from both sides and Bo had the strange sensation that the oceans were parting, clearing a path before her, and that, if she kept going, she would be able to walk right across the water.

Shivering, Bo nestled into Emil's side and they watched the sun sink towards the watery horizon, turning the sky pink and violet. The seagulls had fallen silent and the seals had disappeared in anticipation of the imminent nightfall. Bo felt Emil inhale deeply beside her, then he lowered his rucksack from his shoulder, dropped to his haunches and carefully removed a grey, vase-like container from inside.

He stood up and took a few steps forward so that he was standing at the very tip. Bo watched as he unscrewed the lid; he held the vessel upright for a moment, then tipped it sideways. A cascade of silvery ash flew out and hovered momentarily, seemingly suspended in the pink-infused air before being caught by the breeze and dispersing into thousands of particles across the waves.

'*Farvel, Mor,*' Emil said. 'Goodbye, Mum.' Bo stepped up behind him and stroked his arm, feeling hot tears starting to form at the back of her eyes. She squinted into the sunset, trying to follow the progress of the tiny particles of ash, but they had all vanished into the ether.

'Well, that's it,' Emil said. He returned the empty container to his rucksack and turned to face her. His lips were pale and his eyes watery. Without even thinking about what she was doing, Bo put her arms around his neck and pulled him into a hug, whether it was to comfort him or because she craved comfort herself, she wasn't sure. He stepped closer and she felt his arms circle her waist and his warm breath in her ear.

They clung to each other, the waves splashing at their feet, both savouring the comfort of physical contact. As they began to pull apart his cheek brushed against hers and before she knew what was happening her lips found his and they kissed. His breath mingled with hers and suddenly she was no longer aware of the crashing waves or darkening sky, just a feeling of closeness, as if they were somehow merged with each other, and at one with the sea and the sky. Eventually, she lowered her heels to the ground, put her gloved hands on his cheeks and looked at him intently.

'I'm sorry,' she murmured. 'I didn't mean to do that. I hope you don't—'

'Don't be sorry,' he replied, sliding his arm tight around her waist and pulling her closer to kiss her again.

'The moon's going to be bright tonight,' Bo said, when they finally pulled apart. The sun had disappeared and the sky was dark now, but a luminous white glow shimmered on the horizon over Emil's shoulder. Emil turned and they both watched, but instead of seeing a moonrise, the glow expanded, spreading sideways, taking on a greenish cast. They watched in awestruck silence as the glow intensified, revealing a shimmering arc of green light which ran from east to west just above the horizon.

Bo gasped in amazement. 'I didn't know you could see the Northern Lights from here,' she whispered.

'I've never seen them before,' Emil replied.

'Look, it's moving,' Bo murmured, transfixed by the glowing band of green that had begun to sway, undulating like a curtain in the wind.

They stood motionless, Bo leaning into his body, Emil's arm draped around her shoulder. 'I wonder what causes it,' Bo whispered.

'Danish folklore says it is swans,' Emil said.

'Swans?' Bo repeated, looking up at him, puzzled.

'Swans held a competition to see who could fly the

farthest north,' Emil said, curling her in closer to his chest. 'Some birds became caught in the ice and tried to escape. The movement of their wings flapping produced the waves of the Northern Lights.'

'Oh,' Bo said, on a strangled note. 'That's so sad.' Her face tightened and she dropped her head.

'Why are you crying?' Emil asked, tilting her chin up and wiping away the tears which had begun to roll down her cheeks.

'Because of the poor swans!' she said thickly, peering up at him through the curly strands of hair which had escaped her ponytail and blown across her face. Emil laughed and tucked the curls tenderly behind her ears.

'It's just a story,' he said, with a reassuring smile. 'I'm pretty sure the scientists have a different explanation.'

She half smiled, half winced. 'I know,' Bo whimpered, 'but it's just so sad.'

'I suppose it is,' he agreed, pulling her head in close to his shoulder and rubbing her back, like a parent consoling an upset child. Bo fished a tissue out of her coat pocket and wiped her nose, relieved that her tears seemed to be subsiding.

'Or maybe someone up there,' Emil continued, looking up at the shimmering sky, 'decided to put on a show for Mum.' His words caused Bo to take another heaving breath as fresh tears sprang into her eyes.

'Oh, God!' she whimpered, mortified, putting a hand to

her face to stifle a sob. 'I'm so sorry, Emil. I should be the one comforting you, not the other way round!' Emil let out a low chuckle and nuzzled her hair.

'That's okay,' he soothed. Bo wondered if she should say anything else, but there didn't seem to be the need. Instead she put her arms around his waist and together they stared at the shimmering arc of light until they were so cold they could no longer feel their feet.

Eventually Emil said, 'Shall we go home?' and Bo nodded. They turned away from the luminous horizon and began the long walk back to their bikes.

The blinds were lowered and the sound of Otis Redding greeted them as Bo unlocked the summerhouse door. Florence and Simon were in the kitchen, but neither of them heard Bo's key in the lock or noticed them wiping their feet on the doormat. Florence was sipping wine at the stove, whilst Simon rummaged through the salad drawer in the fridge.

'Simon, babe. What *are* you looking for?' Florence said impatiently, stirring the contents of a simmering pan on the hob.

'Fennel seeds,' Simon grumbled.

'Well, you're not going to find them in there,' replied Florence, and she stepped sideways to pluck a jar from the cupboard.

'Thanks,' Simon mumbled, taking the jar.

'Something smells good,' Bo remarked amiably, aware that her stomach was rumbling.

Florence gave a start and glanced over her shoulder at them. 'Simon's cooking dinner,' she said proudly, stepping across the kitchen to turn the volume control down on the speaker. Behind her, Simon pulled a horrified expression and mimed choking, clutching his throat with one hand.

'You're just in time,' Florence added. 'We were beginning to think you'd done a runner.'

'Nothing like that,' Bo replied, pulling off her gloves and shoving them in her coat pockets. 'We went to Grenen to ...' She stopped mid-sentence, feeling it was not for her to explain the purpose of their trip.

'I scattered my mother's ashes,' Emil stated simply.

Florence's face softened. 'Oh, babe, I'm sorry,' she said sincerely.

'It's okay, really,' Emil replied. 'In fact, it was beautiful. And I was not there alone.' As he said this, he and Bo exchanged a coy smile and Bo instinctively touched the side of his arm.

Florence observed the gesture and her eyes flickered between them shrewdly. 'Well, in that case ...' She trailed off, with a pointed look at Bo.

Feeling a blush brewing and keen to move the subject on, Bo said, 'Have you seen the sky?'

'The sky?' Florence repeated, a quizzical wrinkle forming between her eyebrows. Simon put the jar of fennel seeds on the counter and went over to the window, yanking up the blind to reveal the glowing green sky outside.

'Bloody hell,' he exclaimed, peering out through the glass. Florence padded across the room and stood beside him, open-mouthed.

'Bo, babe,' she said, without taking her eyes off the view, 'pass me my coat, would you?'

They all stood shivering on the front lawn, faces raised towards the bright sky, their breath visible in the freezing air. Conscious of Emil's presence close behind her, Bo instinctively leant backwards and rested her head against his chest, and in response he placed his chin gently on the top of her head and slipped his arms around her waist.

'Beautiful, isn't it?' Bo said, glancing across at the others, enjoying their awestruck wonder.

'Babe, I'm actually speechless,' Florence answered.

A moment passed, then Simon remarked drolly, 'Well, that's a first.' Florence responded with a sharp jab of her elbow into Simon's ribs.

They stood for a few moments longer, huddled close in their respective pairs, until Florence turned to Simon and said, 'Babe, did you turn the hob off?'

'Shit,' Simon hissed, before bounding down the path

and back inside the house. A few seconds later the front door swung open again. 'I think we might have a problem,' Simon said sheepishly. 'The sauce has kind of burnt. It's stuck to the pan and there are black bits floating in it.' Florence tutted and Bo fought to stifle a giggle.

'Shall I take a look?' Emil offered. 'I'm sure it can be rescued.' He released Bo from their embrace and followed Simon back indoors.

'What *have* you done to him?' Bo teased, when the door had banged shut. 'He's like a different person.'

Florence shrugged. 'I haven't done anything, babe, I promise,' she replied, pretending to be affronted. 'Besides, I could ask you the same question,' she added drily. 'No need to ask what happened between you and Emil at Grenen.'

Bo smiled bashfully. 'I hadn't planned it, it just sort of . . . happened,' she stammered.

'Don't worry, babe, I'm not judging,' Florence reassured her. 'How romantic. Having your first kiss under the Northern Lights . . .' She clutched her hands in front of her chest and made a swooning movement.

Bo looked away, grateful that her flushed cheeks were invisible in the dark. 'It was romantic,' she agreed, 'but I'm not sure what happens next. He's going back to Copenhagen tomorrow.'

Florence sighed and stepped closer to loop her arm through Bo's. 'I know what you mean, babe,' she murmured sympathetically. 'But hey, you've still got tonight,' she said, with a meaningful nudge.

The mood at dinner was subdued. Although none of them mentioned it out loud, they all knew that this was to be their last evening together as a four. With music playing softly in the background, they ate Simon's stew in the flickering candlelight.

'This is delicious, Simon,' Bo said.

'I think the black bits definitely add a certain something, don't they?' Simon replied drily.

Beside him, Florence rolled her eyes. 'There aren't any black bits, babe,' she reassured him in a faintly exasperated voice. 'Emil sorted it, didn't he?'

'Still tastes burnt, though,' he muttered darkly. The others murmured their disagreement but Simon looked unconvinced.

'We'll all have to come to your restaurant one day, Emil, don't you think?' Florence said brightly.

'I would love that,' Emil remarked, and as he said it he smiled at Bo.

Bo's heart lurched, but she said nothing. Since she and Emil had set off for Grenen, she had forced herself to focus only on the present moment. The future held nothing but uncertainty, and it was as if she had pulled down the shutters in her mind to exclude everything but the here and now. She knew that *real* life – by which she meant London, unemployment, Ben – was lurking at the edge of her consciousness. She was doing her best to ignore it, just as she had ignored her phone, which had remained switched off in her bedroom all day. Real life meant disappointment, and hurt, and guilt. She knew she could not avoid it for ever, but she was not ready to face it yet.

Real life would have to wait.

The morning light slanted in through the window, spreading across the narrow bed. Bo's body was tucked neatly alongside Emil's, her head nestled in the crook of his shoulder.

'What time do you have to leave?' she whispered sleepily.

'There's a train at eleven,' he answered, tenderly stroking his fingers through her hair. She raised her head and glanced at the watch propped on the edge of the desk beside Emil's metal-framed glasses. At most, they had a couple more hours together. She felt a shiver of apprehension, as if the outside world was trying to intrude.

'Tell me about your life in Copenhagen,' she said, propping her head up on her elbow. She felt a sudden urgency to find out as much as she could about him, not to waste the little time they had left together.

Emil turned his head to look at her, his brow wrinkled in puzzlement.

'What do you want to know?' he asked.

'Everything,' she said, her face earnest, until the absurdity of her words hit her and she dropped back onto the pillow with a groan.

'At the moment, the restaurant *is* my life,' he answered ruefully. 'I work every evening and weekend.'

'That doesn't sound very *hyggeligt,*' Bo said.

'It's not,' he agreed.

'Where will you be for Christmas?' she asked, feeling a stab of concern that he might be spending it alone, or working.

'I will probably visit my dad in Aarhus,' Emil answered. 'What about you?'

'Oh, I'll be at my mum and dad's.' Bo was aware of the sinking feeling at the thought of yet another Christmas in Buckinghamshire, with all the frustrations that entailed, but then she reminded herself of Emil's circumstances. *You're lucky. Be grateful,* she told herself sternly.

'And what about Ben, will you be seeing him when you get back to London?'

Bo shivered, as if the temperature in the room had suddenly dropped. Emil was looking at her intently, and there was a flicker of something in his eyes – fear, or jealousy perhaps. She angled her face away from his.

'You read his text, I take it?' she whispered.

'I didn't mean to, but yes,' he said. 'Ben is your boyfriend, I guess?' he said.

Bo exhaled slowly. 'Yes, well, sort of. It's complicated.' It was a question she had tried her best to avoid thinking about. 'The truth is, I'm not sure, and I don't think he is, either,' she said at last, aware that as answers went, it was hardly satisfactory. But it was the truth. Just as she had never felt fully certain whether she and Ben were a couple, she now found there was just as little clarity in her mind about whether they had broken up.

She squeezed her eyes tight shut and tried to repress the childlike voice that was forming in her head, protesting that she didn't want to go back to the life she had left behind in London, the angst and insecurity, the constant feeling that she wasn't sure where she stood about anything and that she was faking being an adult. How she longed to stay here in the cosy summerhouse, with the tall fair-haired Danish man lying in bed next to her. Somehow everything seemed simpler with Emil, more straightforward, as if there was no need for her to pretend she was something she wasn't. But Emil would return to Copenhagen in a couple of hours and she would be back in London in a few days. Whatever her feelings for Emil might be, it wasn't as if anything could come of this. Could it?

A little later, they went downstairs to find Simon and Florence in the kitchen, waiting to say goodbye. The taxi had pulled up outside, its engine idling. Emil held out his hand to Simon, who pulled him into a bear hug.

'See you later, mate,' Simon said, patting Emil firmly on the back.

'Goodbye, Simon,' Emil replied fondly.

'Bye, Emil,' Florence said, stepping forward to throw her arms around him. 'We'll see you in Copenhagen. At your restaurant,' she said authoritatively. 'Best table in the house, please.'

'I told you, it's not my restaurant,' he reminded her, laughing, 'But I will make sure you get a nice table.'

Outside, the taxi by the front gate beeped its horn. Florence and Simon moved discreetly aside and Bo rose up onto her tiptoes and put her arms around Emil's neck.

'Goodbye, Boughay,' he said, and she felt his breath on her hair.

There was so much she wanted to say but now the moment had come her throat felt tight and she found it difficult to speak.

'You should go,' she mumbled into his shoulder, finally. As they pulled apart, she stared hard at the zip on his jacket, willing herself not to cry. He swung his rucksack over his shoulder and grabbed the handle of his suitcase.

'Oh, don't forget these!' she exclaimed, reaching into her coat pockets for the gloves he had lent her. She held them out towards him and he stared at them for a moment.

'Don't worry, you keep them. You will need them while you're here,' he said.

She stood on the doorstep, watching him walk down the path. Low clouds scudded overhead, and the wind had picked up, threatening rain. He placed his suitcase in the boot then climbed inside the taxi. Florence and Simon came to stand beside her, and they all waved as the taxi pulled away.

Once the taxi had finally disappeared from view, Florence took a step closer and put her arm around Bo's shoulder.

'You all right, babe?' she asked solicitously. Bo nodded, staring hard at the point where the taxi had vanished.

'What a lovely guy. I'm going to miss him,' Florence said, rubbing Bo's arm.

'Me too,' Bo whispered, wiping away the single tear which had begun to roll down her cheek.

Bo couldn't settle to anything for the rest of the morning. She sensed Florence and Simon's concern, their discreet attempts to try to work out whether she wanted to be alone or in company. The truth was, she just wanted to mope, to give free rein to the bittersweet feelings of elation and agony which had been fighting for dominance inside her.

Eventually, thinking that if she spent any more time cooped up indoors she might scream, she pulled on her coat and headed into Skagen. She hoped that a walk in the fresh air might clear her head and give her respite from her inner turmoil, but the more she walked, the more she was plagued by the conviction that she had let something potentially wonderful slip away.

Dusk was falling when she got back to the summerhouse, and Bo felt comforted by the sight of light glowing invitingly behind the window blinds as she walked up the path.

When she opened the door, it took a moment to register that there were three people sitting around the table.

Florence, seated next to Simon, looked up and smiled.

'Hi, babe,' she said.

'Hi,' replied Bo automatically.

The woman sitting opposite them twisted in her chair and beamed at her.

'Surprise!' Kirsten shouted. 'I made it, at last. What have I missed?'

Bo stared at her friend and tried to arrange her face into a smile, but instead she found herself bursting into tears.

Part Three

London

Chapter 17

Bo opened the front door and breathed in the cool, stale air inside the flat.

'Home sweet home,' Kirsten sighed, heaving her suitcase across the threshold.

Bo stooped to gather the messy pile of leaflets, letters and free newspapers which had accumulated on the doormat during their absence. Looking down the hall, she saw the flat with fresh eyes; had the ceilings always been so low? The woodchipped walls so grubby? The summerhouse popped into her mind, with its clean, spacious rooms, tasteful lighting and elegantly designed furniture, and she felt a shiver of shame for the shabbiness of her home.

The journey back from Denmark had been long; their flight had been delayed, and Bo had found herself sinking further and further into gloomy despondency with every hour that passed. She was flying back to uncertainty and confusion on both the personal and professional fronts. Rather than clearing her head about Ben, her time in Skagen had merely added a new layer of complication to her love life, in the form of Emil. She had travelled to Denmark feeling unsure of where she stood with one man; she was returning unsure of where she stood with two. And then there was the small matter of finding a job . . .

The bump of the plane's wheels touching down on the runway at Gatwick had brought with it a jolt of dread, and a faint nausea about what lay ahead. So much for being a grown-up, she thought, as she and Kirsten edged along the seating aisle to disembark from the plane.

Bo shoved the detritus from the doormat onto the hall shelf and yawned.

'Tea?' she asked, unzipping her coat and heading for the kitchen.

'Love one, but we won't have any milk,' Kirsten replied, unlacing her boots.

Bo groaned and turned back towards the front door. 'I'll just pop out and get some,' she said, grabbing her keys.

The afternoon light was fading as she climbed up the stone steps to the pavement. It was early December and several houses on the street were draped in fairy lights, or had Christmas trees twinkling in the window. The festive décor felt incongruent given the mild London weather: leaves still clung to tree branches, and a blackbird trilled from a rooftop as Bo walked past. It was positively summery compared to the rawness of the Danish winter, and it felt almost as if nature itself was reluctant to acknowledge that Christmas was coming. Bo felt the same way, and at the corner shop she bought milk, a loaf of cheap sliced bread and a large box of Maltesers, but ignored the display of mince pies and Advent calendars by the till.

Back at the flat, Bo and Kirsten sank onto the tartan sofa, with the open box of Maltesers on the faded cushion between them. In the glare of the overhead lights, Bo sipped her tea and let her eyes wander around the living room, taking in the dusty grate in the unused fireplace, the peeling woodwork around the windows and the ugly glass dining table and plastic chairs. There was nothing *hyggeligt* about being home, she thought morosely.

Beside her, Kirsten was efficiently sorting the post into three neat piles on the sofa arm: one for herself, another for Bo, and a third for junk. The junk pile was by far the largest, forming a messy tower of pizza menus and estate agents' flyers. She handed Bo a small wedge of envelopes, rested her feet on the coffee table and popped a Malteser into her mouth.

'Pleased to be back?' Kirsten asked, crunching the Malteser between her teeth.

Bo leaned back against the sofa cushion and stared at the long crack in the ceiling which snaked from the overhead light to the cornicing above the window.

'Not really,' she answered, honestly.

Kirsten took a slurp of tea. 'Missing Skagen already?' Then, after a pause she added quietly, 'Or missing Emil, perhaps?'

They had spent Kirsten's first evening at the summerhouse in the living room, sipping wine in front of the fire while Simon and Florence cooked dinner. Bo had tearfully described what had happened during Kirsten's absence. Kirsten had listened in slack-jawed amazement to Bo's account of Emil's unexpected arrival, their growing intimacy during the day out at Råbjerg and Ålbæk, and the dramatic denouement of their embrace under the Northern Lights.

'Bloody hell, Bo! You packed a lot into a few days, didn't you?' Kirsten observed, with evident admiration.

Bo cringed. 'I suppose you could say that.'

'I can't believe I missed all the fun,' Kirsten complained. 'And to think I missed Emil by just a few hours. I haven't seen him since we were kids.' There was genuine regret in her tone. She took a sip of wine, then added with a fondly nostalgic air, 'I snogged his brother once, when I was fourteen,' prompting Bo to giggle, in spite of herself.

The sound of Florence and Simon bickering in the kitchen wafted through the double doors.

'They seem like a nice couple,' Kirsten said.

'They say opposites attract,' Bo replied with an amused shrug. When she mentioned, as an afterthought, that Florence and Simon had been strangers when they arrived at the summerhouse, Kirsten had slapped her forehead in disbelief.

'They must be putting something in the water around here!' she exclaimed.

Simon flew home on Saturday, and Florence left the following day, so by the end of the weekend Kirsten and Bo had the house to themselves. Although she tried to hide it, with the others gone, Bo felt a sense of anticlimax. The summerhouse felt empty and quiet, and Bo missed Florence's bubbly presence and Simon's dry sense of humour.

More than anything else, though, she missed Emil. It was as if the summerhouse was torturing her with memories: wherever she went, images of Emil popped into her mind. She saw him cooking at the kitchen counter, or sprawled out on the sofa reading, or pouring schnapps at the table. Her anguish was compounded by a paralysing uncertainty about what would happen now that he had gone. What was the grown-up way to handle what had happened between them?

She had texted Emil shortly after his departure, wishing him a good trip. He had not replied until late in the evening, saying it had been a pleasure to meet her and hoping she enjoyed the rest of her stay in Skagen. The wording of his message had struck Bo as courteous but formal, and she wondered if its slightly detached tone signalled an emotional withdrawal, or a regret for what had happened between them.

Kirsten had dismissed her concerns and tried to convince her that something had got *lost in translation* in the text message.

'He's probably just tired, Bo,' she said encouragingly. But once the seed of doubt had been planted, Bo found herself unable to stop herself nursing it into a full-blown crisis.

She had to consider the possibility that it had been mere chance that had thrown her and Emil together – she had just happened to be in the right place at the right time, and he had turned to her for comfort when he had no one else. She recalled the desolate beauty of the beach at Grenen, the crashing waves on the sand bar, his mother's ashes glinting in the pink light. They had seen the Northern Lights together, for goodness' sake! Was it any wonder they got carried away by the romance of it all?

Her last few days in Skagen were characterised by contradictory feelings of longing to see Emil again, whilst at the same time desperately wanting to escape the summerhouse and all its bittersweet memories of him.

Now that she was back home in London, however, it felt almost as if her experiences in Skagen had been a dream. Maybe the grown-up response would be to acknowledge that what happened with Emil had been a fling, a holiday romance; fun while it lasted, but destined to fizzle out once real life had resumed.

Bo's rather maudlin reverie was interrupted by the sound of Kirsten crunching a Malteser on the sofa next to her.

'Do you think you might go over to visit Emil. In Copenhagen?' Kirsten probed, as if she had been reading Bo's mind.

'Who knows,' Bo replied.

Not wanting to be drawn on the subject of Emil, Bo distracted herself by going through her mail. She ignored the credit card bills and bank statements in favour of a white envelope with a central London postmark, which she tore open with a feeling of apprehension.

'My P45's arrived,' she said bluntly, placing the slip on the sofa arm and unfolding the accompanying letter. 'And my severance package has been finalised,' Bo read. 'The money should be transferred in the next few days.'

'Drinks are on you, then?' Kirsten teased.

Bo smiled wanly and picked up her tea, feeling, if anything, even more downcast than she had before. The redundancy money was welcome, for sure, but it signified the definitive end of her association with Aspect, and there seemed something callously impersonal about the way five years of her life had been brought to a close with a tax slip and a financial pay-off.

*

Bo's mood didn't improve in the days that followed. Kirsten was back at work so Bo spent her time alone in the flat with little to do other than mull over what had happened in Skagen. The flat felt draughty and cramped compared to the summerhouse and she missed the elemental Danish landscape, the endless dunes, the vast skies and the turbulent sea. She even missed the sound of rain lashing against the windows.

When she was not obsessing over what had happened with Emil, Bo tortured herself about Ben. On both fronts, she found herself unable to achieve any clarity. Instead, a dense mass of confusion and guilt seemed to be lodged deep inside her, like an undigested meal. She had not replied to Ben's last text at the summerhouse, and there had been no attempt at contact on either side since her return to London. She supposed she ought to feel guilty about what had happened with Emil; she knew it made a hypocrite of her, when she had wrongly accused Ben of cheating. Yet part of her protested that it was not straightforward. The terms of their relationship had always been ambiguous. Did sleeping with Emil count as cheating, if she had never been sure whether Ben, definitively, considered them to be a couple?

In the hope that baking might cheer her up, she decided to knock up a batch of brownies. As she whisked and folded, she realised that it was the *hygge* feeling she was trying to recapture, the sense of cosiness, camaraderie and together-ness that had characterised her cooking sessions in Skagen.

But, alone in the poky kitchen in Holloway, it was impossible to muster any feeling of *hygge* contentment.

Bo slid the tray of brownie mix into the oven and slammed the door shut, just as her phone started to vibrate with an incoming call. She grabbed the phone and, seeing the name of a recruitment agency displayed on her screen, set her face into a smile.

'Hello?' she answered.

'Hi, Bo, this is Shelley from Marsh Recruitment, how are you?' a voice chirped down the line. In the background, Bo could hear the buzz of an office, phones ringing, disembodied voices, a distant shriek of laughter.

'I'm fine thanks, Shelley, how are you?' Bo replied, mirroring Shelley's familiar tone, even though they had neither met nor spoken before.

'Good, thanks. Listen' – the social niceties dispatched with, Shelley was getting down to business – 'we've got a *fantastic* job just in, which I thought might suit you.'

Bo felt an instinctive reluctance, but replied, 'Oh, right,' with artificial brightness.

'Marketing exec, good package and prospects. For a really *great* company. Central London location, near Euston,' Shelley enthused. 'It's in a different sector, though. How would you feel about working in food?'

Chapter 18

Bo sat on the tube train speeding her towards central London, on her way to her first job interview in over five years. She was wearing her smart grey trouser suit and a pair of high heels, and had painstakingly blow-dried her hair so that no rogue curls could spoil her look of well-groomed professionalism. She had not worn heels for months and, by the time she had reached the platform at Holloway Road tube station, she could already feel the tell-tale throb of a blister on her left heel. Staring at her reflection in the carriage window opposite, she made a mental note to buy sticking plasters at the earliest opportunity, to avoid the embarrassment of turning up at the interview with a limp.

She emerged from Euston station with forty minutes to spare. A van selling coffee and waffles was parked on the concourse outside the station entrance: a cute, vintage-looking vehicle painted sky-blue, with corrugated metal sides and a wooden serving hatch. Its appearance made Bo think of sun-baked market squares in the South of France. Bo paid for a coffee from the smiling woman behind the hatch, and carried it to a nearby bench. There she sat and sipped her drink, looking out over the lanes of traffic making their stop-start way along the Euston Road.

At exactly eleven o'clock, Bo pushed through the revolving doors of an anonymous concrete office block and took the lift to the third floor. There, a bored-looking girl with fuchsia nails motioned for Bo to take a seat, and Bo obediently lowered herself into a blue armchair next to the water cooler.

She tried to ignore the sinking feeling that had begun to spread through her as she waited. It wasn't just that she felt an almost visceral aversion to being inside the airless, blandly corporate office, but also the fact that it was the headquarters of Petits Pains, a company which operated food outlets in airports and railway stations. Their outlets sold pre-packaged baguettes and baked-from-frozen croissants to customers who were in too much of a hurry to find a more appetising alternative. Petits Pains outlets were just the kind of places that Bo, as a rule, tried to avoid.

But as she stared at a tired-looking pot plant on the floor next to her chair, Bo told herself to keep an open mind. Granted, working in the marketing department of a chain of sandwich bars did not exactly fulfil her youthful ambition of working with food, but she had to be realistic. Her redundancy money would not support her for long, and she needed to find a job.

In a featureless meeting room overlooking the Euston Road, Bo sipped water from a plastic cup while the marketing manager, a plump blonde called Karen, asked about her experience and aspirations. Bo talked about her work at Aspect and described her enthusiasm for all aspects of the design, planning and implementation of marketing campaigns. Karen smiled and nodded approvingly and, forty-five minutes later, Bo stepped out into the December sunshine feeling simultaneously pleased that she had given a good account of herself, and mildly depressed at the thought that she might actually be offered the job.

She had arranged to meet Hayley for lunch in Soho and, as she strode through the elegant Bloomsbury streets, Bo considered her options. Had her marketing career simply lost momentum, or was she in the throes of a full-on professional crisis?

Emil, Florence and Simon had all forged careers out of their creative passions, and perhaps she had absorbed some of their creative conviction by osmosis. Her time in Denmark had offered her a tantalising glimpse of a different kind of career from the one she had known, and made her wonder if it might not be crazy to think she could make a living from doing something she loved. It was as if a spark had ignited inside her, but it risked being snuffed out by the harsh realities of life, and by her need to start earning money soon.

Her professional dilemma occupied her thoughts for the duration of her walk from Bloomsbury to Soho, where she was to meet Hayley. She pushed open the door to the dim sum restaurant on Wardour Street and took a stool at the bar in the window to wait for her former colleague. An efficient waitress with a slick black bob handed her a menu, which she perused idly whilst watching the trendy media-types passing along the pavement on the other side of the tinted glass. After a few moments, a gust of cold air cut through the warm, slightly steamy atmosphere of the restaurant, as the door swung open beside her.

'Hi, Hayles,' Bo said, stepping down from the stool to kiss Hayley on the cheek.

Hayley peeled off her jacket and hung it on the back of her stool. The waitress reappeared promptly, handed Hayley a menu and hovered nearby, waiting to take their order.

'So, how was the interview?' Hayley asked amiably, once they had ordered and the waitress had scuttled away.

'I think it went okay,' Bo replied in a non-committal voice.

'Sounds to me like it went well,' Hayley said encouragingly.

Bo shrugged. 'I s'pose,' she mumbled.

Hayley returned a puzzled look. 'Don't you want the job?'

They were interrupted by the reappearance of the waitress

with their drinks, and Bo was grateful for the distraction. Given Hayley's penchant for gossip, Bo knew that, if she confided in Hayley about her doubts, news of her career crisis would be all around the Aspect office by the end of the afternoon.

'Oh, I don't know,' she murmured evasively. 'I just want to keep my options open, that's all.' Hayley pulled a 'fair enough' expression and took a sip from her glass.

'How's things in the office, anyway?' Bo asked, keen to steer the subject away from herself. Hayley twirled the end of her ponytail and rolled her eyes heavenward.

'It's a *nightmare*,' she said bitterly. 'We've got a trade fair coming up and the directors won't pay for any extra help. Even Claire admits it's too much.' Bo pulled a sympathetic face.

'The Christmas party's next week and I haven't even had time to buy an outfit,' Hayley added, but the merest flicker of Bo's facial muscles drew her up short. 'Oh, sorry,' Hayley murmured sheepishly, 'I didn't mean—'

'Don't worry,' Bo cut in, with a forced brightness, 'I wasn't expecting an invitation.'

A silence followed, during which the waitress returned and placed two rectangular dishes of steaming dumplings on the bar in front of them.

'It's going to be a bit of a low-key do this year,' Hayley went on, in a transparent attempt to make her former colleague feel better. 'Just drinks and a buffet. Company efficiencies, and all that.' Bo nodded expressionlessly. She was mildly surprised to discover that she felt no sadness at all that she was missing out on the Aspect Christmas party.

Hayley chewed on a mouthful of dumpling. 'I've got high hopes for some *quality* romantic indiscretions taking place this year,' she said, glancing at Bo out of the side of her eye. A moment passed, during which Bo sensed that Hayley was waiting for her to say something.

'Oh, yeah? Who's your money on?' Bo asked, her tone studiously indifferent.

Hayley's nose wrinkled and she puffed her cheeks, as if the question demanded serious consideration.

'Well,' she began eventually, 'Dev in tech support has just split up from his fiancée, so he's a frontrunner. And Lorraine is anyone's after a few shandies.'

She paused to take a sip of Coke, before adding as an afterthought, 'But I wouldn't rule Ben out of the running. He's always been something of a dark horse on the romance front, hasn't he?'

Bo felt a jolt of panic seize her stomach. She opened her mouth as if to speak but closed it again, aware of Hayley's laser-beam gaze on the side of her face.

'Actually, Ben said something strange to me the other day,' Hayley went on airily, returning to her food, while Bo kept her eyes resolutely on the window.

'Oh, yeah?' she replied, a little shakily.

'Yeah. We were in the kitchen at the end of the day, getting a beer. I'd been working flat out on the brochure for the fair, and I joked that you were lucky to be out of there, and that you were probably having the time of your life in Denmark.' Bo smiled thinly and took a sip of her drink.

'Anyway,' Hayley continued, 'Ben made that little laugh he does when he's about to be sarcastic and said, "Only if you think playing Scrabble is having the time of your life."'

Hayley pushed her plate away and turned to face Bo once more. 'So I said "How do you know she's been playing Scrabble, Ben?" And he just looked at me like, well, kind of like you're looking at me now.'

Bo had turned to meet Hayley's gaze, feeling her cheeks burn, and time stretched as silence filled the air between them. Eventually, Bo dropped her eyes, exhaled slowly and pushed her own plate away.

'To be honest, I'm surprised you didn't work it out sooner,' she said quietly, staring at her cutlery.

'Well, I had my suspicions,' Hayley replied, 'but I figured it was none of my business.'

Bo's eyebrows shot up.

'I know I like to gossip, but I do have *some* discretion, you know,' Hayley said, feigning offence. 'So how long has it been going on?' she asked tentatively.

'Since February,' Bo replied, before hastily adding, 'but to be honest, I'm not sure it is still going on. It's all got a bit . . . complicated, since I left Aspect.' She glanced across, half expecting to see the glint which habitually appeared in Hayley's eyes when she had learned some new snippet of intelligence. But instead, Hayley's expression was one of concern.

'Out of sight, out of mind, eh?' she asked softly.

Bo's brow furrowed. 'Something like that.'

'Well, for what it's worth, your secret's safe with me. I won't breathe a word to anyone.' Hayley pinched her thumb and forefinger together and mimed zipping her lips shut.

Bo smiled. 'Thanks, Hayls. But like I said, there might not be a secret to keep any more.'

They chatted for a little while longer about work and their respective plans for Christmas, until Hayley glanced at her watch and sighed. 'I'd better get back to the office,' she said glumly.

They stepped down from their stools and began to pull their coats on. 'Just out of interest,' Bo asked, as she tugged at the zip of her coat, 'what gave it away, about me and Ben? Were we that obvious?'

Hayley smiled, the merest glimmer of gratification in her eye. 'It was the way you reacted at your leaving do, when I told you what I'd heard about Milton Keynes.'

'The way I reacted?' Bo repeated, frowning.

Hayley struggled to conceal a smirk. 'Bo, you went white as a sheet, and within five minutes you'd walked out on your own leaving drinks. Then thirty seconds later Ben bolted after you. It was a *bit* of a giveaway.'

Bo grimaced. 'Oh God, don't remind me.'

They stepped out onto the pavement together and made their way to Oxford Street, where they parted with a hug. Bo watched Hayley scurry over a pelican crossing and disappear behind a wall of queuing buses, then she turned left and began to walk towards Oxford Circus.

There seemed a certain irony to what had just happened: that her relationship with Ben, which she had taken such pains to conceal, had been discovered just at the point when it seemed to be falling apart. Now that it was out in the open, it sounded so clichéd – a secret office romance that wasn't such a secret after all. Yet, as she weaved her way through the crowds of shoppers, she had no feeling of regret that they had been found out, but rather a sense of relief. After all, whether anyone at Aspect knew about her relationship with Ben, and what they thought about it, was no longer any concern of hers. It might have mattered, once, but it certainly didn't matter any more. All that mattered was what she and Ben felt about each other, and to be sure of that, she would have to see him face to face.

Chapter 19

Back at the flat, Bo kicked off her heels, changed into her comfiest tracksuit and collapsed onto the sofa with a slice of home-made brownie in one hand and her phone in the other. She had resolved to send a text to Ben suggesting that they meet up, but knew she must choose her words carefully so as to sound neither hostile nor needy. After much thought, she settled on: *Hi Ben. Sorry I didn't get back to you while I was in Denmark. Do you fancy meeting up this weekend? Be good to catch up. Bo x*

She half expected to be fobbed off with an excuse, but his reply – *What did you have in mind?* – though brief, was amenable. She was reluctant to suggest dinner *à deux* in a restaurant. That would carry a certain weight of romantic expectation, as well as having the potential for becoming a mortifying re-run of their last date before she had left for Denmark. Instead, she suggested lunch at a new street food market in Southwark.

Sounds good. See you then, Ben replied.

Saturday arrived cold, crisp and clear. Bo put on an ensemble designed to send the message that she had dressed for comfort rather than to impress: jeans and a polo neck, Ugg boots, and the goose-down jacket she had bought at Aalborg airport on her way back from Denmark.

The food market occupied a sprawling site beside the arches of a rail viaduct in the shadow of the Shard building, and the sound of trains squealing to a halt in London Bridge station could be heard in the distance. It was laid out in an informal, almost ramshackle style, with a mix of permanent sites built into the railway arches, and mobile pitches on the paved outdoor areas.

Bo had arrived early, so she wandered between the pitches, fascinated not just by the enticing array of cuisines on offer – everything from wood-fired pizzas to ramen, Turkish dumplings and burritos – but also by the vendors themselves, many of whom looked no older than herself, and the variety of vehicles they traded from: converted ice-cream trucks, vintage vans and airstream trailers. Some of the vendors had customised their vans with their own artwork, or explained the story behind their food on a hand-written chalk board. The result was a bohemian, festival-like vibe, in which the vendors seemed to be enjoying themselves as much as the customers.

Bo bought a coffee from a man in a purple camper van

and took it to a seating area beneath one of the railway arches. The communal tables gave the space an egalitarian, common-room vibe which, combined with the warm glow of the paraffin heaters, felt cosy and welcoming – *hyggeligt,* in fact. *Emil would approve,* Bo thought, gazing out through the railway arch at the growing crowd of hipsters, urban twenty-somethings and young families. She had just drained the dregs of her coffee when she spotted Ben's tall frame striding through the market, hands thrust in the pockets of a grey wool jacket, striped scarf wound around his neck. She walked out to meet him.

'Hi, Blu-ray. Long time no see.' He gave a boyish grin and she reflexively offered her cheek for a kiss. As his lips brushed against the side of her face she felt a stab of some difficult emotion – longing, perhaps, or regret – but she swatted the feeling away.

'Nice jacket, is it new?' Ben asked, casting an approving eye over her figure.

'Thanks. I got it in Denmark,' she replied, making a quarter-turn and striking a jokey, modelesque pose. 'The Danes say there's no such thing as bad weather, only bad clothing. Turns out they have a point,' she laughed.

'No kidding,' he replied wryly, but without malice.

They stood facing each other in the middle of the bustling market and Bo felt uncomfortably as if she was on a first date, and wasn't quite sure what to say.

'It's starting to fill up,' Bo observed, somewhat unnecessarily. 'Shall we get something to eat?'

They set off on a tour of the food stalls, side by side but not touching, browsing the different dishes on offer, before eventually settling on a van selling Vietnamese rice bowls, with strips of chicken and pork sizzling tantalisingly on an open griddle.

The eating area beneath the arch was much busier now, and most of the seats were taken. They squeezed between the backs of other customers to claim two vacant chairs on one side of a long sharing table.

'Smells good,' she observed, peeling back the plastic lid from her bowl and inhaling the mouth-watering sweet-and-sour-infused steam.

They began to eat, and Bo was conscious of the proximity of those sharing their table, and the way the acoustics of the enclosed space intensified the volume of conversations around them. She began to wonder whether it had been a mistake to suggest meeting here, given the nature of what they had to talk about.

'So,' Bo began tentatively, 'how's work?'

'Better,' Ben replied, with a relieved look. 'The clients have stopped throwing their toys out of the pram, for now at least. I think maybe they're starting to realise I'm not a complete idiot.' He gave a hollow laugh, but Bo was struck by the insecurity behind his comment. She watched him spear a slice of chicken with his wooden fork. 'Still bloody hard work, though,' he mused, 'I've been the last to leave the office every day this week.' He took a mouthful of chicken and chewed.

Bo smiled supportively. 'I'm sure you're doing great,' she reassured him. He returned a coy smile and murmured, 'Thanks,' and, for a fleeting second, she glimpsed a little boy unsure if he had bitten off more than he could chew. It was a vulnerability he didn't reveal very often, and Bo found it strangely endearing. She was surprised to find herself fighting the urge to stroke his hand.

Feeling suddenly bashful, Bo returned to her food while, across the table, two attractive young women squeezed into the seats opposite theirs. They were in mid-conversation, oblivious to the way that, as they shrugged off their coats, Ben's eyes flickered across their bodies in automatic appraisal of their looks. Bo's urge to comfort him instantly drained away, and she stabbed a piece of chicken with her fork.

'So, I had a job interview this week,' she said, in a tetchier tone than she had intended.

'Oh right. What's the job?' he asked, his eyes snapping back to hers. She took a sip of water, deliberating on whether to give a positive spin to her account of the job interview – good company, decent package – or whether to be honest about her reservations.

'Marketing executive. For a food company,' she said

evenly, but even as she spoke she noticed his eyes flicking to the women across the table again. Thanks to the echo-chamber acoustics of the railway arch, Bo could hear every word of their conversation.

'He was on Tinder the whole time,' the long-haired brunette said, scandalised.

'Wanker,' replied her friend.

Ben had evidently been listening to them too, because it took him a fraction longer than it should have to respond to Bo.

'What's the company?' he asked, finally.

'Petits Pains. You know, the sandwich places you see in railway stations.'

A sneer began to form on Ben's lips. 'Mmm, gastronomic stuff,' he scoffed.

'It's a marketing job, Ben. I wouldn't have to eat their food,' she replied snippily.

'Thank God for that.' He gave a snide laugh. Bo could feel the beginnings of a familiar resentment bubble in her stomach. How typical that he expected her to be sympathetic when it came to his career, but was so coolly dismissive about hers.

Bo sat and ate in resentful silence. She heard the brunette across the table say, 'I've blocked his number now,' and her friend sniggered.

'So, how was Denmark?' Ben's question caught her

unawares. She scraped at the last remaining grains of sticky rice coating the inside of her plastic bowl.

'Oh, well. It poured with rain for the first couple of days so we were pretty much housebound. Which was okay, because the summerhouse was very cosy. After that, we went for bike rides, walked on the beach, flew a kite, cooked.' She was speaking quickly, and Ben's puzzled expression made her suspect she was coming across as flustered – defensive, even. She sensed she was sailing into dangerous waters. 'We saw the Northern Lights one night, though; that was pretty cool,' she gabbled. A tiny flicker of jealousy flashed across Ben's face.

'Wow. Sounds amazing,' he said expressionlessly.

'It was,' she agreed. 'And quite rare for Denmark. We were really lucky.'

'Tell me again, who else was there?' Ben asked. His eyes were fixed on the side of her face and, for the first time since they had sat down, she felt certain that she had his full attention, just at the moment she would rather she didn't. She frowned at her empty rice bowl.

'Oh, well, there was Florence, the artist I told you about. Kirsten arrived on Friday. And there were a couple of other friends of Kirsten's mum there too.' Through her peripheral vision, she could see Ben looking at her intently, emanating suspicion.

'Were they artists too?'

'Who?' she stalled.

'The other friends.'

'Um, no,' she said vaguely. 'One was a writer. The other one's a chef.' Ben's face had taken on a mask-like, expressionless quality, and she could feel a warm flush spreading up her neck.

'What were they called?'

'Simon. He's the writer. And Emil.' As she said the name, her gaze dropped.

'Email?' Ben quipped. 'What kind of name is that?'

'Not Email, Emil. He's Danish.' She felt a flicker of indignation and was aware that she was properly blushing now, from her neck to her cheeks. She knew that Ben had noticed.

'And Emil's a chef, is he?' Ben asked flatly.

She nodded. 'In Copenhagen.'

A clatter of cutlery being dropped on the stone floor provided a welcome interruption, and Ben turned away to look in the direction of the noise.

When he turned back, he said coldly, 'Sounds like quite the house party you had out there.'

'Hardly,' Bo protested, with a forced casualness. 'Like I said, we went for walks, did some cooking, played games – you'd have been bored senseless.' She attempted a laugh, but Ben's face was stony.

'Well, you must have been enjoying yourself. You didn't return my call.'

Bo opened her mouth, on the verge of blaming the poor phone signal in Skagen, but then the thought *just tell him* came unbidden to her mind.

'Look, Ben,' she said quietly, 'there is something I should probably tell you,' her eyes coming to rest on a watermark on the table next to her empty rice bowl. 'I kind of had . . . a thing . . . with someone while I was in Denmark.' She glanced across to see Ben blink once, very slowly.

'A thing?' he repeated. 'What kind of thing?'

Bo swallowed. 'Like, a romantic kind of thing,' she said, cursing herself inwardly for her evasiveness, like a child trying to dodge a telling-off.

His eyes narrowed. 'Who with? The writer or the chef?' There was a harshness to his tone.

'Emil. The chef,' she whispered, staring hard at the water stain.

'Right.'

She allowed herself a fleeting look across at him. His jaw was clenched and he was staring into the middle distance.

'So, let me get this straight,' he said, his voice sceptical, and louder now, 'having jumped on the plane to the middle of fucking nowhere in Scandinavia and thrown yourself under the nearest Danishman' – Bo winced but he kept talking – 'you text me to apologise for wrongly accusing *me* of cheating. Then, when I accept your apology, you give me the cold shoulder again, don't return my call, and I hear nothing from you until two weeks after you're back.' He gave a derisive snort. 'Classy, Blu-ray. Really classy.' Bo cringed. He was making no effort to lower his voice, and Bo was acutely aware that the women opposite had fallen silent to eavesdrop.

'That's not how it happened,' she whispered meekly. Ben rolled his eyes. 'You make it sound like I did it just to get back at you!' she protested.

'Well, didn't you?' he snapped. Along the table a hipster-ishman with a beard looked over his shoulder at them.

'No!' she insisted vehemently. She dropped her voice and in a hushed, measured tone said, 'The way things had been going between us, I wasn't even sure if we were still together when I left for Denmark. All that stuff with Charlotte, remember?' Ben let out a derisive snort. 'Milton Keynes. And that photo on Facebook. What was I supposed to think?' Her eyes were shining defiantly.

He glared back. 'Maybe you were supposed to think about who you trusted more, me or a jumped-up office gossip like Hayley,' he said spitefully. 'And I told you there was nothing going on in that photo. But you had to go and prove a point by shagging the first man you met in Denmark.'

Bo slumped in her seat, feeling drained and defeated. 'Look, I didn't do it to prove a point. It was just one of those things. It just happened.' She resented the way he was wilfully twisting her words to make her behaviour seem vindictive and vengeful.

Ben was staring into the middle distance again, his face set in a snide smile. 'A holiday romance. How lovely for you. While I was back home working my bollocks off.' He had crossed over into self-pity and, all of a sudden, her residual guilt evaporated, and indignation rushed in to take its place.

'It's not my fault that you're having to work hard in your new job,' she replied. 'I only went away because I'd been made redundant, remember? Whereas you got a big fat promotion. Poor you,' she said sarcastically. He shot her a sideways look. 'And besides, it's not like we were ever a *proper* couple. You're conveniently forgetting that you never wanted anyone to know we were together.'

Ben rolled his eyes wearily in a *not again* expression. An air of mutual dissatisfaction and recrimination had settled over them and they lapsed into silence. Bo fiddled with her water bottle. Ben pulled out his phone and stared at the screen.

They sat there for a while until eventually Ben placed his phone on the table and said, 'So, I guess you'll be flying back to Denmark soon, then, to visit your Viking.' Bo bridled, but let the jibe pass.

'I don't know yet,' she replied airily.

'A chef, too. Quite a catch, for a foodie like you.'

'That's right,' she shot back. 'He works at just the kind of restaurant you like, come to think of it. Michelin stars. Expensive.' Bo hated the tone of her voice, sour and petty, but she sensed they had passed a point of no return and it seemed too late to try and retain her dignity.

'Well, in that case, I guess you won't need me to take you out any more,' he muttered, draining his bottle of water.

She stared at him hard for a moment, then said quietly, 'No, I guess I won't.'

Chapter 20

Bo threw herself onto her bed and stared at the ceiling. She knew she ought to cry, but the tears wouldn't come; rather than sad, she felt numb and empty. Her gaze settled on a cobweb in the cornicing, and, as her eyes traced the pattern of its dusty threads, she replayed her conversation with Ben at the food market. Although she was in no doubt that their relationship was over, she wasn't entirely sure which one of them had ended it. It was as if they had stumbled into a stalemate through mutual pique and wounded pride, and breaking up had been as much a way to save face as a conscious choice.

There had been a few excruciating moments following their quarrel during which they remained at the crowded table under the railway arch, neither of them knowing quite what to do. Bo had been torn between an urge to walk off in a huff, and a desire to part on good terms. In the end, they had left the table together and walked out through the market in silence. When they reached the main road, Ben had mumbled, 'See you around,' and given her a cursory peck on the cheek, which Bo had met with a tight smile and a perfunctory, 'Take care.' As break-ups went, it had been neither apocalyptic nor amicable, just awkward and unsatisfactory.

Bo closed her eyes and tried to force the image of Ben's retreating back from her mind. Uncomfortable though it may have been, the break-up ought – surely – to make her life simpler. At least now she could work out how she felt about Emil without the nagging guilt that she was betraying Ben. She rolled sideways, pushed herself upright on her mattress and took out her phone.

Hey Emil, she typed. *How are you? I've been thinking about you a lot since I got back. Hope you're well. Bo x*

Her thumb hovered above the send button, but something inside her urged caution. It was not just that it felt opportunistic and callous to contact Emil so soon after breaking up with Ben. There was also the lurking suspicion that she might have made too much of what happened in Denmark, that she had got carried away like a lovesick schoolgirl and that, if Emil had thought anything could come of what had happened, he would have been in touch by now.

It had been a fortnight since she returned to London and, the more time that passed, the less certain she was of her feelings about Emil. After all, how well did she really know him? They had only spent a few days together and, although some of her memories of him were as vivid as if they had happened yesterday, when it came to his life in Copenhagen – his *real* life – her knowledge was hazy, to say the least. She couldn't picture his apartment, or his friends, or how he spent his free time. She had no idea what his reaction would be upon receiving a text from her. Would he simply ignore it or – worse still – feel obliged to send a polite *thanks but no thanks* reply? She pressed delete and let her phone drop onto the duvet.

Over the days that followed, Bo sank into a depression that was tinged with self-pity. She moped around the flat in her pyjamas, on the basis that there was no point getting dressed when she had nowhere to be and no one to see. She dwelt obsessively on the twin preoccupations of Ben and Emil, alternating between feeling resentful and hard-done-by, and berating herself for bringing about her own predicament. Some of her friends had invited her out, via a Whatsapp chat entitled *Xmas drinkies!!!* but her heart sank at the prospect of dragging herself into the West End for an evening of enforced sociability at some overpriced bar. Besides, she knew she would end up talking about her love life and her redundancy, and recoiled at the prospect of her friends' outraged sympathy on both counts.

But when Kirsten started bringing home bags of gifts

and wrapping paper, and tactfully enquired whether Bo was ready for Christmas, Bo realised she could wallow no longer. She had brought back a few gifts for her family from Denmark: bottles of Aalborg aquavit for her father and brother-in-law, and scented candles infused with aromas of the Scandinavian landscape for Lauren and her mother. But, with Christmas only a week away, there was more shopping still to do.

Bo had always enjoyed Christmas shopping; she loved lingering over window displays, and found something seductively alluring about the notion that life could be transformed by the acquisition of a few luxuries. But this year, as she wandered, aimless and uninspired, through the gifts section of John Lewis, the whole enterprise struck her as hollow and crassly materialistic. She grew increasingly fraught as she moved between the lavish displays, unable to summon enthusiasm for anything she saw. Everything seemed so unoriginal and predictable: toiletries sets, pointless desktop gadgets, or quirky gifts themed around gardening or golf.

She had begun to despair of finding anything to buy when, wandering into the kitchenware department, she paused in front of a shelf of stoppered glass storage jars. Seized by an idea, she grabbed a selection of jars and put them in her basket: rather than buy some generic, clichéd gift, she would give home-baked Danish treats, something simple and unpretentious, but made with love. Combined with the aquavit and the candles from Denmark, it would feel like giving the gift of *hygge*. The thought made her smile as she stood with the other frazzled shoppers in the long queue snaking towards the tills.

When Kirsten returned from work that evening, she found the flat heady with the aroma of ground spices and sugar, and Taylor Swift blaring from the speaker dock. Bo was in the kitchen in a flour-streaked apron, washing up at the sink whilst singing along to 'Never Ever Getting Back Together'.

'Blimey, you've been busy, haven't you?' Kirsten observed, looking at the rows of walnut-sized cookies cooling on racks on the kitchen worktop. 'Are those *pebernødder?*' she asked. 'I haven't eaten those for years.'

Bo looked over her shoulder from the sink and nodded. 'I found a Danish cookery blog. Try one,' she urged. Kirsten popped a cookie into her mouth and chewed while Bo watched nervously, like a contestant on a cookery show awaiting the judge's verdict.

'Just as I remember them,' Kirsten said approvingly.

The following day, Bo made *romkugler*, rum-flavoured truffles dusted in coconut flakes. Like the *pebernødder*, they were characteristically Danish: simple and unpretentious, but deliciously moreish. She carefully decanted the truffles and cookies into the jars, to which she attached handmade labels with red ribbon. Feeling pleased with herself, she took some of the leftover truffles and a cup of tea to the living room.

Dusk was falling and the room was in semi-darkness so, balancing her tea and saucer of truffles, she jabbed at the light switch with her elbow. In the harsh light from the overhead bulb, she felt a pang of embarassment for how shabby and slovenly the room was. Old newspapers were strewn around, empty mugs stood on the coffee table, and the place hadn't been dusted for weeks. She did a quick, efficient tidy-up, clearing away the dirty mugs, tipping the rubbish into the wastepaper basket and straightening the sofa cushions. Then, seized by a sudden urge to make the room feel more . . . Danish, she returned to the kitchen, dug a multipack of tea lights out of the drawer and found nine glass ramekins stacked in precarious towers at the back of one of the cabinets. With the blinds lowered, the overhead light off, and the flickering tea lights in their improvised holders, the living room felt infinitely cosier and more *hyggeligt*. The soft yellow candlelight rendered the dust invisible and dulled the sofa's garish tartan. Bo sank onto the sofa and propped her feet up on the coffee table, feeling pleased with her domestic prowess.

Out of nowhere a memory popped into her mind from Skagen, of Emil telling them about the concept of *hygge* in the summerhouse, explaining to a sceptical Simon that it wasn't just about soft furnishings, it was about taking time to appreciate what you have, to be grateful and to think about the things that really matter. Time had been the first casualty of her London lifestyle, she realised. Life had become so frenetic, so focused around proving herself at work, that she had not allowed herself to wonder whether the lifestyle she was chasing was one she actually wanted. Now, with time on her hands thanks to her redundancy, the conviction was growing that she knew what made her happy – that she'd always known, but somehow she had lost sight of it along the way. She wanted more from her career than office drudgery. She wanted to be challenged and stimulated by her job, and to feel she was connecting with people, and bringing pleasure to their lives, in however small a way.

The electronic trill of her phone's ring tone brought her reflections to an abrupt standstill. *Marsh Recruitment – Shelley* flashed up on the screen. A jolt of some uncomfortable emotion passed through Bo, and she set her mug down on the coffee table.

'Hi, Shelley,' she said, trying to mask her apprehension.

'Hi, Bo. I'm calling with good news,' Shelley trilled gleefully. Bo could hear the sounds of the office in the background: conversation and ringing phones. 'Karen from Petits Pains has just called. They'd like to offer you the job!'

In the silence which followed, Bo was conscious of the clarity she had felt moments earlier draining away.

'Wow, really?' she stalled. 'I wasn't expecting to hear anything till January.'

'Well, they must have liked you because they've made

273

their minds up already,' Shelley chirped, in a tone that suggested Bo ought to feel flattered.

'Wow,' Bo repeated, expressionlessly, feeling uncomfortably as if she was letting Shelley down by failing to match her enthusiasm. Perhaps sensing that something was needed to clinch the deal, Shelley began to read out a summary of the terms on offer, the salary, holiday entitlement and bonus scheme, while Bo listened in silence, staring blankly into the middle distance.

'Do I have to let them know before Christmas?' Bo asked, once Shelley had finished. There was a silence, during which Shelley's surprise and disappointment that Bo had not accepted on the spot was palpable. When she eventually answered, Shelley's voice was pitched several tones lower than before.

'That would be helpful,' she responded coolly.

Having promised to get back to Shelley in the next couple of days, Bo hung up and collapsed against the sofa cushion, her mind a fog of doubt and indecision. The tea lights continued to flicker, but the flat no longer felt *hyggeligt*, it felt claustrophobic. She went over to the window and peered behind the blind. The sky was battleship-grey and it would soon be getting dark, but Bo was seized by a desire to be outdoors, to let the cold winter air clear her head. She blew out the candles and pulled on her goose-down jacket and Emil's gloves, and headed out into the afternoon gloom.

The street lamps were beginning to glow orange, and car headlights swooped past as she meandered through the streets of her neighbourhood. She had no destination in mind, but hoped that the process of walking would bring some order to her thoughts. Minutes earlier, she had been sure that she knew what she wanted from her career, but now that the choice had been put before her, her confidence was crumbling. She was torn between whether to stick with the security of the familiar, or trust her instincts and try and forge her own path. The conviction was growing that this was some sort of test of her mettle, a chance to prove her maturity. The trouble was, she was not at all certain which was the grown-up thing to do: to accept the job and buckle down to a corporate career, or take a risk and follow her dream?

Chapter 21

At four o'clock on Christmas Eve, Bo walked up the sloping driveway to her parents' front door, which was resplendent with a festive holly wreath. Despite her mild misgivings at the prospect of spending four days with her family, it was a relief to leave London, and all its associated pressures and responsibilities behind. Reminding herself of her resolution to be grateful, and not to take her family for granted, Bo took a deep breath and pressed the doorbell.

Barbara answered the door, casually elegant in a lamb's-wool sweater and loosely tailored trousers.

'Hello, darling,' she said, giving Bo a kiss and reaching out to take her overnight case. Bo removed her coat and shoes in the porch and went inside.

'The house looks lovely, Mum,' Bo said, knowing how much time and effort Barbara devoted to festive décor every year, transforming their home in a characteristically tasteful,

John Lewis sort of way. A garland of pine fronds had been woven between the staircase banisters and, as she passed the front-room doorway, Bo glimpsed the handsome spruce tree wreathed in lights and matching purple and gold baubles.

'Waitrose have just delivered,' said Barbara, before adding in a heavy voice, 'they substituted your father's port.'

Bo grinned. 'Oh dear. How's he coping?'

'He'll live,' Barbara replied tersely.

The spacious kitchen bore testament to the recent supermarket delivery. Every surface groaned with the traditional accoutrements of Christmas gluttony: an enormous polythene-wrapped turkey, packs of smoked salmon, jars of condiments, family-size boxes of biscuits and assorted wedges of cheese. Seated on a stool at the kitchen island, amidst a mountain of carrier bags, Clive was peering dubiously at the label on a bottle of port.

As soon as he caught sight of Bo, he put down the bottle and broke into a smile. 'Ah, here she is,' he said, rising from his stool at the kitchen island and leaning across a boxed panettone to kiss her cheek.

'Hi, Dad,' Bo said.

'Wine?' he asked convivially.

'Actually, I'd love a tea.' Her father looked mildly disappointed, as if her not drinking made his own yearning for a glass harder to justify, but he dutifully carried the kettle to the sink and began to assemble the tea things.

'So, how was Denmark?' Clive asked, once the three of them were seated around the island, sipping tea.

'Amazing, thanks,' Bo replied, taking a nibble from one of Barbara's home-made mince pies. She gave a picture-postcard account of the highlights of her trip: the cosy summerhouse, the shifting Råbjerg dune, the colliding seas at Grenen, and the Northern Lights, purposely avoiding any mention of what had happened with Emil.

'Sounds beautiful,' Barbara sighed, standing to pull an apron over her head, getting ready to tackle the vegetables in preparation for the Christmas meal. Clive looked faintly sceptical and muttered about the astronomical levels of tax and the high cost of alcohol in Denmark, as if these were serious shortcomings which ought to be borne in mind.

As soon as Barbara set to work peeling the potatoes, Clive poured himself a glass of Merlot and launched into an anecdote about the golf club's Christmas dinner-dance which he had compered the previous weekend. Bo smiled indulgently as her father, his eyes gleaming, described his address to the retiring club president, and how the evening had almost ended in disaster when the batteries in his microphone had failed. The story had a well-rehearsed quality and, judging by Barbara's thinly veiled boredom, was one that her mother had heard several times already.

Bo drained her tea, grabbed a peeler from the cutlery

drawer and went over to the worktop to help with the mound of Maris Pipers. 'What time's Lauren coming tomorrow?' she asked.

'About eleven,' replied Barbara. 'They'll set off after the twins have opened their stockings. Lauren said they've hardly slept all week,' she warned.

Clive, who was already on to his second glass of wine, assumed a look of dread. 'I hope you've brought your ear plugs,' he joked. With a pang of guilt at her disloyalty to her niece and nephew, Bo grimaced.

After an evening curled up on the sofa, watching a period drama on television, Bo said goodnight to her parents and went up to bed. The guest bedroom was, as usual, spotlessly clean and tidy, and smelt faintly of lily of the valley. There was something innately comforting about being back in her childhood bedroom, the familiar ticking sound from the cooling radiator, the feel of the thick cotton bedding against her skin, the unstinting, well-appointed comfort of it all. She was about to doze off when a gentle creak drew her attention. The bedroom door inched open and her parents' little black cat padded proprietorially into the room, its tail raised in greeting.

'Hello, Nancy,' Bo murmured, patting the duvet invitingly. With a chirrup, the cat jumped up onto the bed and turned in circles a few times, before curling up in a neat crescent beside her. Bo switched off the bedside light and, with one hand resting on the warm body of the purring feline, was soon fast asleep.

Bo woke up on Christmas morning to the sound of the shower running in her parents' en suite. She put her arm down by her side, but the cat had vanished during the night, leaving just a round indentation in the duvet where it had slept. It was eight o'clock and, although she was tempted to drift back to sleep, a sense of daughterly obligation forced Bo out of bed and down the hallway to the bathroom.

By the time she had showered, dressed and made her way downstairs, a harassed-looking Barbara was arranging smoked salmon onto tiny triangles of brown bread in the kitchen, while Clive was bringing in firewood from the garden in a show of making himself useful.

'Can I do anything, Mum?' Bo offered, pouring herself a coffee from the filter machine.

'Lemon wedges,' Barbara replied distractedly, grinding black pepper over the smoked salmon. Bo obediently found a lemon in the fruit bowl and cut it into wedges to place around the edge of the oval platter, which her mother promptly covered with cling film and placed inside the fridge.

Clive deposited the wicker basket full of firewood on the kitchen hearth and, with the self-righteous air of one who has done his bit, plucked a bottle of champagne out of the fridge.

'You're starting early, Dad. It's only half nine,' Bo teased.

'Just something to steady my nerves before the *terrible twins* arrive,' he replied, looking stoic. At the worktop, where she was forcing stuffing beneath the turkey's skin, Barbara tutted.

'You'll join me, won't you?' Clive looked at Bo pleadingly.

Sensing that her father needed moral support, she said, 'Go on then, it is Christmas.' Clive beamed, dropped sugar cubes into two flutes, added a dash of bitters and topped it up with champagne. They clinked glasses and Bo took a sip, savouring the cocktail's ice-cold fizz in her throat.

Just after eleven, Lauren and her family pulled up in their Volvo four-by-four. The twins tumbled out of the back seat and made a beeline for the front door and the presents they knew awaited them inside. Bo had to dodge sideways as they tore past.

Barbara trailed in their wake, calling, 'Amelie, Freddy, don't forget to take your shoes off!'

'Looking good, sis. I'm liking the curls,' Lauren said, giving Bo's hair a playful flick as they embraced on the driveway.

'Thanks. Thought I'd go *au naturel* for a bit. Give the straighteners a rest. Happy Christmas, Nick. How are you?' Bo said, turning to her brother-in-law, who was unloading a seemingly endless collection of cases and bags from the boot of the car.

'I'm good, thanks, Bo. Happy Christmas,' he mumbled distractedly.

Inside, Clive escaped to the kitchen to knock up another round of champagne cocktails while the twins tore around the ground floor, flushed with excitement, ignoring Lauren and Barbara's attempts to calm them through a combination of admonishment and distraction. Once the car was unloaded, the twins had both visited the bathroom, and the adults had been handed drinks, everyone assembled in the front room.

'Who'd like to open some presents?' Barbara asked, clapping her hands together like an enthusiastic teacher. With a chorus of shrieks and squeals, the twins scrambled down from the sofa and, within minutes, the beige carpet had disappeared under sheaves of torn wrapping paper.

Amidst the chaos, the adults passed their gifts around. Bo's *hygge*-themed presents were received with enthusiasm; the scented candles and aquavit were sniffed appreciatively, and the jars of home-made treats were complimented and cooed over. When Bo unwrapped her present from Lauren she broke into a broad grin.

'An *aebleskiver* pan! Thanks!' she exclaimed, holding up a deep-set frying pan with a base filled with circular indentations.

'You're welcome,' answered Lauren, faintly nonplussed. 'What's it for? The instructions are all in Danish.'

'Pancake balls,' Bo replied.

'Sounds painful,' Clive chortled from his armchair by the fireplace. Barbara shot him a prim look.

'They're like a cross between a pancake and a doughnut, basically,' Bo explained enthusiastically. 'I found a recipe on a food blog. I've been dying to try them.'

They sat down to lunch at a table sumptuously laid with a red damask tablecloth, a silver candelabra and Barbara's best china. Crackers were snapped, drinks were poured and plates heaving with turkey and its accompaniments were passed around. A pleasurable quiet descended on the room as everyone began to eat. Even the twins fell silent in their booster seats, eagerly stuffing chunks of roast potato and shreds of turkey into their mouths.

'So, Bo, any news on the job front?' Nick asked, blinking at her across the table. Although she knew the topic of work was bound to come up during her stay, she had hoped to avoid it until after Christmas dinner, at least. But Nick's question riled her less than it might have, had she not been feeling light-headed after two champagne cocktails and a glass of wine.

'Well, I was offered a job last week, actually,' she answered, guardedly.

'That's fantastic, darling. Why didn't you mention it before?' Barbara said, looking simultaneously hurt and relieved. Bo gave an apologetic shrug, and braced herself for what she knew was coming next.

'What's the job?' Lauren asked from the other side of the table, where she was dabbing gravy from Freddy's chin with a napkin.

'Marketing executive for Petits Pains. The food company,' Bo replied.

'Wonderful news, Bo. Congratulations,' Clive said proudly from the head of the table, raising his wine in her direction. Mirroring his gesture, the others made to pick up their glasses.

'Actually, I turned it down,' Bo said hastily, before they could complete the toast. A silence descended on the table, with the exception of the twins who, having eaten their fill, were embroiled in a dispute over a paper crown from one of the crackers.

'Why?' Lauren asked, seizing Freddy's hand as he was about to lunge for a clump of Amelie's hair.

'It just ... didn't feel like the right job for me,' Bo answered cagily. Seemingly oblivious to the escalating conflict between his children, Nick assumed a look of brotherly concern.

'Do you think that was wise?' he said, rather pompously. Bo glimpsed Lauren's leg twitch as she kicked him underneath the table, but he ignored the hint. 'It's tough out there in the job market at the moment. A bird in the hand, and all that.'

Bo felt her mask of benign nonchalance begin to slip. She

took a fortifying sip of wine. 'Actually, I'm thinking of a change in direction,' she said, aware of a trembling sensation the pit of her stomach. The adults all looked at her expectantly and, sensing Lauren's momentary lapse of attention, Freddy leaned sideways and snatched the paper crown out of Amelie's hand, ripping it in half in the process.

'I want to work with food in a more hands-on role,' she explained cautiously, sensing bemused looks being exchanged around her and decided that, having gone so far, there was nothing to lose by full disclosure.

'I've been thinking about setting up a street food business, actually.'

'A street food business?' Barbara replied, dubiously. 'You mean, like a burger van?'

Bo let out a nervous titter. 'No, not a burger van, Mum. Coffee and cakes. Pastries. Brownies. That kind of thing. I want to bake, not flip burgers.'

She looked around the table, awaiting her family's reaction, but was met with looks of blank incomprehension. The stunned silence was only broken by Amelie furiously launching her plastic beaker at Freddy's head, and the ensuing howls of outrage provided Bo with a welcome respite from her family's concerned scrutiny. Lauren chastised the twins while Barbara rifled around on the dining table in a frantic search for two replacement crowns.

It took several minutes to placate the twins and, when the

conversation eventually resumed, as if by mutual agreement, the topic had moved on to Lauren and Nick's forthcoming skiing holiday.

After lunch, the twins were wedged between a snoozing Clive and Barbara on the sofa in front of the Christmas movie, while Nick assembled garish plastic toys on the carpet, teasing tiny twists of wire out of cardboard packaging and cursing at instruction booklets. Bo and Lauren, as family tradition dictated, tackled the meal's messy aftermath in the kitchen.

'So how long have you been planning the street food idea?' asked Lauren, filling the sink with soapy water.

'Not long,' Bo replied quietly, stacking dirty plates in the dishwasher. 'I've only been thinking seriously about it since I got back from Denmark.'

Lauren seemed intrigued. She lowered the first batch of greasy roasting tins into the bubbles and set to work with the scouring pad. 'Where would you work?' she asked. She sounded curious rather than sceptical.

Bo slammed the dishwasher shut and picked up a clean tea towel. 'There are loads of street food markets all over London now. It's still early days, though. I'd need to do my research.'

Lauren rinsed the roasting tin under the hot water and handed it to Bo.

'Sounds like a lot of work,' Lauren observed.

Bo shrugged. 'I reckon I can handle it. I know it's a gamble, but I've realised I don't want to work in an office any more.'

They stood side by side at the sink, Lauren scouring and Bo drying, in contemplative silence. The sound of a sentimental Disney ballad drifted down the hallway from the living-room television, above the background drone of Clive snoring.

Lauren's unexpected open-mindedness had fostered a feeling of closeness, and Bo felt her guard dropping.

'I envy you, you know,' Bo said eventually. 'It must be so nice, not having the pressure of deciding what you want to do with your life. Not having to worry about explaining a gap on your CV, or whether you'll be able to afford next month's rent.'

'My life's not all milk and cookies, you know,' Lauren said, her voice tight. 'Don't get me wrong, Nick and I have a lovely lifestyle, but being a mum to twins isn't exactly easy.' Lauren was staring into the sink but Bo sensed that her sister was close to tears.

'Oh, I know that, I didn't mean—'

'I haven't had more than five hours' sleep a night for nearly three years,' Lauren cut in. Her hands, Bo noticed, were trembling. 'And that's not just Monday to Friday. It's *every* day. I can't even go to the toilet without one or other of the twins banging on the door to get in' – she had turned to face Bo, and a flush was rising in her cheeks – 'let alone go off on holiday on my own, on the spur of the moment.'

The allusion to her Danish trip stung, and Bo's first instinct was to point out that she only went away because she had lost her job, and to remind Lauren that she and Nick were about to head to the Alps for a week. But, instead, she said gently, 'I hadn't realised. You make it look so easy.' Lauren's shoulders sagged and her head dropped.

'Sometimes there's nothing I would like more than to go off to an office every morning,' Lauren explained. 'To sit at a desk for eight hours a day, with other grown-ups to talk to, and not have to listen to *Peppa Pig* on a loop – and to get paid for the privilege! That sounds like heaven to me.' Lauren gave a mirthless laugh.

Bo dried a roasting tray in shamefaced silence. 'I'm really sorry, Lauren. I guess I never really thought about it like that.' She gave Lauren's arm a rub, Lauren returned a watery smile and they stood in sisterly silence for a few moments.

'I think you should give it a go,' Lauren said finally.

'Give what a go?' answered Bo, confused, thinking for a split second that Lauren was talking about motherhood.

'The street food idea,' Lauren replied.

'Really?' Bo looked at her sister in astonishment.

'If you don't do it now, you might not get the chance again,' Lauren urged. 'Don't wait till you're tied down with kids.'

From nowhere, Bo felt a sob rising in her chest, but the tears which suddenly brimmed in her eyes were tears of gratitude, rather than of sadness.

Bo went to bed that night buoyed up by her conversation with Lauren. Articulating her ambition out loud had helped to clarify her thoughts and her street food idea was beginning to feel like a real possibility rather than just a fantasy. For the first time, she had a clear sense of what she wanted her business to be. Inspired by her experience in Denmark, her ethos would be rooted in the values of cosiness, simplicity, and making time for simple pleasures; her mission – to offer a taste of *hygge* in the midst of the frenetic life of the capital. The thought made her smile. Emil would appreciate the sentiment, she was certain.

She closed her eyes and had a sudden vision of herself and Emil on the sand bar at Grenen as his mother's ashes floated into the ether above the crashing waves. With an intense stab of guilt, she realised how self-absorbed she had been since her return from Denmark. She had been so preoccupied with her own problems that she had overlooked the stark reality of Emil's situation. This was his first Christmas without his mother and, regardless of whether anything would come of what had happened between them, she wanted to let him know she was thinking of him.

She picked up her phone, found his contact details and typed: *Happy Christmas, Emil. I know today must have been hard for you. Bo x*

Chapter 22

Lauren and her family set off on Boxing Day morning for Nick's parents' house in Surrey. Their departure was a whirlwind of fractious toddlers, misplaced car keys, and snippy exchanges.

Once the car boot was finally packed, Bo helped to settle the twins.

'Ready for round two?' she joked, leaning into the back of the Volvo to strap Amelie into her car seat. Lauren returned a conspiratorial smile across the back seat.

'More turkey. More tantrums. Can't wait,' she replied drily, clicking Freddy's seat belt into place.

They all exchanged farewell hugs and kisses on the drive.

'Have the twins got enough snacks for the journey?' Barbara asked anxiously, peering through the window at Freddy, who was demolishing a mince pie messily in his car seat.

'They'll be fine, Mum,' Lauren reassured her, with a tiny sideways smile at Bo.

'Right then, let's go,' Nick said, a little tetchily, and pulled his car keys from his jeans pocket.

'Maybe I could come down to Berkshire in the new year?' Bo said, as Lauren opened the passenger door and climbed into the plush leather seat. 'It would be nice for us to spend some time together.'

Lauren held her gaze and smiled. 'I'd love that.'

Bo spent the remainder of her stay in her bedroom, researching the street food scene on her parents' iPad. Barbara poked her head around the bedroom door intermittently, offering cups of tea and fretting that Bo might be ill.

'I'm fine, Mum, don't worry. I've just got stuff to do, that's all,' Bo said, as Barbara placed the back of her hand against her forehead to check for a fever. She noticed her mother's eyes flicker to the screen on her lap, which was open on a page about a street food market in King's Cross, but nothing was said about it at dinner that evening. Although she was grateful for their discretion, Bo suspected that her parents hoped that, if left alone, her street food idea would fizzle out of its own accord.

Emil had replied to her text on Christmas night, apologising that he had not been in touch sooner and explaining that he had worked in the restaurant up till

Christmas Eve, before flying to Aarhus to spend a few days with his father. They continued to message each other over the days that followed, sending politely chaste messages, as if neither of them was quite sure how intimate they were allowed to be. Bo desperately wanted to tell him she had split up with Ben, but could not think of a way of mentioning it which would not sound crass and opportunistic.

Instead of addressing how they felt about each other, they talked about work. She told Emil about her street food idea, although she held back on revealing her plan for a *hygge*-themed menu, worried that he would find it phony (she might have a Danish-sounding name, after all, but that didn't give her the right to sell Danish food). Emil was full of enthusiasm and encouragement and, in turn, revealed that he had been asked by his employers to help set up a new restaurant in Copenhagen. It would offer a simpler, more pared-down menu, whilst still adhering to the New Nordic cuisine ethos of using native, seasonal ingredients in inventive ways. He added, almost as an afterthought, that he had been offered the role of head chef.

That's amazing news! Congratulations! she wrote. She wanted to add, *I'm so proud of you*, but lost her nerve, fearing it might sound presumptuous.

With December drawing to a close, the topic of their respective plans for New Year's Eve arose. Bo was relieved to hear that Emil would be spending the evening with his brother and sister-in-law at his flat in Copenhagen, rather than at a party. She wasn't sure what a Danish New Year's Eve party would consist of, but she suspected copious amounts of schnapps would be involved and that there would be a lot of pretty, long-legged blondes. The very thought of it made her irrationally jealous. When Emil asked after her plans, she told him she would be going to a party with friends, *some girls I went to school with,* she clarified, hoping he would read between the lines and understand that she was not going to be seeing in the New Year with Ben.

The question of whether they would make arrangements to see each other again hung over them, unspoken. January was going to be a busy time for them both and, whether it was because neither of them had the confidence to ask, or because they both sensed the timing was not right, neither of them broached the subject.

In the event, New Year's Eve was a dispiriting evening of cheap wine, supermarket party food and forced jollity with people Bo quickly realised she no longer had anything in common with. Rattling back to Holloway on the tube in the early hours of the new year, doing her best to ignore the carousing of other revellers in the carriage, it occurred to Bo that she would rather have spent the evening sharing a meal with friends than in the poky kitchen of a flat in

Walthamstow, sipping wine from a plastic cup and shouting to be heard over a thudding drum beat.

It was a relief when the festive period was over and Bo could, at last, devote her time to thinking about her business plan. She spent hours hunched over the laptop at the dining table, scribbling notes in a pad. She had found an online guide to setting up a mobile catering business, which covered everything from street trading laws to start-up costs and advice on branding. But her research, though fuelling her conviction that street food would be the best way for her to try her hand at a career in catering, also made her realise how many challenges lay ahead.

First and foremost, she would need a vehicle to trade from. A scan of the selling sites swiftly put an end to her dream of buying a cute vintage van of the type she had seen at Euston station. Retro-charm, she discovered, came at a premium. She balked at the idea of buying a no-frills catering van, having read that the food markets and festivals allocated pitches – in part – based on the appearance of the vendors' vehicles. Besides, it was important to Bo that her mobile café be consistent with the Danish aesthetic of elegance and style. Serving her cakes and coffee from a white-box-on-wheels van did not fit with her brand image at all.

She searched the sites again with scaled-back expectations, scrolling past the adapted airstreams and Gypsy caravans and ignoring the functionally ugly burger vans, seeking something that would combine vintage charm with a modest price tag. Eventually, an image of a converted horse-box slid onto her screen. It had a wooden serving hatch in its corrugated-iron side and, although tiny, it had a quirkily vintage look. She clicked on the listing to check its specifications. Although compact, it had everything she would need in terms of water, electricity and storage. Most importantly, it was within her budget. Bo closed her eyes and indulged in a daydream, imagining herself in a pink apron, serving brownies through the horse-box's hatch at a trendy London food market. The daydream came to an abrupt end, however, when it occurred to Bo that, if she went ahead and bought a horse-box, she would also need to buy a car with which to tow it.

Sipping coffee on the sagging sofa of a Berkshire soft-play barn a few days later, Bo explained her quandary to Lauren. 'A horse-box is no use to me without a car, but if I buy the horse-box I won't be able to afford a car as well,' she said morosely. Around them, the walls echoed with children's screams, and the *Frozen* soundtrack blared from wall-mounted speakers.

'I could speak to Nick if you like,' Lauren volunteered. 'Maybe we could lend you the money for a car?'

Bo puffed out her cheeks and stared absently at Amelie and Freddy, who were pelting each other with coloured plastic balls in a giant pit. Although she couldn't admit it to Lauren, she didn't like the idea of being indebted to her brother-in-law. She wanted the street food business to be hers alone and she suspected that Nick would assume some kind of quasi-proprietorial interest in the business if he had helped to fund it.

'Thanks, Lauren, that's really kind, but I couldn't ask you to do that,' she said. 'I'll find some way round it, I'm sure. Something will come up,' she concluded brightly, trying to sound more optimistic than she felt.

In the second week of January, Bo was halfway through an online food hygiene course when she received a text message from Florence.

Hey babe, long time no see! How've you been? Fancy a trip to the seaside? Come down to Hove for a day! LOADS to tell you x

Bo smiled at her phone screen. She had a sudden flashback of Florence sitting opposite her at the marina café in Skagen, chatting good-naturedly, and had a pang of longing to see her again.

Would LOVE to come down and see you. I've got lots to tell you too.

I'll show you a proper British day at the seaside, give Skagen a run for its money, Florence promised.

A flurry of texts followed, in which they agreed that Bo would come down to Hove that coming weekend.

Saturday arrived, chill and blustery. Bo spent the train journey to the south coast thinking about the horse-box she had seen on the selling site, and toying with menu ideas, until the train's rocking motion lulled her to sleep. Florence met her on the platform at Brighton station, waving excitedly from behind the ticket barriers in her knitted bobble hat. The sight of her impish grin made Bo instinctively break out into a smile.

They drove along the seafront to Hove in Florence's clapped-out Fiat Punto. It was the first time Bo had seen the sea since Denmark, and although the built-up British resort lacked the bleak desolation of the Danish coastline, the sight of the brooding, steel-grey sea nevertheless gave her a thrill of excitement.

Florence deftly manoeuvred the Fiat into a space on a street lined with white-painted Victorian terraced houses. Seagulls screeched overhead as Bo followed Florence inside and up a cramped stairwell to the first floor. There, Florence twisted her key in the lock and gave the front door a firm shove with her shoulder.

'Chez moi,' she said mock-grandly. Inside, a cluttered hallway opened into a living room which, even on a grey day in January, felt bright and cheerful. Two handsome sash windows gave an airy feel to the room, which was at the same time quirkily shabby and effortlessly chic. The walls were painted in a bold cobalt blue and a 1950s-style orange sofa faced the fireplace across a coffee table made from a recycled wooden pallet attached to industrial castors.

Paperbacks and old sketchpads jostled for space on the alcove shelves and a battered 1930s leather club chair squatted against the wall between the windows.

'This place is great,' Bo murmured admiringly, taking a few steps further inside and placing her bag on the small wooden dining table tucked against the wall.

'Hello, Bo,' a voice said from behind.

Bo turned to see a smiling, bearded man rising from an antique wing chair which she had not noticed, it having been concealed from her view by the open door.

'Oh!' she exclaimed, momentarily poleaxed.

'Simon . . . I didn't realise . . . Florence hadn't . . .'

Bo fired a questioning look at Florence, who was smirking like a mischievous child.

'She wanted to surprise you. So, *surprise!*' Simon replied drolly, waving both hands theatrically like a chorus-girl. He stepped towards her and they exchanged a kiss.

'The beard threw me. I almost didn't recognise you.' Bo laughed, glancing at his hirsute jawline.

'Florence's idea,' he replied with a faintly pained look. 'She thinks it makes me look *cuddly*.'

'Well, cuddly is an improvement on *sulky*,' Florence teased, with a playful wink at Bo.

Bo stood in astounded silence for a few seconds then, as her brain began to process what she was seeing, said, 'I had no idea you two . . . I mean, how long . . . when . . .'

'Since we got back from Denmark,' Florence replied, taking pity on Bo's befuddled state. 'I was in London and called Simon to see if he wanted to meet for a drink and . . . well . . . here we are.' She gave a happy-go-lucky shrug then said, 'I told you we had lots to catch up on, didn't I, babe?'

'You did,' Bo agreed.

Bo sat down beside Simon on the orange sofa while Florence made tea in the kitchen.

'Still working on the novel?' Bo asked brightly, noticing the open laptop on a little table next to the wing chair.

Simon's brow clouded. 'Second draft,' he said, as if that explained everything.

Florence reappeared with a tray of steaming earthenware mugs.

'He says he wants to see me,' she said, placing the tray on the coffee table and lowering herself into the club chair, 'but I think really he just comes here to write.'

Simon looked shamefaced. 'Two birds with one stone, and all that,' he mumbled apologetically. 'Besides, it shouldn't be too much longer now.'

Florence rolled her eyes in an exaggerated *heard it all before* gesture, but Bo sensed affection behind the exchange, and found the thought of Simon and Florence still bickering about his novel obscurely comforting.

'Has he let you read any of it yet?' she asked, playing along. Florence snorted.

'Course not.'

Bo had brought home-made Daim chocolate muffins, in homage to their stay in the summerhouse, and the three of them sipped tea and ate muffins, chatting about their plans for the year ahead. Florence was preparing for an exhibition, working on a series of pieces inspired by coastal flora. She jumped up from her seat to fetch a porcelain tile delicately embossed with a seed head of dune grass.

'Oh wow, it's beautiful,' Bo murmured, tracing the cool, shiny surface with her fingertip.

'Thanks,' Florence beamed. Bo leaned against the buttoned backrest of the orange sofa. 'Well, funnily enough, I've been thinking about a career change, since I got back from Denmark.'

'Oh, yeah?' Florence replied, intrigued. Then her brow clouded. 'I hope you're not going to ask to borrow my Wonder Woman costume?'

Bo giggled, set her tea down on the coffee table, drew her phone out of her bag and called up the photo of the converted horse-box.

'You buying a horse, babe?' Florence asked, dubiously.

Bo shook her head, and told them about her street food business idea and how it had come about as a result of her time in Denmark; that she had been inspired by the *hygge* ethos of making time for simple pleasures, and thought it was a natural fit for a mobile coffee-and-cake business. 'At least, that's the plan, if I can find a vehicle to trade from. That's where the horse-box comes in,' she concluded, a rueful smile playing around her lips.

'I love it, babe, it's a brilliant idea,' Florence cooed, and even Simon looked quietly impressed.

A little later, they went for a walk along the seafront. The white dome and flashing lights of Brighton pier seemed to hover about the water in the distance, and the stony beach crunched and slid under their feet. Simon went to the water's edge to skim stones against the surf.

'So, no need to ask how things are going with you two,' Bo said, slipping her arm inside Florence's as they made their way along the shingle.

Florence broke into a grin. 'No one's more surprised than me, babe,' she replied. 'Turns out Simon's a bit of a secret softy underneath that gruff exterior.'

'Not a psychopathic serial killer after all, then?' Bo teased.

'Well, if he is, maybe he's just learnt to hide it better,' Florence replied.

Bo laughed, but she didn't think Simon was hiding anything, in fact, quite the reverse. His furrowed brow had vanished, and he seemed more relaxed, more open, as if the repressed rage which had seemed to lurk beneath the surface had been worn away by Florence's good-natured optimism.

'And what about you?' Florence returned, with a

significant look. 'Heard anything from Emil since you got back?'

Bo smiled coyly. 'Yeah, we've been in touch,' she replied carefully. She could see Florence's eager expression out of the corner of her eye. 'He's got a new job. He's setting up a new restaurant, so . . . who knows?' She trailed off.

Bored of stone-skimming, Simon drifted back to join them, and the three of them walked along the beach until the chill wind and lowering sky led them to take refuge in a brightly lit chippy.

They sat around a Formica table eating battered cod and salty chips with their fingers.

'We should ask Pernille if we can go back, don't you think?' Florence said, dousing her fish with malt vinegar. 'Maybe in the spring, when the weather's nicer. Get Emil along too. It would be like a reunion.' Florence's eyes sparkled with excitement.

'I'd love that,' Bo replied wistfully, 'but I can't think that far ahead at the moment. I've got a business to launch, remember?'

'Bo's Buns,' Simon said, absent-mindedly, munching on a mouthful of battered cod.

'Say what, babe?' Florence said, licking vinegar from her fingers. Simon swallowed his mouthful.

'A name for your business: Bo's Buns. Just a suggestion,' he added modestly.

Bo laughed. 'Thanks, Simon. It's catchy. I like it, but I've already decided on a name.'

The others looked at her expectantly.

'Hygge and Kisses,' she said.

Chapter 23

On Sunday morning, the buzz of an incoming text startled Bo out of a dream. She swung her arm sideways and rifled across the bedside table for her phone.

Are you around today? Barbara wanted to know. Bo rubbed her eyes groggily and glanced at the clock. It was nine.

Yes. Why?

Don't go anywhere. Dad's coming over.

Bo stared at the screen, mildly perturbed by the seeming urgency of her mother's words.

When the doorbell rang an hour later, Bo padded apprehensively down the hallway to find Clive standing on the front doorstep. He was wearing his weekend corduroys, with a navy scarf tucked neatly inside the collar of his Barbour jacket.

'I was half expecting to find you in pyjamas,' he said with an amiable smile. Bo was conscious of a wave of relief passing through her; her father's demeanour did not suggest he was the bearer of bad news.

'Hi, Dad,' she said, standing aside to make room for him to pass, but Clive stayed put.

'Actually, you might want to slip some shoes on,' he advised, glancing at her fluffy slippers. Puzzled, Bo pulled on her Uggs, grabbed her coat and keys and followed him up the stone steps, past the wheelie bins and onto the pavement.

'Where are we going?' she asked, mystified. There was no sign of her father's Lexus on the street.

'I suppose that's up to you,' answered Clive, fishing a key from inside his jacket pocket and handing it to her.

'What's this?' she asked, bemused. Clive chuckled and guided her by the elbow along the pavement.

'Graham at the golf club has been looking to get rid of it for a while. He used to take it fishing, but he's had to chuck that in. His arthritis has been playing up. Poor bugger.'

Bo sensed that her father was in danger of digressing. 'Get rid of what, Dad?' she said, keen to steer him back on track. Clive drew to a halt a few houses further down the street.

'This,' he said, gesturing towards a dark green Land Rover parked by the kerb.

A moment's silence, then, 'I don't . . . is it . . . Dad, what's going on?' Bo felt simultaneously excited, confused, and like she was about to cry.

'Barbara and I thought you might be able to make use of it,' replied Clive. Bo opened her mouth but no words came out. 'Lauren phoned us,' Clive explained, his blue eyes crinkling. 'Told us you need some wheels for the business, but that you'd be too proud to ask. It's fully insured. Consider it an early birthday present.'

Bo stared, speechless, at the car in front of her. It was a boxy model, over ten years old, with a few scratches on the paintwork and a dent in the bumper, but it looked sturdy and dependable. Overwhelmed, Bo burst into tears.

'There, there,' Clive whispered, putting his arm around her heaving shoulders.

'Sorry, Dad, it's just ... thank you!' she sobbed, wiping her eyes with her sleeve.

'It's quite all right,' Clive said soothingly. He waited while Bo fished a tissue out of her pocket and blew her nose, then said, 'Right, you need to take this old girl for a test drive, and I need a lift home. So pull yourself together and let's get going.'

First thing on Monday morning, Bo opened up her laptop and scrolled through the selling site, praying the horse-box had not been sold. Upon finding the listing still active, she seized her phone to dial the vendor's number and, by lunchtime, was hurtling up the A1 on her way to Hertfordshire for a viewing.

Rough gravel crunched beneath her tyres as she steered the Land Rover past a complex of agricultural buildings towards a neatly maintained farmhouse. She parked the Land Rover and climbed out onto the drive, stooping to pat the black-and-white collie which had appeared from nowhere and begun to sniff eagerly at her shoes. The front door of the farmhouse swung open and a fifty-something man in wellies and an anorak stepped out. He introduced himself as Steve, shook Bo's hand and, with the collie trotting at his heels, led her across the courtyard.

'It was our son's idea,' Steve explained, as they walked past a stable block, from which a row of hay-munching ponies observed them benignly.

'He persuaded us to pay to have it adapted into a mobile coffee shop,' Steve said, squeezing past a rusting iron trailer at the entrance to a corrugated-iron shed. 'Had all these dreams of touring the festivals, earning a living as he went.' Steve shook his head, emanating the faintly resentful demeanour of a parent who had been left to clear up their child's mess.

'Course he lost interest as soon as the summer was over, and now he's gone off travelling.' Bo felt obscurely like she ought to apologise to Steve for his son's behaviour, as though by dint of her age, she were somehow guilty by association.

Inside, Steve tugged at the corner of a tarpaulin sheet, which fell away to reveal the horse-box, its curved roof and tongue-and-groove panelled exterior coated in a thick layer of dust and cobwebs.

'I'll open her up for you,' Steve said, flicking through a jangling bunch of keys before releasing the padlock on the rear doors. Bo gingerly climbed onto the footplate and went inside. The interior was compact – if she stretched out her arms she would touch both walls with ease, but there was room for a coffee machine on top of the counter and space for a fridge beneath. She ran her hand along the serving shelf, feeling the knots and grain of the wood.

'Can I open this?' Bo asked eagerly, pointing at the hatch. Steve nodded, so she slid the metal panel out and up until the supporting struts on both sides clicked into place. A spider scuttled through the opening and vanished over the edge of the serving shelf and she leaned forwards to peer through the hatch, indulging the fantasy that she was not standing in a dusty outhouse, but serving coffee and cakes at a bustling food market. Then she turned to look at Steve through the open rear doors.

'I love it,' she said.

At the table in the farmhouse kitchen, Bo went through the paperwork with Steve, then, with a trembling hand, wrote out a deposit cheque, with the promise that she would return

Clara Christensen

to collect the horse-box as soon as she had found somewhere to store it. She drove back to London in a state of mild shock. Somehow, everything else she had done in preparation for launching the business – the online courses she had completed, the licences and permits she had applied for – all had an abstract, theoretical quality about them. It was only now that she had stood inside the half-ton of wood and metal, leaned against its counter and checked inside its cupboards, that the whole enterprise began to feel like a reality rather than a fantasy.

Bo collected the horse-box the following weekend and there followed a few enjoyably productive days during which she had it cleaned and re-sprayed sage-green. She ordered a *Hygge and Kisses* banner to display above the serving hatch, a matching apron, and purchased a second-hand coffee machine and fridge. Within a week of going to view it, the repainted horse-box stood gleaming in a rented garage in an industrial estate off Holloway Road.

In February, Bo heard that she had been awarded a regular morning pitch on a train station forecourt in north London. She spent two days baking, and checking and re-checking that she had enough cups and paperware. She barely slept the night before, terrified that she might sleep through her alarm (which was set for five-thirty), and drifting in and out of fitful dreams in which she turned up at the pitch only to discover she had forgotten her stock, or that she was wearing her pyjamas. The hours stretched and it was a relief when her alarm finally went off and she could, at last, throw her clothes on and begin to load her boxes of baked goods into the back of the Land Rover.

It was still dark when she pulled onto the station's concrete forecourt just before seven o'clock. She attached her *Hygge and Kisses* banner to the roof, arranged her pastries in neat pyramids beneath glass cloches, and placed her chalkboard menu on the serving shelf. Then she waited.

At half past seven it started to rain: fat, icy droplets which bounced noisily off the roof of the horse-box. Although Bo did her best to maintain a cheerful disposition, it felt as though she were invisible to the grim-faced, umbrella-wielding commuters rushing to or from the station platforms. She shivered and pulled the zip of her goose-down coat up to her chin. Gazing through the hatch at the rain-soaked forecourt, she was forced to acknowledge that the reality of running a *hygge*-themed catering business might not always feel very *hyggeligt*. She returned home just before lunchtime, shattered and disheartened, with almost as many *aebleskiver*, *snegles* and muffins in the back of the Land Rover as she had set off with six hours earlier.

On her second morning, however, the sun shone weakly, and a modest but consistent trickle of customers wandered up to the hatch. Despite her best efforts to engage them in conversation, most of her customers seemed determined to make as little eye-contact as possible, and the majority ignored her glass dome-covered displays and ordered just coffee. But as the days passed, Bo was gratified to note that she was starting to attract regular customers, even getting to know some of them by name, and that she was selling food as well as coffee. Occasionally, customers would comment on the name of the business, asking what *hygge* meant, or how to pronounce it. She fixed a handwritten sign to the panelling on the side of the van, to explain that *hygge* was the Danish concept of well-being and cosiness, and meant taking time to enjoy simple pleasures, like coffee and cake.

In early March, just as the daffodils were beginning to flower in the garden behind the flat, Bo received a call from the organiser of a food market in south London, to say that there had been a last-minute cancellation, and offering her a pitch that coming weekend.

Bo felt almost identical amounts of excitement and apprehension as she drove down to south London early on the Saturday morning. The market, on Clapham Common, comprised a farmers' market selling everything from French cheeses to artisan breads, and a street food market. When Bo arrived at nine o'clock, the site was already a hive of activity, with traders efficiently assembling their tents, hooking up power generators, and setting out their produce. A teenager in a high-vis jacket flagged her down and directed her to a pitch next to a voluble man selling Cornish pasties.

The first customers began to arrive around ten and within an hour there was a queue at the horse-box which snaked across the grass.

'Make sure you leave them room for a pasty at lunchtime,' her neighbouring vendor joked, eyeing the generous portions of *aebleskiver* being passed through the hatch.

At half past eleven Bo looked up and, to her astonishment, saw Ben browsing one of the market stalls. The market was crowded now and a cluster of other customers surrounded him. It was only when Ben began to move away and started talking to someone over his shoulder that Bo realised he was not alone. He took a few steps away from the market stall and a woman appeared from behind him; a petite, mousey-haired woman in a grey coat. It was Charlotte. Bo felt a pulse of panic at the realisation that they were heading her way, and had an overwhelming urge to crouch down behind the serving counter, but the long line of customers at the horse-box meant hiding was not an option.

Through her peripheral vision, she monitored Ben and Charlotte's inexorable progress towards the horse-box. There was an unmistakable intimacy in their body language: their arms brushed against each other's as they walked, and their strides were in step. It was Charlotte who noticed her first. Ben's attention had been drawn by a stall selling bottles of organic beer, but there was no mistaking Charlotte's fractional double-take, and the discreet nudge of Ben's ribs with her elbow. She whispered something, he looked across and, in the fleeting moment when Bo met his gaze, Ben's dismayed look exactly mirrored her own. She forced her attention back to the job in hand, whilst acutely aware that Charlotte and Ben were wandering over to join the back of the queue.

'Fancy seeing you here,' Bo said with an artificial brightness, when they finally stepped up to the hatch.

'Hi, Bo,' Charlotte said, a little sheepishly.

'So, the rumours are true then,' Ben said, scratching the back of his neck uncomfortably. 'I heard you'd had a change of career.'

Bo gave a light-hearted shrug. 'I guess you could say that,' she said breezily.

Ben's eyes were lingering on her torso, which she found faintly disconcerting, until she realised he was reading the text on her branded apron.

'*Hygge and Kisses. Spreading a little hygge-ness, one slice of cake at a time,*' he read aloud. Charlotte let out a little bleat of nervous laughter, which the others both ignored.

'*Hygge.* That's Danish, isn't it?' Ben asked, his brow furrowing. He pronounced it hidge, but she decided not to correct him.

'That's right,' she said, keeping her tone purposely neutral.

Ben gave a little, tight smile.

'What can I get you?' Bo said, conscious of the line of people waiting behind him.

'I'd love a latte and a chocolate brownie, please,' replied Charlotte gratefully.

'Same for me,' Ben added, with the slightly reproachful air of one who didn't want to be overlooked. While the coffee machine hissed and gurgled, Bo put two brownies into a cardboard container and placed it on the serving counter.

'These look amazing,' Charlotte murmured.

Ben glowered.

'That'll be five pounds, please,' Bo said genially.

Ben drew out his wallet and passed a note through the hatch. Then, with a smile which failed to reach his eyes, he picked up the cardboard container and walked away, leaving Charlotte to trail after him.

'Talk about awkward,' Kirsten said, cringing, when Bo described the encounter to her in the flat that evening. Bo swung her legs up onto the sofa cushion and stared thoughtfully at the ceiling.

'You know, it really wasn't as bad as it could have been,' she said, in a tone tinged with surprise. 'If anything, he seemed to be more uncomfortable than me.' She looked across at Kirsten, who was eating a microwave meal straight from the plastic container at the dining table.

'Do you think he'd been lying to you, then, when he said nothing was going on?'

Bo sighed wearily. 'Honestly? I don't know. It might have been going on for months, for all I know. But even if it was, I think I'm just . . . not that bothered.'

'Well that's got to be a good thing,' Kirsten said matter-of-factly. 'And at least Ben got to try your chocolate brownies eventually,' she added drolly.

'He had to pay a fiver for the privilege, though,' Bo pointed out, a mischievous smile playing around her mouth.

On the coffee table, Bo's phone beeped. She sighed and leaned sideways to pick it up.

'Oh my God,' she exclaimed, staring at the screen.

'It's not from Ben, is it?' Kirsten asked, with an alarmed look.

'No, it's from Florence,' Bo answered, her face lighting up in a smile. 'She and Simon are getting married!'

Kirsten stared, open-mouthed, while Bo replied to Florence's text with a succinct, *YOU'RE WHAT?!*

A phone call followed, during which Bo and Kirsten listened on speakerphone while Florence described the events of the previous weekend. Simon had finished the second draft of his novel, she explained breathlessly, and they had gone out for dinner in Hove on Saturday night to celebrate. 'A nice restaurant, too – I should have realised something was up.'

Bo and Kirsten smirked.

They had been walking back to Florence's flat along the beach afterwards when it started to rain. 'And I mean *really* rain . . .' She paused for emphasis. 'It was like Skagen all over again. Blowing off the sea horizontally.'

They had sought shelter behind a row of beach huts and it was there, huddled together under a flimsy umbrella watching rivulets of water stream off the huts' wooden roofs, that Simon had turned to Florence and said there was something he'd been wanting to ask her.

'He'd planned it all, bought a ring and everything,' Florence said, sounding simultaneously flattered and incredulous. 'He'd been counting on a clear moonlit night, but instead he got lashing rain and both of us looking like drowned rats.'

Bo and Kirsten *aww*-ed in unison.

The wedding was going to be in Sussex in early May, she said.

'Nothing fancy, just a big barn party for all our friends,' said Florence.

'So soon!' Bo exclaimed.

'You know me, babe, once I've made my mind up to do something, I like to get on with it. You can both come, can't you?'

'Of course!' Kirsten said avidly.

'Wouldn't miss it for the world,' Bo agreed. There

followed a high-spirited chat which covered the obligatory topics of the newly engaged: the dress ('nothing flouncy'), the hen night ('don't care as long as there's plenty of booze') and the honeymoon ('probably Butlin's. We're both skint'). They were about to say their goodbyes when Florence asked Bo if she would consider baking something for the wedding day.

'Nothing fancy, we don't want a white-tiered monstrosity. Cupcakes, perhaps? We'd pay you, obviously.'

Bo said she would be honoured. 'No need to pay me, though,' she insisted and, before Florence had a chance to protest, offered to bring the horse-box too, on the basis that it would be good publicity for the business.

'You're on, babe,' Florence agreed unhesitatingly.

Lying in bed that night, Bo texted Florence to ask if Emil knew about the engagement and whether they planned to invite him to the wedding.

Yes, Simon texted him and of course we're inviting him! came the reply. *It wouldn't be a Skagen reunion without him!*

Bo's heart felt like it flipped in her chest. She stared at the phone for a moment then, with a purposeful intake of breath, she composed another text.

Hi Emil. Great news about Florence and Simon, isn't it? Do you think you'll be able to come to the wedding?

She set her phone back down on the bedside table and

closed her eyes, resolving not to look at it again before the morning. But when the phone buzzed a few minutes later, she sat bolt upright and snatched the phone so fast she knocked a box of tissues and a bottle of water onto the floor.

Chapter 24

Eight a.m. on the day of the wedding saw Bo and Kirsten speeding along the M25, a tower of cardboard cupcake trays stacked on the back seat of the Land Rover, and the horse-box trailing behind. Bo had hooked her iPod up to the stereo and turned the volume up high to drown out the noisy thrum of the Land Rover's engine, and was singing along enthusiastically to 'Single Ladies (Put a Ring on It)'.

In the passenger seat beside her, Kirsten sipped tea from a thermos and winced in the early summer sunlight.

'How come you're so perky?' Kirsten groaned. 'It should be against the law to be up this early on a Saturday.'

Bo crunched the gears and assumed a self-righteous look. 'I slept till seven this morning. That's a lie-in for me, these days.'

Kirsten yawned into the back of her hand. 'The ceremony's not till two,' she protested half-heartedly.

'I know,' answered Bo patiently. 'But I'll need time to set up.'

They arrived at the reception site in Sussex just before ten. A hand-painted *WEDDING* sign on the grass verge guided them through an open five-bar gate onto a rough track.

'Wow. When she said it was no-frills, she wasn't exaggerating,' Bo observed, peering through the windscreen at the ramshackle wooden barn in a field up ahead. She slowed to a crawl, mindful of the Land Rover's ageing suspension and the deep potholes pock-marking the track.

Several cars and vans were parked on the grass and the site was busy with people rushing back and forth carrying furniture or flowers. A row of portable toilets was being lowered into position from a flatbed truck and, by the entrance to the barn, a balding man was unloading lights and a sound system from the back of a van labelled *Have I Got Grooves for You*. It took Bo several minutes to locate Florence among the mêlée, finally spotting her standing beside a Transit van in a T-shirt and leggings.

Bo wound down her window and leaned out. 'Happy wedding day!' she shouted. 'Shouldn't you be doing bridal stuff? Hair and make-up, or a manicure?' Bo asked, as Florence trotted over.

Florence snorted dismissively. 'Oh please, I have no intention of looking like a drag queen on my wedding day. Besides, there's too much to do here. Everything's a bit last-minute, as you might have noticed.'

On the grass in front of the barn, an array of gazebos of varying sizes and designs had been erected to form a makeshift marquee. Bo pulled the car onto the grass and clambered out. Beneath the colourful fabric of the mismatched tarpaulins, a disparate assortment of seating including deckchairs, plastic garden recliners and beanbags had been laid out on rugs, creating an effect which felt like a cross between a youth club and a hippy commune.

'Simon! Bo and Kirsten are here,' Florence shouted across the tented area. From the far side of the space, where he was manoeuvring a wicker sofa into position, Simon looked up and waved.

'Do you want to see the cakes?' Bo asked, gesticulating towards the cardboard cupcake tray on the back seat of the car.

Florence clapped her hands excitedly.

Bo carefully removed one of the trays and lifted the lid. She had baked vanilla cupcakes, iced with buttercream and dusted with edible gold glitter. Each one was decorated with a tiny flag attached to a cocktail stick reading *I Do; Mr & Mrs;* or *Just Married*.

Florence squealed with delight. 'Bo they're *gorgeous*,' she cooed, and grabbed Bo around the neck in a one-armed hug. 'Oh, that reminds me, babe,' she said suddenly. 'There's something I wanted to give you. Wait there!'

Florence winked and ran across the track to her car. She

returned carrying a slim package wrapped in plain brown paper.

'It's just a little something to say thank you for doing the cakes,' she said breathily.

Bo tore open the paper to see a framed pencil drawing of a seascape, in muted shades of green and grey.

'Oh! It's Grenen!' she exclaimed, recognising the curved sand spit tapering into the sea, lapped on both sides by tumbling waves.

'It's a sketch I did last summer. I thought you might like it,' Florence said modestly.

'It's beautiful, Florence, I'll treasure it,' she stammered, and they hugged again.

It was gone eleven when Florence and Simon finally set off to get ready for the ceremony. Bo had moved the horsebox into position between the barn and the tented area and was unhooking it from the Land-Rover.

'Anyone want a lift to the hotel?' Florence offered, climbing into the driver's seat of her Fiat.

'Yes please,' Kirsten called. 'You don't mind, do you, Bo?' she asked apologetically.

'Course not. No need for you to hang around here. I'll see you at the hotel in a bit.'

Kirsten grabbed her overnight bag from the Land Rover and ran gratefully over to Florence's car.

Bo watched the Fiat bump its way along the uneven

track, then glanced at her watch. Satisfied that she had plenty of time, she connected the generator and opened the hatch. She wrote *Congratulations Florence and Simon* inside a pink heart on her chalkboard and placed it on the serving counter, and had just begun to rinse the coffee machine filters in the sink when she heard a familiar voice behind her say, 'What's on today's menu?'

A jolt of something like electricity surged through her and she turned to see the top half of Emil framed in the rectangle of the open hatch. He was dressed in a pale grey suit with a lilac shirt unbuttoned at the neck. His face was lightly tanned and there was a dusting of freckles across the bridge of his nose.

'I guess that depends,' she replied demurely. 'What were you hoping for?' But her offhand tone was betrayed by the reflexive way her hand went to smooth her hair. Emil tilted his head back to look at the banner on the roof.

'*Hygge and Kisses*,' he read with careful deliberation. 'In that case, could I have a kiss, please?' Bo stepped forward and stooped, placing her elbows on the wooden serving counter, with her chin propped on the heel of her palm so that her head was level with his.

'Only if you promise not to tell any of my other customers,' she said in a confidential tone. 'Otherwise they'll all be wanting one.'

She closed her eyes and, when Emil's lips met hers, it

was as if all the angst and doubt she had felt since they parted in Skagen suddenly evaporated, and all that mattered was the here and now, and that they had found each other again.

The wedding ceremony took place in the function room of the hotel. Florence looked radiant in a vintage tea-dress, clutching a hand-tied bouquet of wild flowers, while Simon beamed beside her in an elegantly tailored navy suit.

Afterwards, back at the barn, they sat down to eat at two long, parallel rows of tables upon which tea lights flickered inside glass holders. Bo was seated next to Simon's cousin, a dour chartered surveyor, with whom she made polite but somewhat stilted conversation, whilst being acutely conscious of Emil opposite her, engaged in courteous small-talk with an elderly relative of Florence's. A few places further down the table, Kirsten was engrossed in a lively exchange with a friend of Simon's, a bookish type in his early thirties. Bo noticed how Kirsten became increasingly flushed and giddy as the meal went on, breaking out into peals of laughter and flicking her hair off her shoulders coquettishly.

When Bo rose from the table after the meal, Emil did the same, offering to help her serve coffee and cupcakes.

'I've never had an assistant before,' she remarked,

unlocking the rear doors of the horse-box. He stepped up onto the footplate, stooping slightly so that his head did not knock against the top of the door opening.

'Wow, it is ... small in here,' he noted, leaning sideways so that Bo could open one of the wall-mounted cupboards. Bo retrieved a bag of coffee beans then slammed the cupboard door shut.

'Don't you dare criticise my horse-box,' she warned. 'Besides, you say small, but I prefer cosy. *Hyggeligt*, even.' A playful smile hovered around her mouth. 'Now make yourself useful and grind some coffee beans.'

Emil operated the coffee machine while Bo served cupcakes through the hatch. Once all the guests had been served, they poured themselves a glass of champagne and wandered back to the makeshift marquee, passing Kirsten and Simon's friend, who were sitting together on a garden swing, deep in conversation and seemingly oblivious to everyone around them.

They sank onto an ancient velour sofa and Emil put his arm around Bo's shoulder. She instinctively nestled in closer to his side, feeling suddenly sentimental and light-headed. For a few minutes they sipped their champagne in silence, listening to the sounds of laughter and music from inside the barn.

'When are you going back to Copenhagen?' Bo asked at last, keeping her eyes on the insects that swirled in loose helical shapes above the grass, their wings shimmering and sparkling in the golden evening sunlight.

'Tomorrow afternoon,' Emil answered. She nodded once, slowly, and silence seemed to fill the space between them. 'But I will be back in London in July,' he added in an incidental, almost offhand way. Bo sat up straight and turned to face him, her expression incredulous.

'You will? How come?'

'For work. The restaurant is taking a summer residency at one of the hotels. Just for two weeks. A *pop-up,* I believe is the correct name.' He smiled at her shyly, and Bo stared back, stalled between excitement and trepidation.

'And will you be working *all* the time you're here?' she asked tentatively, hoping her tremulous voice would not give away how much hung on his answer.

'It will be a lot of work, yes,' he acknowledged sombrely, and Bo looked away, feeling her eyes start to prickle. 'But that is why I have arranged to stay for an extra week afterwards.'

There was a fractional delay while Bo digested the meaning of his words. Then she turned abruptly to face him, and found that he was smiling.

'An extra week?' she repeated.

He nodded.

'And you won't have to work?'

He shook his head. 'It will be a holiday,' he said, and his

eyes twinkled behind their metal-framed glasses. 'In fact I was wondering if you'd be free to show me some of the London sights . . .?'

Bo felt like her heart was about to burst. 'I'd love to,' she said. 'Have you ever been to Holloway?' and she leaned over to kiss him.

'Check out these two lovebirds!'

Bo turned to see Florence swaying towards them, woozy and pink in the face.

Emil and Bo shuffled along the sofa and Florence collapsed tipsily onto the cushion beside them, causing a spring somewhere beneath them to emit a comical *boing* noise. Florence didn't seem to notice.

'I would ask whether you're both having a good time,' she said, 'but I think I already know the answer.'

'We're having a very nice time, thank you,' said Emil. 'But more importantly, are you?'

Florence snorted. 'Bloody *brilliant* time, thanks, babe. I should get married more often. Cheers!'

She held out her champagne flute and the three of them clinked glasses.

On the path in front of them, a bespectacled man in a three-piece suit staggered past, slopping red wine over the side of his glass. 'That's Simon's literary agent,' Florence whispered, as if she were divulging sensitive information. 'Simon thought it would be a good idea to invite him.'

They all watched the agent stumble up the steps to the portable toilets.

'Did Simon ever let you read his book?' Bo asked curiously, after the man had disappeared inside the Gents.

Florence grinned. 'Yep.'

'And? The suspense has been killing me. Were we right about the Scandi noir?' she asked keenly.

Florence chuckled. 'I'm not sure I'm at liberty to tell you,' she replied demurely, ignoring Bo's imploring look. 'Let's just say, it's not what I was expecting.'

It was hardly a satisfactory answer, but Bo recognised she was unlikely to get anything more out of Florence on the subject tonight.

Whoops and shrieks emanated from the barn, where the disco was in full swing.

'Just think,' Florence said, 'only six months ago none of us had met. And look at us now. Weird, isn't it?'

Bo nodded. 'It is a bit.' She was conscious of the warmth of Emil's thigh against hers, and the beginnings of a wave of sentimentality which made her throat constrict. It occurred to her that for the first time in ages, she felt completely at ease, not just with the people around her, but with herself. For the moment at least, life felt exactly how it was *supposed* to.

'I blame you, Emil,' Florence said abruptly, leaning across Bo to fix Emil with narrowed eyes.

Clara Christensen

'Blame me?' he repeated, alarmed, 'For what?'

'All that *hygge* nonsense at the summerhouse. Making us *appreciate the simpler things* and telling us to *be grateful.*' Florence wrinkled her nose in pretend disdain. 'We were all quite content to be miserable until you and your *hygge* arrived. And now look at what it's led to.'

'I agree. Who needs *hygge* in their life anyway?' Bo concurred, sniffing purposefully. Emil laughed and rubbed his hair with one hand.

'I apologise,' he said. 'I just thought it would help us get to know each other.'

'Well, you weren't wrong about that, babe,' Florence sighed, leaning across Bo to pat his knee affectionately. 'Oh look, here comes my husband.'

Simon was making his way between the chairs and tables towards them. He had loosened his tie and there was a rosy glow to his cheeks.

'What are you all doing out here?' he asked. 'The party's just getting going.' He grabbed Florence by the wrists and levered her upright. She groaned tipsily, and he put his arm around her waist to support her.

'I've requested a song just for you, Bo,' Simon added, a smile hovering around his lips. 'I told the DJ to put on something really classy, for a friend of ours with impeccable musical taste.'

'Oh, right,' Bo replied guardedly, sensing his sarcasm. As

330

if on cue, the opening notes of 'The Promise' by Girls Aloud boomed out of the barn. Emil and Florence sniggered.

'Good choice,' Bo said wryly, pushing herself up from the sagging sofa. 'It's one of my favourites.' She took Emil's hand and, with the setting sun casting long shadows behind them, and the promise of a night of jubilant celebration ahead, the four of them walked across the grass and disappeared inside the barn.